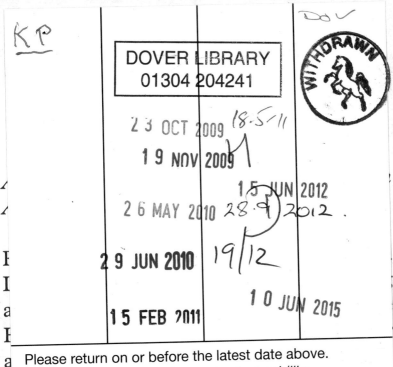

as well as with a particularly vicious thug –
then Leonie disappears...

FIRE BELOW

FIRE BELOW

by

Dornford Yates

Dales Large Print Books
Long Preston, North Yorkshire,
BD23 4ND, England.

British Library Cataloguing in Publication Data.

Yates, Dornford
  Fire below.

    A catalogue record of this book is
    available from the British Library

    ISBN   978-1-84262-654-2 pbk

First published in Great Britain by Ward Lock Limited, 1930

Copyright © by Robin Humphreys and Camilla Kirkpatrick

Cover illustration © Mary Evans Picture Library

The moral right of the author has been asserted

Published in Large Print 2009 by arrangement with
Robin Humphreys and Camilla Fitzpatrick,
care of A P Watt Literary, Film & Television Agents.

Dales Large Print is an imprint of Library Magna Books Ltd.

Printed and bound in Great Britain by
T.J. (International) Ltd., Cornwall, PL28 8RW

CONTENTS

To the Inner Temple
Whose amenities I had the honour to
share with famous men

CHAPTER 1

The Lion's Mouth

It is by George Hanbury's desire that this book has been made. Speaking for myself, I went into the business of which I am going to tell in much the same spirit as that in which a host turns out on a snowy night to bring in some one of his guests whose car has broken down. In a word, I set out in some annoyance, because I had other things to do: and once being in the venture, I think everyone will agree that I could hardly withdraw. No knightly emotions inspired me at any time, and, though I strove to conceal it, again and again I was frightened out of my life. The mistakes we made need no pointing out and were, I think, unpardonable: at least on one occasion my own infirmity of purpose cost us extremely dear: and that in the end we came out no worse than weary is due not so much to our persistence as to that inscrutable agent, the way of a maid.

When, one spring evening in Wiltshire, I told my friend George Hanbury that before the summer was out my wife and I should visit Austria, he threw back his head and laughed.

'I suppose you know best,' he said: 'but, now that you're married, I should recommend some less exacting vicinity. Deauville, for instance.'

Though he spoke in jest, I felt the truth of his words.

Austria seemed to be fated to be my cockpit. Three times I had visited that country and each time met with adventure of an uncommon sort: these encounters had been as exciting as any young man could have wished, but they had not been free from peril, and when a man marries, I think he loses the right to take his life in his hand. George had each time been with me, and I must confess that we courted what danger we found, or at least, being in the quarrels, made no attempt to withdraw. Still, the trouble was not of our making, and since outside that country our lives had been very peaceful, it was easy to look upon Austria as the lion's mouth. For that reason I would not have gone there, still less have taken my wife, but, as luck would have it, I could not help myself.

The year before, I had had the honour to marry Leonie, Grand Duchess of Riechtenburg, and though she had dropped her title and always showed her displeasure if she was treated as other than a commoner's wife, she had not parted with the duchy which she had quitted to marry me eight months before.

The duchy lay in Carinthia, and though its great house was gone, a hunting-lodge, lately restored, made a fair residence during the summer months. While much of the property was wild, there were some ten or twelve farms, and since there was no bailiff, I think only an indifferent landlord would have been willing to continue to stay away.

'We must go,' said I. 'Both of us. You see, there's the Anger estate.'

George raised his eyebrows.

'Headquarters Littai?' he said.

I nodded.

'Leonie hopes,' I said, 'that you'll come and stay.'

'I'll come with pleasure,' said George. He drank what was left of his port and lighted a cigarette. 'But I warn you that I shall go armed.'

'You can wear chain mail,' said I, 'so long as you come.'

George smiled. Then he fingered his chin.

'And I'll tell you another thing. I'm not going to Riechtenburg.'

'Make your mind easy,' said I. 'Riechtenburg's off our map.'

'I'm glad of that,' said George. 'There's nothing the matter with the country, and Vigil's the best-looking city I ever saw. But I prefer to forget them. Possibly when good

Prince Paul has drunk or kicked himself into a timely grave, I may be disposed to take another look at the place. But I doubt it. Some of the hours I spent there were very crowded, and not with "glorious life", either. No, I don't want to go back.'

'I'm with you,' I said, and meant it.

Had Leonie so chosen, she could have married Prince Paul, the ruler of Riechten-burg. They had, indeed, been betrothed for four or five years, but she had broken her engagement when he ascended the throne. For this she may be forgiven – the man was vile. Both George and I had met him and done him more than one service while he was heir to the throne, but his Highness had never liked us, and had we not left the country as soon as he became Prince, I think he would have used his position to do us ill. That my subsequent marriage had inflamed him there could be no doubt, and since there was happily nothing to take my wife into his realm, the thought of revisiting the country had never come into our heads.

Only two friends we had there – Sully, the Lord President of the Council, and Marya Dresden of Salm, who had been my wife's lady-in-waiting and faithful confidante.

The Countess Dresden was young and possessed great personal charm, and though her life was not easy – for the Count had charge of Riechtenburg's foreign affairs –

she never failed to distinguish the role she was called upon to play. At least, so said Sully, and he was a very good judge. But now her husband was dead, to his country's loss. No doubt she mourned him; but the Count had been her elder by thirty-one years, and, while she had been in all things a dutiful wife, the marriage had been made to serve some political purpose and had been, I fancy, little more than a matter of form. Had he lived, she would before now have been our guest: indeed, the date of her visit had been agreed when to our great disappointment his death had disordered her plans. But she was to come to Littai and stay with us there for a month, and we had some hope of bringing her back to England when autumn came in.

With George's promise, then, the prospect we had wished was complete, and we thought no more of the matter, but turned to the end of the hunting and the call of the season in Town.

Some three months later – to be exact, on the second day of July – Leonie and I came to Littai, travelling by road. Her maid and my servant, Bell, brought our baggage by train. For a week we stayed at a farm in the village itself, and then removed to the lodge three miles away.

The lodge stood in a valley above a tumbling stream and made a more pleasant dwelling than many a larger house. A little terrace in front was shaded by chestnut trees, and there our meals were served three times in the day, for the weather was very fine and the nights were warm. The stabling was good, and a mighty coach-house was there to shelter the Rolls – this to Bell's great content, for, though a body-servant, he cherished the car and many a time had passed the night on her cushions, because she was in some strange garage whose people he did not trust.

Of our two guests George Hanbury was the first to arrive, and, though we had been very happy, the light of his pleasant countenance did our hearts good.

George was a man of my age, that is to say, twenty-six, fair and blue-eyed. His manners were easy, he wore a lazy air, and his nature was gay: his wit was as quick and ready as mine is slow: and his friendship was like a rock which no weather, fair or foul, can ever change. To Leonie he was devoted, and she was most fond of him, and I think our relation went far to refute the proverb that three is no company.

With George came Rowley, his servant. The latter and Bell, ex-soldiers, had served us for some four years and had shared the adventures of which I have spoken above. They were true men.

If the lodge was retired, we lived in luxury.

Jameson, an English butler, controlled a most willing staff, six decent saddle-horses stood in the stalls, and, since George had come out by road, we had two cars. The handsome country we had very much to ourselves, and, as we were all fond of fishing, hardly a day went by when we did not prove some water, while, if the estate did not claim us, we usually spent the day by the side of some stream.

So for two careless weeks. Then came a telegram to set our nerves tingling and shatter our peace of mind.

Leonie Chandos Littai,
Dare not come
Marya.

The day was Monday, and on Wednesday we were to have met her ten miles our side of the frontier of Riechtenburg.

Dare not come...

That we should be greatly concerned was natural enough. Marya Dresden was no coward, nor was she given to crying before she was hurt. Little wonder, then, that we found her message pregnant with serious news, and, what was worse, we had not a shadow of doubt that the trouble now beset-ting the Countess had sprung from her friendship with us, if not direct from her purpose to stay in our house. Such interference was monstrous, but, as I have said, Prince Paul was by nature ignoble and I can think of no practice to which, if it served his hatred, he would not have stooped.

We could not call upon Sully, for he was gone to Vichy to take the cure, and when we had posted to Meagre, our nearest town, and had telephoned to Vigil to be told that no reply could be had from the Countess' house, we were alarmed in earnest for the well-being of our friend.

'We must telegraph,' said I. 'She may have shut up the house.'

'I can't believe that,' said Leonie.

'Neither can I. Never mind. We must send a wire. If we get no answer tomorrow I must go to Vigil to see what's what.'

Leonie drew in her breath.

'Let me go, Richard,' she said. 'After all, I'm still the Grand Duchess, and Paul would never dare to–'

'Not on your life,' said I.

'I agree,' said George. 'Besides, we shan't go in by the hard, high road. Yes, I'm going, of course. And Rowley is coming with us, while Bell sits tight at Littai and never lets you out of his sight.'

'I don't like it a bit,' said Leonie, finger to lip.

'If we watch our step,' said George, 'there's

not the slightest reason why Prince Paul or anyone else should know that we're there. Besides, we haven't wired yet, and we may very well get an answer to lay our fears.'

But though we telegraphed twice, no answer came: and at six o'clock the next evening I bade Bell turn out the Rolls.

I never remember setting out with so vague and loose an idea of what I was going to do, and though, for Leonie's sake, we tried to evolve some plan, our endeavours came to nothing because of the manifold chances of what we might find amiss. We were, in so many words, going into the dark, and until we were in touch with the Countess, we could not so much as determine our line of retreat. For all that, we early decided that Rowley must stay with the Rolls upon Austrian soil and that, ere we went over the border like thieves in the night, we must choose some spot close to the frontier where they could lie hid: for so, in case of pursuit, we should have a present refuge which was better than any fort and would carry us out of danger at eighty-five miles an hour.

At this, Leonie besought me to take with us Bell, declaring that if I would do so, she would leave the lodge, which was lonely, and return to the farm: and after a little I consented, on condition that she took with her Jameson and one of the grooms and never went out unattended until we came back.

Now from where we stood to the frontier was a matter of less than four hours in a fast-going car, but since, because of the guards, we dared not enter the country except by stealth, it seemed likely that the rest of our journey would have to be made afoot. This meant a long delay, for Vigil lies twenty-five miles from the border of Riechtenburg, and, even if we should be able to arrange to be carried so far, to enter the city by day seemed out of reason, for we had been there but last summer and were generally known by sight.

I, therefore, reminded Leonie that, though I would send her news as soon as I could, if we were to exercise caution, our movements must be very slow, and I am glad to remember that she did not protest, but only smiled and nodded and slid an arm round my neck.

Then food for two or three days was put into the car and a suitcase with changes of linen and other such stuff, and at half past six we ran through the village of Littai to which my wife was to follow before night fell.

We had a map and a compass and all of us carried arms, and, though no words were spoken, I think we were all four thinking of other times when we had gone out in like manner and wondering what fortune we should meet with before we came back.

The evening was very fine, and the roads

were clear, and by half past nine we made Bariche, a village some fifteen miles from the nearest frontier-post. There we took in petrol, and ten miles further on I brought the car to rest by the side of the road.

Now while I had driven, George had been studying the map, and at once he set out his conclusions, illustrating his points by the light of the dashboard lamp.

'We're here, and there's the frontier, running due north and south. Turn south, and we meet the river. Turn north, and we meet the hills. I'm no damned antelope, but from what I've seen of that river I don't fancy a dip in the dark. I mean, too much excitement is bad for me. Very well. That reduces us to the mountains. Now that looks a likely place – I make it about twelve miles off. The road nearly touches the border and then curls back. If we could park the Rolls there... What's more, there's a bridle-path marked, running almost out of that bend clean over the hills.'

I wrinkled my nose.

'A bridle-path means a sentry – perhaps a post.'

'Exactly,' said George. 'But we've got to be over those mountains by break of day, and unless we've some line to follow – well, I'd rather have a dart at the river. We may be drowned, but it's only got a couple of banks.'

'The river's hopeless,' said I. 'It's far too

21

swift. But I'm afraid of that path.'

'So am I,' said George. 'But I'm still more afraid of losing my way in the mountains and being shot by a sentry as soon as it's light.'

'So be it,' said I, and, with that, I let in the clutch.

George was, of course, perfectly right.

To find our way across the mountains would have been easy by day; but by night we could never have done it, for, for lack of sight, we could not have chosen a line and should have spent half our time retracing our steps. All the same, I was not at all easy about the path, for this was no doubt a way that was favoured by smugglers and therefore more carefully guarded by night than by day.

Half an hour later we came to the spot George had chosen and the end of the bridle-path, to find it by no means private, for a farm was sunk in a hollow not sixty yards off, and though the house was silent, I heard the kick of some horse against the wood of his stall.

We went some three miles further, but found no kind of cover in which to bestow the car, so with a lot of trouble we turned her round, to see if we could do better upon the way we had come.

We had repassed the farm and had left it two miles behind when we came to a track on the left-hand side of the road. The track was rough and narrow and promised the poorest shelter, but in desperation I took it, to see where it led.

I had hopes it would lead to a quarry or into a wood or at least, to some dip or hollow where Rowley could take his chance. But it led to none of these things. It led to the farm.

When I saw the familiar buildings, I could have cried out with rage, for the waste of time was shocking, and the thought of reversing in darkness for nearly a mile and a half was enough to break any man's heart. Then I saw a way out of our plight, which, if we could only take it, would turn our loss into gain.

We were now at the back of the farm, the front of which was commanding the bridle-path. If the farmer would harbour the Rolls, no covert could be more convenient, for, if we returned in haste, we could enter the farm from the front and leave by the back and be well on the way to Littai before we were found to be gone.

At once I told George this notion, and five minutes later the farmer had been awakened and was listening to George's words.

The tale he told does not matter, and indeed I did not hear him, for Bell and I kept out of sight: but I think he alleged that the car was not fit to proceed and desired to leave her and his chauffeur until he had done some business and had the time to return.

To this the farmer consented with a very good grace and started to get on some clothes before coming down. Whilst he was making this toilet, we thrust some food into our pockets and Bell made up a small bundle and put on his overalls. This, because any disguise was better than none, and since he could speak no German, he stood in more need of assistance than George or I.

Ten minutes later we took the bridle-path.

We had gone, I suppose, some three miles – and these, so severe was the gradient, might well have been six – when we heard the dull roar of water that falls in a hollow place. As we rounded a bend, this sound became gradually louder until it was very clear that we were approaching some bridge.

'The frontier for a monkey,' breathed George. 'And now for the post.'

We went on gingerly.

Except by consent of the guards, I am very certain no smugglers use that path; and, indeed, I think we owed the absence of any patrol to the gulf which Nature had fixed in the midst of the way.

As we rounded the last of the bend, we saw the dim shape of a building, and when we had slunk very close, we made out the truth.

Before us lay a ravine, quite twenty-five feet across and God knows how deep. In this the water was tumbling with a sullen bellow of rage, as though resenting the prison which it had made for itself. Upon either side of the gulf stood a low, white lodge, each housing, no doubt, the opposing frontier-guards. And between the two lay a foot-bridge some six feet wide.

Now the bridge was well built of twin girders let into the rock, and though there was no hand-rail, a man might have made the passage without a thought. But the space between the girders was empty, and the floor of the bridge was gone.

I suppose this was made of loose boards which the guards laid down each morning and took up at night, and that when they were gone, the sentries took their rest, for no light burned in the dwellings and the Austrians' door was shut. Be that as it may, the bridge was useless except to an acrobat, and the bare idea of attempting to cross on a girder made my hair rise upon my head.

After a little discussion, we decided to climb up stream.

This proved no easy matter, for, though it was wooded, the mountain rose very sheer and we made the slowest progress for nearly an hour. Then we must have passed over some crest, for all of a sudden we found that the ground was falling and the roar of the torrent had sunk to a steady, crisp rush.

With every step, this change became more apparent, and when the wood gave way to a level stretch of meadow, I could have thrown up my hat.

Two minutes more and we stood upon the bank of the stream.

The night was starlit, and after the black of the forest we seemed to be able to see extremely well.

The torrent was something wider than it had been at the bridge, and its bed was littered with boulders great and small. Between these it thrust its way without much fuss, displaying none of the fury it showed below. Indeed, I was surprised at its patience, until I had found a stick to use as a sounding-rod.

So far from my touching bottom, the stick was whipped out of my hand, and when I had found another and had braced it against a stone, we found to our consternation a depth of nearly four feet.

To ford such a head of water was out of our power, and though by day we might have picked a way over by leaping from rock to rock, we dared not attempt by night so horrid an exercise.

I saw George glance at his watch and heard him draw in his breath. Then–

'There's a light, sir,' said Bell. 'Up stream.'

Before we could turn, however, the light was gone, and Bell at once divined it had been the flare of a match. As though to confirm his finding, the light reappeared and flickered for two or three moments before going out.

'There may be a bridge,' said I, and led the way up stream as fast as I could.

Before three minutes were gone we had crossed the little clearing and come again to the trees and, with the trees, to a darkness that hampered our steps, but, before I had taken six paces into the wood, I saw before me the glow of a cigarette.

At once I stopped and stood peering, for the cigarette seemed low down and I could not see the smoker, although I could smell the smoke.

Then something moved on the ground three paces away, and I saw that two men were grappled and were fighting like beasts, while the cigarette lay smoking a few feet away.

The heavy rustle of the water smothered what noise they made, and the seeming silence of the struggle lent it the air of the fights that are shown on the screen. Indeed, it was like to have ended as some of these do, for all of a sudden I saw the flash of a knife.

At once I sprang forward and seized the one that had drawn, to find he was uppermost and had his man by the throat.

Bell had a torch in his pocket, and I called for a light.

Both men had the look of gypsies, and the one I had seized was cross-eyed. This blemish was certainly against him, but no excellence of feature could have redeemed his looks. I have never seen evil so written in any man's face: and he eyed me with a malignancy that made me tighten my grip. This, I confess, with repugnance, for I might have had hold of some beast, so long and so thick was the hair which covered his arm, like a close-fitting sleeve. He showed no sort of surprise, but only a snarling resentment of my interference with his plans, and he never so much as loosened his grip on the other's throat.

'Let go,' I said sharply, 'and drop that knife.'

For a moment we eyed one another. Then the man spat in my face.

I suppose he was blind with rage, for he must have known that I was powerful and that he was at my mercy if it pleased me to strike.

Be that as it may, I hit him on the point of the jaw with all my might and then stepped over his body to bathe my face.

When I got back, the other was sitting up and answering George's questions humbly enough. He was twice the age of his assailant and though he still looked a fine fellow, was obviously past his prime.

'Smugglers,' said George shortly. 'I can't understand half he says, but it seems that he brought the money and Lord Chesterfield didn't bring the goods. Sheer robbery with murder, of course. What's much more to the point, you've killed the right man. This wallah comes out of Riechtenburg, and he's perfectly ready an' willing to lead us back.'

'I haven't killed him,' I cried.

'No, sir,' said Bell, rising. 'His heart's all right.'

'More's the pity,' said George. 'He'd be greatly improved by death. Never mind. Chuck his knife in the water, and let's get on.'

Two minutes later we were again under way.

It soon became clear that we were approaching a fall, and when we had covered a mile, we must have rounded some shoulder, for the noise became suddenly louder and the air began to grow chill. Five minutes later we saw how the water came down.

This was one great leap from a cliff some fifty feet high, and even by night the sight was very handsome – a mighty sheaf of white foam against the black of the rock.

I am glad to think I had time to see its beauty, for the next moment George was shouting to make himself heard, and fall and cliff and thunder have made me a dreadful nightmare from that time on.

Our way lay under the fall.

I will not dwell upon our passage, which I think took a month from my life. Though I daresay there was no danger, the path was most narrow and ragged and drenched with spray, while the darkness and the monstrous concussion bade fair to dishevel the wits. When I was across I was shaking like any leaf, and it is still a mystery to me how any man heavy-laden can pass that way.

So we entered the country which we had sworn to avoid.

Our way was now much more simple, for while we could still hear the fall, we struck the bridle-path which we had left at the bridge, and, just as the sky was paling, we came out on a pleasant upland to see open country below us and far in the distance a tiny pinprick of light.

I knew this at once for the level-crossing at Vardar, because I had been by that way.

'What could be better?' said George. 'You go through Vardar for Vigil. Now all we want is a road. I think we can stick to the roads till half past five. I mean, we shall go so much faster.'

Our guide brought us down to a road in ten minutes' time and would, I am sure, have led us to Vigil itself, for, though he was a man of few words, he was plainly deeply grateful for what we had done. When we bade him good-bye, he uncovered and, pointing to heaven, said quietly that God would always save us, if He would only be gracious to hear his prayers and that if we were upon some venture, his wife would 'make a novena' for our success. Then he told us that his name was Ramon and that he was a smith by trade, with a forge in a village called Gola, some three miles off: 'and there,' said he, 'you will find me if ever you stand in need, for from now I am at your service by day as by night.'

We thanked him and bade him tell no one that we had met, and, with that, we shook hands and parted, full of goodwill, for honesty sat in his eyes and a child could have seen that he meant every word that he said.

We had now two hours before we must make ourselves scarce, and since, by the map, we were twenty-six miles from Vigil, we started along the road as hard as we could.

It was light ere we came to Vardar, and this made us think it was foolish to show ourselves in a village which might be awake, while to use a level-crossing whose keeper was about his business was to court the observation we wished to avoid. We, therefore, took to the fields and were lucky to attract no attention but that of a little girl who was herding some cows.

We had passed beyond Vardar and had come to the railway line when the murmur of an oncoming train suggested a means of progress of which we had never thought.

On all sides the world was stirring and in less than an hour now the round of village and country would have begun, and though, had we kept to by-roads, I am sure that we should have been safe, the importance of concealing our presence from those it might interest magnified every risk. Add to this that we were weary and footsore, for, though we were all very strong and 'as hard as nails', in the ordinary way we did but little walking, but spent our time in the saddle or on the front seat of a car.

When, therefore, I saw the metals which would lead us directly to Vigil, still more than twenty miles off, the idea of obtaining a lift leaped into my mind. Could we but board some freight train, to leave it again before it ran into the city, we could then withdraw to some wood and take our ease: this, with a quiet mind until it was dark, for so an hour after nightfall we could be at the Countess' house, as ready as rest could make us for whatever should then befall.

When I made this proposal to George, he leaned against the rough fence and wiped the sweat from his face.

'It's dazzling,' he said. 'My feet weren't made for walking: they're not the right shape. I want to lie down and stay down for several hours. But not yet. I must have some more miles behind me before I rest. And that's not the will to win: it's arithmetic. I don't know how far we've come and I don't want to: but I know that the next stretch I

do has got to be short. I can go on now –
somehow. I suppose I've got into my stride.
But this is the sort of effort I can't repeat.
Damn it, my legs'll come off.'

I think he spoke for us all, for the thought
of another forced march was scarce to be
borne. But when I pursued my suggestion,
he cut me short.

'All sorts and shapes go by train. Why
don't we go to a station and damned well
take our tickets in the ordinary way?'

'Because,' said I, 'because in this cursed
country every station platform is a regular
beat of the police.'

'So it is,' said George. 'I'd forgotten. Well,
show me a slow-going train, and I'll do what
I can. But I don't want to get run over.'

I climbed the fence, made my way through
some bushes and looked up and down the
line.

A furlong ahead was a wood which swallowed the metals up; but I saw that the
ground was rising, so that if there was there
no cutting, a train which was bound for Vigil
would be going uphill. Whether, even so, its
pace would allow us to board it, I could not
tell, but I had often watched freight trains
that seemed to go very slow, and the wood
would afford us cover until the moment
arrived.

Ten minutes later we were sitting beneath
its trees.

A quarter of an hour went by before we heard a train coming from east to west, but, before we could see it, we knew it for a passenger train. Indeed, it roared by as though it were going downhill, and George's face was a study as he stared in its wake.

Presently he moistened his lips.

'Let's be clear about this,' he said. 'Perhaps the expression "run over"'s a little loose. What I meant was "I don't want to be damaged". Either by way of mutilation or battery, or dragging. Trains are rough things.'

If I laughed, I agreed with him.

Thirty minutes later a very different rumble suggested the train we wished, and, when at last it appeared, we saw that it was a freight train in very truth.

At once we took up our positions, each standing behind some tree, but as it drew near we very soon saw it was hopeless to endeavour to get aboard.

Its engine was certainly toiling, but, though I cannot pretend to judge its speed, I doubt if a man could have boarded it from a platform, and only a fool would have tried from the permanent way.

We watched it pass in silence.

Then–

'There's nothing for it,' said George. 'We'd better get on. There's the line to guide us, and there's nothing the matter with this wood.'

We pushed on dismally.

We had gone, I suppose, half a mile, when we heard a man's voice.

This came from the railway line and seemed to be very near, but a heavy growth of bushes was preventing our view. Very glad of this cover, we stopped, proposing to wait till our neighbours should go their way; but though the man stopped speaking, nobody moved.

Cautiously I stole to where the bushes were thin, to see the guard's van of the train and one man down by the metals and another leaning over the door.

As I looked, the first man turned and began to walk up a rough path towards the head of the train, and, after a little, the other opened his door and let himself out.

I watched his leisurely movements with my heart in my mouth.

Once down, he pushed back his cap and stared up the line: then with a muttered curse he began to trudge after his fellow by the side of the train.

At once I told George and Bell, who were waiting for me to move, and thirty seconds later we were across the metals and stealing up the permanent way.

Now when the train had passed, we had noticed a motor-car, shrouded, of course, by tarpaulins, on a truck by itself. So fast as the guard would allow us – for we dared not overtake him, in case he should hear our steps – we made for this truck, and, scrambling beneath the canvas, climbed into the car.

This was a *coupé de ville*, brand new, capacious and, to judge by its cushions, very well done.

Our luck had come in.

We let down the windows and waited.

After perhaps ten minutes we heard the men returning and almost at once the train began to move.

'Take the time,' said George. 'For half an hour I guess we can put up our feet.'

I felt for a switch, found it and turned on a light.

Six o'clock.

'And very nice, too,' said George, leaning back in his seat. 'This is the way Jorrocks travelled to Handley Cross.' He raised his voice. 'Bell!'

'Sir,' said Bell from his place in the driver's seat.

'There's a paper stuck on to the windscreen. That'll be the consignment note. See if it says who's brought this very good car.'

I saw Bell peer at the paper and saw him start.

Then he looked round – with a ghost of a smile on his face.

The car was consigned to Prince Paul of Riechtenburg.

Now in boarding the train we had taken one obvious risk – the risk of being carried into Vigil, or at any rate further than we wished. But no man can 'have it all ways', and, after all it was no good our going to Vigil if, when we reached the city, we could hardly stand up for fatigue. Still, I must confess that when forty minutes had passed, but the train showed no signs of stopping or even of slackening speed, I began to grow very uneasy and almost to wish myself back in the sheltering wood.

For such apprehension I had, I think, just cause.

Riechtenburg is ancient and modern as is no other country that I have ever seen. Immemorial habits and customs march with the mode. Abuses are not apparent, but it would be strange indeed if no tares sprouted in so rare a field of wheat. There survives one dangerous abuse. While law and order are honoured, the old back stairs which led from arrest to sentence have never been shut; and the stranger that is taken that way may give up hope.

Leonie, George and I had offended Prince Paul – lay under the man's displeasure, for what it was worth. Beyond the borders of Riechtenburg, his displeasure was nothing worth: but in his own country, where he was the 'Colonel-in-Chief' of every Department of State – well, Madame Dresden was in trouble, and all the sin she had done was to stay our friend.

If we were to help the Countess, we must clearly avoid the condition of having to help ourselves. Once we were known to be in Vigil, we could no more save Madame Dresden than we could raise the dead. More. We should have our work cut out to save our own skins.

Now I do not seek to imply that every citizen of Vigil knew us by sight: but the police of the city knew us, and, as strangers are very rare there and we had no sort of disguise, our appearance was perfectly certain to be remarked. And once we had been noticed, official cognisance was only a matter of hours.

The freight yard of Vigil's station was, therefore, almost the last place in which we should choose to alight, for, strangers apart, any unauthorized person was sure to be challenged at once.

It follows that when another ten minutes had hastened by, we were all three thoroughly alarmed, 'for, by thunder,' said George, 'we didn't bargain for this. They're sure to have this car off the moment we dock, and once we're bolted, they'll pull us down in an hour.'

By now we were out of the car and were looking under the canvas to see what we could. But none of us knew the railway, but only the road, and even as we were peering, the rising walls of a cutting began to obscure our view. We were waiting in some impatience for the grass-grown walls to subside, when the engine let out a screech and we rumbled into a tunnel which might have been the entrance to Hell itself, for, another train happening to pass, the noise was frightful and a volume of filthy smoke offended our eyes and throats.

Now the tunnel would have made such fine shelter that, noisy and foul as it was, we would thankfully have alighted before the train had emerged, but, though it promised to be endless, we seemed to be running downhill and our speed to be increasing with every yard. What was worse, I had now no doubt that we were fast descending to the level of Vigil itself and were actually threading the hills that keep the aged city to north and east. If that were so, we should presently issue from the tunnel clean into the station yards, for the latter lay under the hills north-east of the town.

And so we did.

As the train ran into daylight the brakes were applied. The next moment we banged across points and lurched to the left. Then we heard shouts and whistling and the crunch of steps upon the ballast and the hissing of steam, and two minutes later the train was brought to a standstill in an atmosphere of excitement which showed there was something amiss.

Here let me say that if ever three men were unlucky I think it was we, for I afterwards learned that the driver of the train was in error in not slowing down before, *that he should have passed through the tunnel at five miles an hour,* that had he not had a clear run, we must have been smashed and that, as it was, he overran the point at which the train should have rested by more than a quarter of a mile.

Such negligence drew to the train the attention of every employee that heard or saw it arrive, and, to judge from the scrambling and hubbub, our passage into our siding was watched and attended by most of the station's staff.

This reception was trying enough, but when I perceived we were running alongside a platform my heart sank into my boots, for so long as the train was not berthed, they could not discharge the car, but once they could take her off, I was sure that, as George had said, they would do so without delay.

Something had to be done – and done at once.

I turned to Bell.

'The consignment note,' I said. 'Get it off the windscreen as best you can.'

He was back in the car before I had George by the arm.

'Bluff,' said I. 'We must bluff them. You and Bell and I have come down in charge of the car – by royal command. Engineer, tester and mechanic, specially sent. We supervise the off-loading and deliver to the palace ourselves. You must do the talking – you're better than me. Take a high line.'

'It's a chance in a million,' said George. 'Give me the note.'

With his words the train stopped with a jerk and I turned to Bell.

'Come,' said I. 'We're under Mr Hanbury's orders and we're going to off-load the car. Take notice of no one, and if anyone gets excited refer him to me.'

Then I took a deep breath, pulled aside the canvas and slid down on to the rails…

We had the car uncovered before an official arrived, and before two minutes were past I think he was sorry he came.

George was magnificent.

He vouchsafed no explanation – there were the Royal Arms on the doors of the car, and had the bonnet open and Bell had found a duster and was rubbing the silver plate. He did not so much as produce the consignment note. But he fell upon the man as a panther falls upon its prey.

He cursed the line and the driver and he cursed the pace we had come: he cursed the platform and the station and the tunnel through which we had passed: he cursed the

41

absence of helpers and skates and ramps; and he shouted and stamped till the fellow, now thoroughly rattled, began to reflect the censure and to scold his astonished underlings into some show of life.

In that moment the trick was won.

Men fell over each other to fetch the ramps, and when no skates were forthcoming, no one dared say as much, but a superintendent was sent for to break the news. George fed upon the delay with a hideous zeal, and when out of pity I said we could do without them, he turned upon me and rent me till the blood came into my face. When two superintendents arrived without any skates, he gave such an exhibition of insolent rage and scorn that, though I had feared their arrival, I think they would sooner have questioned the devil himself, and I have never seen the saying 'Attack is the best method of defence' so vividly justified.

The truck being long, we were able to manoeuvre the car and, by exercising great care, to bring her on to the platform without any skates, but this delicate operation gave George such a scope for contumely, that by the time it was over both superintendents had gone and the helpers stood huddled together like frightened sheep.

When he called for petrol, his demand was frantically echoed a score of times, and four or five went running to fetch the fuel; and water was brought before he had thought to ask it, on the ground, no doubt, that prevention is better than cure.

The car was of German make and bore a good name, and though I had never used one, its engine seemed simple enough. Indeed, the latter started without any fuss, but I had to endure a volume of execration, because I had used the self-starter instead of taking the trouble to swing the crankshaft by hand.

We let her run for five minutes while George passed about the car, pointing out invisible scratches and breathing out dreadful threatenings against everybody concerned. Then he asked the whereabouts of the palace and took his seat at the wheel and ordering Bell and me to sit by his side, drove the car out of the freight yard and into the streets.

The temptation to leave the city and take to the countryside was very strong, for so we could have rested all day in some remote spot, yet have been in Vigil without effort as soon as night fell: but that would have laid us open to a charge of stealing the car, and would have made us the quarry of a hue and cry so shocking to contemplate, that after a hasty discussion we decided that we had no option but to drive to the palace at once.

We did not relish such a visit, but the day

was young, and the palace was guarded by sentries and not by police, and once the car was safely within the forecourt, all that we had to do was to beat a retreat.

Indeed, what danger there was lay in the streets we must use, and I think we should have done better to leave the car at the station when once she was off the truck: but, as I have shown, we had had no time for reflection, and when one is using shock tactics it is easy enough to be carried away oneself.

'But we needn't all go,' said George. 'In fact it's far better that I should appear alone. Where shall I drop you and Bell? And where shall we meet?'

This conclusion was plainly sound. Bell and I could do nothing, for George, who could speak like a German, must play the hand. The question was where we could shelter the livelong day.

I think our late misadventure must have disordered my wits, for not until then did I suddenly see the folly of wasting the hours which had fallen clean into our lap.

We had come to help Madame Dresden, and here we were at her gates a full day before our time.

'Go by the Lessing Strasse,' I said. 'It's sure to be empty now, and Bell and I can go over the garden wall.'

'Of course,' said George. 'And with luck I should be with you in a quarter of an hour.'

Danger is a curious thing, and I have often proved that the ground which one seeks to avoid may be crossed in safety, while the quarter one has never suspected is the covert of Peril itself.

All the way we saw but one policeman, and he was busy discussing the size of some fruit: no notice was paid to our passing, and we met with no sort of check: the Lessing Strasse was empty except for a watering-cart; and Bell and I were within the Countess' garden before George was out of the street.

I did not like his going to the palace, still less his going alone, but, recalling his success at the station, I felt that his wit could be trusted to bring him safe through. He would then have to walk half a mile by the riverside, but, since it was not yet eight, I could not believe that he would be so unlucky as to meet with someone that knew him in those ten minutes of time.

I, therefore, gave my attention to the back of the house, for though Madame Dresden might be gone, her servants knew me by sight and I was depending on finding some of them there. Indeed, if the house was empty I did not know what we should do, for I knew no other source of which we could make inquiry with any hope of success.

The heavy shutters were closed and this had an ominous look, but since the weather was hot and the rooms faced south, I hoped very hard that the windows they hid were open and the shutters themselves fastened against the heat of the day.

Desiring to learn the truth, I bade Bell stay under cover and crossed the lawn, for the garden was very private and not at all overlooked.

I had left the grass and the gravel surrounding the house and was halfway up the steps which led to the terrace, when, as though by magic, the shutters of the salon were parted, and a man stepped on to the terrace, duster in hand.

It was the Countess' butler.

For a moment we stared at each other. Then–

'Good morning, Carol,' I said. 'Where is Madame?'

'Madame is abed, sir.'

I thought very fast.

'Is the salon empty?' I said. 'I'd like to write her a note, but I must not be seen.'

He found me paper and pencil and stood to the door.

I wrote as fast as I could.

Dear Marya,
Carol knows I am here, but no one else. Walk in the garden before breakfast – as soon as you can.

Richard Chandos.

As I sealed the envelope–

'Madame must have this at once, Carol.'

'Immediately, sir. I shall tell her maid that I found it beneath the front door.'

'That's right.'

As I stepped on to the terrace, he left the room.

I was upon the edge of descending the steps when the clack of shutters thrown open came to my ears.

I shrank back instantly. I had put my faith in Carol, but I had no mind to put it in anyone else.

As I stood waiting, I heard more shutters opened and then the flick of a duster being emptied into the air.

The servants were about their business, and my retreat was cut off.

I stood back in the salon, chafing.

Then I heard a sudden rustle, and there was Marya Dresden beside me, with a dressing-gown over her nightdress and her small feet in slippers and fright in her eyes.

'What is it, Richard?' she breathed. 'Why are you here? Don't say Leonie–'

'She wanted to come,' said I. 'But I couldn't risk that. But you didn't think we'd sit still and watch you drown?'

Marya stared and stared.

'"Watch me drown"?' she repeated. 'My dear, what on earth do you mean?'

I took out her telegram and gave it into her hand.

As she read it, a hand went up to her head. Then– 'I never sent this,' she said.

CHAPTER 2

High Misdemeanour

Madame Dresden's words were so confounding and had unmasked so abruptly such a flood of sinister light that it took me a moment or two to focus the new situation and generally marshal my wits.

'You never sent this?' I repeated.

She shook her head.

'Did you send any wire?'

She nodded, twisting her hands.

'On Monday. I said *Expect me Wednesday as arranged.*'

'That's right,' I said slowly. 'And that telegram was taken, but this was sent. I must say Prince Paul is well served.'

Madame Dresden had me by the arm.

'It was sent to bring you,' she breathed. 'He–'

'It was sent to bring us both, Marya. It was sent to bring Leonie and me. Thank God I had the sense to spoil that.'

'But it's brought you, Richard. It's brought you into his power.' She clapped her hands to her face. 'Oh, my God, why on earth did I send that wire? Everyone knows he's rabid at Leonie's loss. He won't have her Regiment at the palace, and–'

'You can't blame yourself,' said I. 'If one can't trust the Post Office – well... If I were you, Marya, I should leave Vigil for good. And Riechtenburg. I mean, the fellow's not safe.'

'I know,' she said. 'I never see him now, but I hear a good deal. It doesn't affect the country – Sully sees to that. He's really afraid of Sully–'

'Who is away just now.'

Marya caught her breath.

'You must go,' she cried. 'You must go. With Sully out of the country and Grieg–'

'Grieg?' I cried sharply. 'What of Grieg?'

The man was our implacable enemy – had nearly been the death of George Hanbury and would have killed me.

'Three days after Sully was gone, the Prince took Grieg back. Not into the Army: he's been given some job in the police.'

There was a little silence. Then–

'You're right,' said I. 'We must go.'

'"We"?' says she. 'I thought–'

'George Hanbury is with me. And Bell.'

'But how can you go, Richard?'

'As we came,' said I. 'By night. Till then we

must lie up somewhere, and–'

'Here, of course,' cried the Countess. 'And then I can drive you–'

'Not on your life,' said I. 'You're deep enough in. I take it you're ready to go this afternoon.'

'My big baggage has gone,' she said.

'Then today you must leave for Salzburg, and leave by train. We'll come and get you there as soon as we can.'

'I can't go till I know you're safe.'

'You must,' said I. 'Don't you see you must keep to what you said in your wire? If you don't they'll know in an instant that we've been in touch with you.'

'How can they know that you haven't telephoned?'

'We did,' said I. 'And were told there was no reply. And we sent you two wires.'

The Countess stifled a cry.

'It shows the lengths,' I continued, 'our friends are prepared to go. Happily they don't know we're here. And if you don't alter your plans, there's no reason why they should. I assume they don't know that you were to travel by road.'

'The servants know, Richard. I have told the chauffeur that he is to take me to Bariche and then return.'

I bit my lip.

'Then you must go by road. You mustn't alter one jot of the arrangements you've made. Once you're out of the country, that's different. You must take in petrol at Bariche and drive straight on. Don't go to the lodge – stop at Littai. Leonie's gone to the farm.'

'But you and George,' cried the Countess. 'I can't leave you here. I mean, I'm in no danger, but you…'

'You certainly are,' said I. 'And you'll go in up to the neck, if they can establish liaison between you and us. Can you trust your servants, Marya? I mean, you're most certainly watched.'

'I trust Carol,' she said, 'and my maid.'

'What of your gardeners?'

'I have only one, and he is gone to some flower-show and will not be here today.'

'Then we will stay in the garden until you are up. Can you have the shutters shut? Because then I can cross the lawn.'

'At once,' said she. 'You promise you will wait till I come?'

'I promise,' said I. 'And don't worry. We'll give them a run for their money – but nothing else.'

'Please God,' says she softly.

Then she smiled her old, charming smile, slipped through the salon, and stood with her ear to the door. For a moment she waited, listening. Then she waved a slim hand and disappeared.

Two minutes later I heard the shutters closed.

I found Bell where I had left him under the trees.

Now George was not yet due, for, though what had passed since we parted has taken some time to tell, I could hardly expect him till five minutes more had gone by. But what I had learned from the Countess had made me very uneasy on his account, and when twenty minutes had passed, but he had not appeared, I was ready to swear that he had been laid by the heels.

Then there was a sudden scramble, and he came over the wall.

When he had heard me out, he told me his tale.

'I drove the car into the forecourt, parked her bung in the middle, stuck the note back on the windscreen and then got out. Then I strolled to the guard-room and walked inside. When I told the sergeant, he said that it wasn't his business and that I must speak to the porter at the head of some entrance steps. Well, that didn't suit me at all, so I picked up the telephone and asked to speak to the mews. The sergeant began to bristle, but I said that I'd travelled all night to deliver that car and that any sort of obstruction I should report to the Prince. That fixed him, and though he looked pretty surly, he let me be. I don't know who spoke from the mews, but I said that the car was in the forecourt

52

and advised them to come round and get her and wash her face. Then I stalked out of the guard-room and out of the palace gates. Very childish, you know, but my respiration was better the moment I got outside.

'Well, the riverside wasn't crowded. I only met six people and a couple of vans. Nor was the Lessing Strasse. Not crowded. But it wasn't empty, my son. Two fellows were standing talking at Marya's door. One was a red-headed footman, and the other – well, he had a broom and barrow and should have been sweeping the street. I couldn't get over the wall while they were there, so I casually crossed the Strasse and walked straight on. I meant to stroll round the block and then see if they'd gone. But I got an idea and went further… *The Lessing Strasse is the only street that's been watered.* If you remember, we saw the watering-cart. More. It's also the cleanest street of the five I took the trouble to try. The others weren't foul, but there's not a loose leaf in this. *And the wallah with the broom is still sweeping.* When I last saw him he was brushing the trunks of the trees.'

'Observation and collusion,' said I.

'That's right,' said George. 'We're obviously expected. And I'll lay you a bank to a biscuit that Marya won't be permitted to leave the country today.'

'Why not?' said I.

'Because she's the decoy. Once she's gone,

there's nothing to bring us. So we haven't lost our labour. They damned well meant to keep her until we came. They may let her go if they get us, but I guess they want Leonie, too.'

'You're not very cheerful,' said I.

'I don't feel very cheerful,' said George. 'Ever since you said "Grieg", I've had that sinking feeling you read of in books. I can bear the police – with an effort: provided he stands well back, I can even stomach Prince Paul: but Grieg as Chief Constable makes my blood run cold. Never mind. Let's clean the outside of the platter. What's the matter with that tap?'

There was a tap in the bushes to serve the gardener's needs, and, thanks to the gear Bell had carried, we were able to make a rough toilet which did us a world of good.

Then we ate some food and began to discuss the position, which, perhaps because the flesh had been served, proved to be less depressing than it had seemed. Indeed, comparing it with that which we had expected to find, we counted ourselves well off, for we were in touch with the Countess, and though she was under surveillance, she was under no sort of arrest. Provided, therefore, that our presence was not suspected, we had, all four, a good chance of leaving the country that night, for she had a car and we knew the way to go, and though some women would have jibbed at passing beneath the fall, Marya Dresden's courage was of another sort.

Now she had told her chauffeur that we should meet her at Bariche at three o'clock. At two o'clock then, or soon after, she must drive out of Vigil and take the Austrian road. If George was right, she would be stopped at Elsa, the principal frontier-post. Once stopped, it was all-important that she should waste time – for leave before dark we could not – yet give no cause for suspicion by what she did. She must, therefore, protest and argue and endeavour to telephone, and, after that, she must drive to another post and seek to go by. When it was dusk, she could return to Vigil, as though disheartened by her failures to pass the guards, and then we could all leave together and drive for the bridle-path.

We were going over this plan and debating its weaker points, when we saw my lady coming with a posy of flowers she had picked.

She was very good to look at, and the plain black dress she was wearing suited her very well. Her fine short hair was golden, and her skin like that of a child, and when we rose out of the bushes I shall always remember how pretty a picture she made.

She stood very still, with her delicate lips parted and the bright flowers caught up to her breast, and her head half-turned to the house, as though she were fearful that one of the servants would come. The trees were thick with foliage, but little shafts of sunshine that had found their way past the leaves were striking her slim figure and playing with the silk of her stockings and the lights in her beautiful hair.

George stepped to where she was standing and put her hand up to his lips.

'It's as well we came,' he said quietly. 'I may be wrong, but I don't think Pharaoh is going to let Israel go. Your house is watched, Marya.'

'That's because they expect you,' she said.

'No doubt,' said George. 'But until they've seen us roll us, they won't let you go. And I don't like your red-haired footman. He may be all right, but half an hour ago he was having a word with the police.

Marya caught her breath. Then–

'That's the chauffeur,' she said. 'He's the only one with red hair.'

George and I looked at each other.

Our precious plan was crumbling. We dared not trust the Countess to a man in the enemy's pay.

'Bell must drive her,' said I. 'It's the only way.'

'And you?' said Marya, quietly.

When we told her what we proposed, she shook her head.

'I will not go without you,' she said. 'I am in no danger – on that we are all agreed.'

'You're in very grave danger,' said I. 'You are harbouring misdemeanants, for that's what they'll make us out.'

'The car is closed,' said the Countess. 'If Bell is to drive, you two can sit inside and you will not be seen.'

'At what time is it ordered?' said George.

'At half past one.'

'It's out of the question,' said I. 'Do as we say, and–'

'One moment,' said George. 'If she doesn't use her own chauffeur, there'll be the devil to pay. The chauffeur will report it and the man in the street will report it, and they'll telephone to Elsa and tell them to see who's driving and what it means.'

'Then they mustn't go to Elsa,' said I. 'They'll have to lie up in the country until it's dark.'

George shook his head.

'When they don't fetch up at Elsa, the hunt will be up.'

This was true. The Countess must play out her part. She had only to take one step which was not consistent with an effort to get to Bariche to be suspected at once.

Staring before me, I could not think what to do. If only we could put on the clock…

'There is Carol,' said Marya, suddenly.

She made her way to the lawn, and the butler came towards her across the turf.

For some moments they spoke together.

Then he returned to the house, and she strolled up to a border and added some blooms to her posy before she came back. At last she strayed to the bushes behind which we stood.

'They have telephoned from the palace, to say that his Royal Highness will give himself the pleasure of calling upon me at tea time this afternoon.'

'The devil he will,' said George. 'What does that mean?'

Marya shrugged her shoulders.

'It's one way of stopping my going. Because I am in mourning, I cannot be commanded to Court, but that he should pay me a visit is natural enough. Of course, I can make no excuse.'

'That's right,' said I. 'You can't refuse to receive him, and, rather than stop you at Elsa, he's chosen this way.'

'Prince Charming as ever,' said George and sucked in his breath. 'Afraid to declare himself, he uses his damned precedence to cramp his hostess' style. Ask us to meet him, Marya. And then watch him toy with his shrimps.'

'Hush,' said I, laughing. 'He's playing clean into our hands. All she's got to do now is to cancel the car and send a wire to Littai saying "Expect me tomorrow instead of to-day". Then she entertains his lordship, and we all clear out together as soon as it's dark.'

'And till then?' said Madame Dresden. 'You must have food and–'

'We have food with us,' said I. 'Whatever you do, don't try to bring any out. That would give us away in an instant. Go and forget all about us, till after the sweep has gone.'

'Promise me you will stay here,' she said. 'I could not bear to think that you were not within my gates.'

We gave her our word, partly because she would have it and partly because we knew not where else to go.

'That's right,' she said quietly.

The next moment she was gone.

The day did not pass so slowly, for we were all very tired, and two of us slept at a time while the third kept watch. It follows that when it struck four we had each had some five hours' sleep, and, though we were sick of tap-water and would have sold our birthrights to be able to smoke, we felt refreshed and heartened and ready to 'force the game'.

We had, I think, good reason to be content. Our presence was unsuspected, and we had been granted the respite we so much desired. When it was dark, we had but to turn out the car, and we should be five miles off before its departure was reported by the spy in the street: and, before it was gathered that we were not going to Elsa, we should be

59

over the border and nearing the Rolls. The thing was child's play.

Such is the bliss of ignorance. Could we have seen the cards outrageous Fortune was about to draw from her sleeve, our faith would have turned to consternation and there would have been no health in us.

To this day I have not learned at what time the Prince arrived, but I know it was nearly five when I saw him walk on to the terrace and down the steps.

Marya Dresden was behind him, with a hand to her mouth. *And by his side was a wolf-hound with its eyes on its master's face.*

As I gazed, the man peered about him. Then he looked down at the dog and nodded his head...

Now, had the dog made for the bushes, we must have been discovered before we had time to think, but, though it sprang forward, it first dived into a border which it began to search.

'The trees,' breathed George. 'Isn't there one we can try?'

The trees were well-grown and stately, but, though I stand over six feet, the lowest branch I could see was far out of my reach. More. What branches there were were not splayed, like those of an oak, but rose with the trunks, so that only by reaching some fork could a man get any lodgement for hand or foot.

I laid hold of the trunk of the tree beneath which I stood.

'Up on my shoulders,' I said, addressing Bell.

George hoisted him up in a twinkling, and almost before I had felt it his weight was gone.

'Next,' said I. 'That's the style.'

But George did not move. And when I looked round, there was the wolf-hound standing, three paces away.

The dog was young and nervous, but he had an inkling of what he was meant to do, for though he did not give tongue, he let out a growl at my movement and laid back his ears.

'Still as death,' breathed George. 'It's our only chance.'

I heard the Prince raise his voice.

'What is it, Aster?' he cried.

There was no mistaking the nervous suspicion of his tone. He had brought the dog, in case we were in the garden, to find us out.

As the dog bayed in answer, something sprawled through the air from above my head, landed among the bushes and fled for the lawn. At the critical moment Bell had dislodged a cat.

With a whimper of excitement, the dog was gone in a flash…

I had George up in an instant, but when he leaned down to help me, I could not reach his hand.

I whipped to another tree whose branches were not so high, but the cat, which had doubled, ran up the trunk as I got there, and I found the dog leaping beside me and barking as though possessed.

Before I could turn, I heard footsteps and Marya's voice.

'No, if you please, sir – I beg you. I do not want the cat killed.'

'Rot,' said his Royal Highness. 'I hate the brutes. Good dog, Aster. Wait till I find a stone.'

I slipped behind a tree-trunk and hoped for the best.

'Sir, I beseech you,' cried the Countess. 'This is my garden, and I cannot permit even you, sir, to use it so.'

The Prince took no notice at all, and an instant later he was before the tree, panting, and I flat against it, behind.

'Where is she?' he cried to the wolf-hound. 'Where's the – gone?'

Then he side-stepped and saw me, and started back with an oath.

At once I stepped forward.

'Sir,' said I, 'I don't think you heard Madame Dresden. She wishes the cat let alone.'

The man was white as a sheet.

'I knew you were here,' he said thickly. He struck at the leaping dog and pointed to me. 'Seize him,' he cried. 'Seize him.'

The dog, perplexed and bewildered, slunk to my feet. When I put down a hand, he licked me and wagged his tail.

The Prince was trembling with rage.

'This is treason,' he said. 'If you touch me—'

'Don't be a fool,' I said shortly. 'You know why I'm here. To take Madame Dresden to Littai.'

'Then why didn't you come openly?'

'How d'you know I didn't?' I said.

His Royal Highness stamped his foot.

'Don't talk to me,' he raved, and added a filthy oath. 'You've the damned insolence to come here—'

'You brought me,' said I, 'by a lie. You suppressed Madame Dresden's wire and sent another instead. Your service is so putrid that you didn't even know I'd arrived, but you knew I would come – if not today, tomorrow, provided only that you kept Madame Dresden here. So you did her the dishonour of inviting yourself to tea.'

This blunt indictment shook him, as well it might, and when I had done, he was biting his nails like fury, for lack, I suppose, of words.

There was a moment's silence. Then he broke out.

I will not set down his outburst, which, for abuse and incoherence, would have disgraced a groom that was in his cups, but he offered no sort of denial to what I had said.

When he had done, I spoke.

'I tell you I have come to take Madame Dresden to Littai. Will you give orders that we are to be suffered to pass? Now – on the telephone, to Elsa.'

'"Suffered to pass"? We don't deal like that with traitors. We–'

My temper was getting frayed, and I cut the man short.

'This talk of traitors and treason is so much trash. I'm not a subject of yours.'

'No, but *she* is,' he cried, pointing to Madame Dresden. 'She's my subject. And I find you here in her garden, when I visit her unattended and–'

Something moved behind him, and he swung round to see George standing, with fire in his eyes.

'Do you charge that lady with treason?' said George, quietly. 'Because if you do, I'll give you the best of reasons for charging me with assault.'

The Prince recoiled, as though he had seen a ghost.

'Steady, George,' said I. 'What's the good? He'll take it back now and sign a warrant tonight.'

'Go on,' said George, sharply. 'Do you charge her with treason, or no?'

His Royal Highness muttered 'No.'

'Then beg her pardon,' said George. 'Turn

round and beg her pardon for daring to make a suggestion which you knew to be false.'

For a moment the man stood uncertain. The spirit was plainly unwilling, but the flesh with weak.

Then he turned to the Countess and bowed.

'I – I apologise,' he said thickly, speaking between his teeth.

White-faced, but very calm, Madame Dresden inclined her head.

'Lip-service,' said George. 'And here's danger. What do we do?'

As if in answer, the Prince made as though to go by.

'Not yet,' said George shortly. He slid a hand into his pocket. 'Stand where you are.'

'By God,' said the Prince hoarsely, and went very grey.

'Neither move, nor cry out,' said George coolly. 'Don't say I didn't warn you. Bill, I asked you a question. What do we do?'

'We go,' said I. 'In five minutes, with any luck.'

With that, I went to the Countess and spoke in an undertone.

'There's no help for it,' I said. 'Send Carol to summon his chauffeur and, if he has one with him, the footman as well. Send them down here. Say he's hurt his foot or something, and he wants them to carry him out. Then yourself get ready to go. Hat and coat and just your things for the night. The instant you're ready come to the terrace steps.'

'And he?'

'We must take his car. He and his men must be held here until we go.'

'I am desperately afraid, Richard. Is there no other way?'

'I can see none,' said I. 'In the moment he found us here, the fat was burnt. If we cannot get some sort of start, we're all of us done.'

'Very well,' said she, and hastened towards the house.

Now the last thing we wanted was trouble, that is to say, resistance, however slight. To be sure we were all three armed, but while a pistol is always an argument, it loses its force when a man is afraid to fire.

That the Prince would give no trouble, I knew very well, for the man was an arrant coward and would have yielded an empire rather than risk his skin; but though I had little doubt that we could hold up his men, I feared that if they saw his distress, the instinct of bounded duty would compel them to put up a fight.

In vain I looked round for some lodgement, where he could stand at our mercy, yet out of sight.

As I turned to call Bell from his perch, I thought of the tree…

I know his Royal Highness demurred, but,

if I ever listened, I cannot recall what he said. We were pressed for time and I fear we were none too gentle, but once George and I had hoisted him up the trunk, he saw the wisdom of taking Bell's outstretched hand.

An instant later he was lodged in a mighty fork, some twelve feet above the ground, and though with a little discretion he could have scrambled down, I think that he had no stomach for that sort of exercise, for he never moved a muscle, but clung to a branch with his face clapped against the bark, as though in peril of being washed off by some wave, declaring that he was slipping and that we should have his blood upon our heads.

As Bell slithered down to the ground–

'I advise you,' said George, looking up, 'to make no noise.'

With his words, the two servants appeared and, Carol directing them, came clattering down the steps and running across the lawn.

'Their coats and hats,' I breathed. 'We must take his car.'

'Good,' said George. 'You and Bell get out of sight and leave it to me.'

When the men were close to the bushes, he cried out, 'This way,' and once they were under cover, he stepped from behind a tree-trunk and held them up.

Their surprise was ludicrous, and they looked from the pistol to each other as though they were dreaming some dream.

'Put up your hands,' said George.

They did so dazedly.

'Now whether I hurt you,' said George, 'will depend upon you. But I want your coats. Bell, take them off. And their hats.'

To strip them took but an instant.

'Now their boots,' said George. 'Cut the laces. They mustn't be able to run.'

In less than two minutes Bell had their boots in his hands.

'And now turn round,' said George, 'and stand with your face to the wall. March.'

As the men obeyed, I saw a slight figure appear at the head of the steps.

'And now don't move,' said George. 'I'm going to stand here and watch you, and fire at the first that moves. I mean that, mark you. I'm not going to speak again.'

By now Bell and I were wearing their hats and coats, and I took the dog by the collar and gave the sign to withdraw.

We did so in silence, only pausing to hide the boots in a clump of stocks, and when we were all in the salon, I closed the bolted the shutters and shut the windows behind.

'Where's the telephone?' said George. 'We must cut the wire.'

'In the hall,' said the Countess, and ran before...

As Bell took her dressing-case–

'I don't like to leave Carol,' she said. 'You

see, he's involved.'

'Right,' said I. 'Let him put on my hat and coat. And follow in ten seconds, please. I'm going to start the car.'

One minute later the Countess and George and Carol were sitting back in the car we had used that morning, Bell and the dog were beside me, and I was driving all out for the Austrian road.

Our going was none too private. I saw no man that I could have sworn was a spy, yet half a dozen that might have been watching the house, but we met with no sort of obstruction, and if we aroused suspicion, I never saw it declared. I would never have believed it so simple to steal a royal car, but I think that those that were there had not noticed the Arms on the doors and, our livery being plain blue, were not expecting the presence which we had so hurriedly left. When we came to the busier streets, our fortune took on another still more convenient shape, for such police as saw the car coming made haste to clear the way, and the zeal they showed was so active and the compliments they paid were so grand that I could have burst with laughter, while Bell, whose reserve was prodigious, was shaking with mirth.

When we were clear of the city, George leaned out of a window and spoke in my ear.

'Are you going for Elsa?'

'No,' said I. 'I dare not. I believe we've an excellent chance, but supposing we fail…'

'Right,' said George. 'Where then?'

'I'm damned if I know,' said I. 'How long before it's dark?'

'Nearly three hours,' said George. 'It's not yet a quarter past six.'

'Get the map off Carol,' said I. 'It's in my coat. We must dodge across country to Vardar and find some place to lie up.'

I was eager to leave the main road and knew we should find a by-road some five miles on that would take us over the railway and into the hills. I, therefore, wasted no time, and the car being very willing and, in view of its heavy body, unusually swift, we had climbed a steep hill and were approaching the by-road before ten minutes were past.

Now, though I slowed up for the turning, I was not expecting traffic upon such a road, and, anxious not to lose time, I certainly cut my corner more fine than I should. And this was very nearly the end of us all, for there was another car coming and taking, as luck would have it, more than its share of the way.

Thanks to our excellent brakes, a smash was avoided with two or three inches to spare, and, from having come to a standstill, the cars were slowly beginning to draw abreast, when a man leaned out of a window to shake his fist in my face.

I shall never forget that moment or the bitterness which it held, for when a poor wretch 'hath nothing', it is very hard to surrender 'even that which he hath'. In that instant our half hour's start, so hardly won, sank to a few poor moments and what disguise we had was changed to a startling announcement of what we had done.

The man at the window and I had met before.

That scowl, that square jaw, those small eyes – I had reason to remember those features to the day of my death. For they were Grieg's features – the features of the man who had tried his best to kill me and now had 'some job in the police'.

His scowl slid into a stare, and I heard him cry out. And that was all, for I was gone as fast as my gears would let me and had pushed the car up to sixty before thirty seconds had passed.

I spoke to Bell.

'Can you see him?'

'Oh no, sir. The last I saw he was turning. We must have a good minute's start.'

'A good minute...'

'Tell Mr Hanbury to guide me. He's got the map.'

As I spoke, George put out his head.

'Take the first to your right,' he said. 'And then the first to your left. And keep your foot right down. We're leaving a trail of dust

71

about three miles long, and unless we can leave him standing it's simply a paper-chase.'

Now, dust or no, I was very certain that we had the faster car. Provided, therefore, that we met with no serious check, I judged we should shake off pursuit in nine or ten miles. If then we could only vanish *within reach of the bridle-path*, we still had a chance of escaping that very night.

I was less afraid of a check than of losing our way, for we were now over the railway and at this time of year the flocks were upon the hills; but the country was unfamiliar and very blind, and the roads seemed devoid of signposts of any sort. Though the map was true, George was now forced to read it at lightning speed, and to decide in an instant which was the way we sought, and though he was careful never to hold me up, but to give me directions as coolly as though we were riding to hounds, I knew as well as he did that, except he knew the country, no man born of woman could guide a car going so fast.

We flicked through a nameless village and over a hunchback bridge; we were checked by a yoke of oxen passing from gate to gate, each second seeming a minute until the road was clear; for a mile and a half we flung up a twisting lane, so girt and narrow that had we met but a hand-cart we could not have passed; we dropped down into a valley, sped by green water-meadows and switched to the right; we sang up a serpentine hill and into a range of beechwoods that ran for a lady's mile; and we swung to the left at crossroads where – hardship of hardships – a signpost had been blown down.

Of such was that nightmare drive, and when, after thirty minutes, we came to a sudden thicket with a track leading into its heart, I was as ready as George was to, so to speak, go to ground.

Indeed, before he had spoken, I had set my foot on the brake, for if we had come as we wished, we could not be far from the frontier and we might go another ten miles before we found shelter like this.

One minute later we were deep in the wood.

At once I stopped the engine, and all of us sat very still, but all the sounds we could hear were those of the countryside, the twitter of the birds about us and the splash of a neighbouring rill and somewhere, a long way off the lowing of cows.

'Blind leading the blind,' said George, quietly. 'We've beaten Grieg, but I've no idea where we are.'

The daylight we had so much deplored was now the best friend we had, for unless we had found our bearings before night fell, we could not hope to be out of the country by dawn.

We, therefore, sent back Bell to destroy any traces there might be of our entrance into the wood, while the rest of us left the car to follow the track afoot. This soon gave into a meadow which sloped to an idle stream, but on every side rose woodland and we might have stood in some courtyard, for all the way we could see.

We saw no sign of habitation or even of husbandry, and, as soon as Bell had come up, we made our way through the meadow and over the stream. This was happily shallow, and George carried Marya over without a word.

Strangely enough it was our crossing of this water that first brought home to me the truth that we were fugitives, and I still remember the shock of that apprehension and the curious hunted feeling that gripped my heart.

By our treatment of the sovereign we stood guilty of a high misdemeanour, and while two hours ago only some trumped up charge could have been made against us – if, indeed, we were to have been dealt with by any competent court – we had now unmasked against us the heaviest artillery of the law of the land, and if we were taken, nothing on earth could save us from some most miserable fate. The thought that the Countess would share our punishment was insupportable; for though we were all guiltless, and though to this day I cannot see what choice we had but to hold up his Royal Highness and take his car, Marya Dresden had shrunk from such a trespass and had only abetted our action against her will.

For an instant, looking upon her slight figure, I felt the cold breath of panic.

For her sake only we *must* make good our escape. Failure was not to be thought of. By some means, before dawn came, we must stand upon Austrian soil.

It was now past seven o'clock, and the sun was low.

It was therefore arranged that the Countess, with Bell and Carol, should stay in a little dell which ran down to the stream, while George and I set out to find some landmark which we could recognise. Failing this, we must question some peasant, to learn our way, but we hoped to be able to find it without such help, for fear of leaving traces which Grieg who would soon be behind us would be glad to pick up.

We did not like splitting our party, yet felt it most important that the Countess should save her strength; besides, we had not yet determined to abandon the car, for if we should find that we were miles out of our reckoning, we might have no choice but again to take to the roads.

As fast as we could, we climbed to the top of the woods, to discover our view obstructed on every side; and when we had plunged to a valley and had struggled, panting, to the crest of another ridge, there was nothing but woodland before us which two miles ahead swelled into a range of hills. There were mountain and glade and forest and the flash of a stream, but never a road or so much as a curl of smoke, or even cattle straying to argue a neighbouring farm.

'No good,' said George shortly. 'If we go any further we'll probably lose ourselves. Besides, time's getting on. We must go back and try the track.'

By the time we were back in the dell, it was nearly eight o'clock, and the sun was down.

Now, the track running roughly east – that is, away from Vigil and towards the frontier we sought – it seemed best that all should take it, for, come what might, we should not be going directly out of our way, and since we had lost near an hour, we dared not make use of the car for which every village by now would be on the lookout.

So Bell and I put off our borrowed plumes, and the former gave Carol his overalls to cover his butler's dress.

A moment later our anxious march had begun.

Here, I should say that, while George and I had been gone, the dog had strayed into the shadows and had not come back. This was as well. We had only taken him with us to save the poor brute from the vengeance his raging master would have been certain to take, and since there was no name upon his collar, we hoped he would soon be attached to some happier home.

Half an hour went by before we sighted a farm, and the rest of us lay in the bracken, while George went on with Carol to learn the truth. When they came back, George had the map in his hand, but we could not see to read it, and Bell had to bring out his torch.

The farm was the home-farm of some Baron Sabre's estate, upon which, of course, we had been wandering ever since we left the car. As near as we could make it, the bridle-path we were seeking lay twelve miles off. And that was as the crow flies.

There was a dreadful silence.

Then–

'What's twelve miles?' said Marya. 'Come on. We're wasting time.'

I will not set out our progress, for though I shall never forget it, fleeing on foot by night is a business which anyone can picture, and one mile differs but little from that which has gone before; but we very soon decided that we must take to the roads, for, after a spell across country, the Countess for all her spirit began to flag. Besides, it was easier so to keep our way. After eight dragging miles we fell in with a country cart of which the driver was, happily, drunk as a lord. We, therefore, bundled him into the back of his gig, and Carol drove the Countess, while George and Bell and I took it in turns to ride and to shamble behind.

On the farther side of Vardar we left the cart, and, taking the road we had trodden the morning before, hastened along in silence towards our goal.

The time was now two o'clock, and the bridle-path was less than a mile away. I will swear we had been seen by no man, and though two cars had passed us, they had both gone by at high speed and had not seemed to be searching the countryside. If Marya could but continue, our race was as good as won.

From the mouth of the bridle-path to the waterfall was by no means difficult going, but very steep, and I judged that this lap would take us an hour and a half. That meant that day would have broken before we had reached the Rolls, but, once we were over the border, we did not care, for time would be of no moment, and if it seemed best to lie in the woods till dusk – well, what was a few hours' hunger to a few years' lying in jail?

Indeed, we were all exultant, for the strain of finding our way was overpast, and the knowledge that the two hours of darkness that still remained were more than enough to see us out of the country made us a cordial which was rarer than any wine.

Speaking for myself, my weariness seemed to have left me, and the spring came back into my steps and as I turned to look back at the light of the level-crossing on which we had gazed near twenty-four hours before, I saw the humour of our venture and found it rather amusing to have 'singed the King of Spain's beard'.

Then Bell, who was leading, came back to say that ahead were lights which were not those of a dwelling, yet did not move.

The slightest reconnaissance was sufficient to teach us the truth.

The lights were those of two tenders, belonging to Riechtenburg troops. They were standing not twenty feet from the mouth of the bridle-path. This was picketed. I could see the movement of soldiers about a fire. And when I crept closer, I heard a sergeant reporting how he had placed his men.

'In addition to that, sir,' he concluded, 'there are the visiting patrols. I will take my oath that no one can pass our line.'

'Very good,' said his officer. 'And, damn it, mighty quick work. How long is it since we got here?'

'Just twenty-five minutes, sir,' was the proud reply.

CHAPTER 3

In Hiding

Regret was vain. But if it was vain, it was bitter as the salt of the sea.

Our mistakes stood out as glaring as shadows thrown upon a screen, and, prime among them, our folly of leaving the car.

That error was, of course, prodigious, and how we came to make it I do not know; but I think that to Grieg must go the credit of making us lose our race.

Our meeting with the man so shook us as to magnify out of reason the risk we ran of pursuit; and so we swerved from our objective, and, turning from the vital business of gaining the bridle-path, made sure of the trifling matter of covering up our tracks.

Be that as it may, we were beaten, and, though for one frantic moment I was for making an attempt to pass the sentries, the Countess' exhausted condition forbade so forlorn a hope.

Now if we were not to be taken as soon as day broke, we must instantly seek some shelter and indeed be gone into hiding within two hours, for, if troops had been sent to guard the frontier against us, it went without saying that the country would be scoured to find us and that the drive would begin the moment the daylight came. We, therefore, tried to consider which way we had better go, to find ourselves in a very sea of troubles, with nothing to show us which way we had better turn.

Between where we stood and Vardar the country was very open and dotted with farms, and the nearest shelter we knew was the wood in which we had rested by the side of the railway line. And that lay some six miles off – a distance which, without Madame Dresden, I doubt if we could have covered before it was light. Yet, had we been able to make it, what sort of bulwark was a wood when the country was up against us and troops were out? Then, again, we had none of us eaten for nearly twelve hours and, if we avoided capture by lying hid, where was our food to come from, and how could we live? Finally, though it was summer, the nights were fresh, and Madame Dresden, already in need of succour, could never stand an exposure such as not even the peasants were called upon to endure.

We had all but given up hope, when I remembered Ramon, the smith whose forge was at Gola, three miles away.

One minute later we were hastening

towards the village we could not see.

I must confess that I had small hope of success.

I was sure that the man was grateful, but we were about to set him a task which he could not perform. To harbour and feed five strangers in the teeth of the law... Here was work for a noble, with a mansion and trusty servants to do as he said. A village blacksmith could no more do it than fly. Still, he might take in the countess, and Carol might pose as his workman and, being a man of the country, pass unremarked as a helper attached to the forge.

These and such thoughts thrust into and out of my brain, though, what with the shock of disappointment, the danger the dawn was bringing and our weariness of body and soul, I found myself unable to think to any purpose and very soon gave myself up to the business of reaching Gola and finding the forge.

This we did at a quarter past three, and none too soon, for the cocks were already crowing, and the grey of the dawn was stealing over the hills.

The village was very small and seemed to have but one street, but the forge was the first of its houses and stood by itself. For this we were very thankful, for the smith must be awakened, and we had no wish to rouse neighbours upon whom we had no claim.

He must have been a light sleeper, for as I stood back from the oak upon which I had rapped, a window was opened above me and somebody put out his head.

'Ramon,' says George, 'we're in trouble. If you would like to help us, come down and open your door.'

'I come,' said the other quietly, and disappeared.

Not until we were in the kitchen and Ramon's wife was chafing the Countess' hands, did I understand what the latter had undergone. She was by no means fragile, but the strain of the last ten hours had brought her to the edge of collapse, and though she still smiled, she had the air of a runner that has run himself out. Her needs required no statement, and, before we had told her story, Bell was helping the smith to kindle a fire and Carol had been sent to the larder for brandy and milk and bread.

The warmth of the fire revived her, and, thinking it best to leave her to the care of the woman alone, we asked the smith to take us into the forge. And there by the glow of the coals, to the wheeze of the aged bellows we told that good man the truth.

He showed no surprise at our story, still less any fear, but when he heard that I was Leonie's husband, he seemed to regard me as her consort and so entitled to share the esteem and affection in which she had always been held. Indeed, he would have it that the Prince was afraid of a movement to set up my wife in his stead and so was scheming to put us both out of the way, 'for that,' said he, 'would be treason, and you have just told me, my lord, that he gave your conduct that name.'

I shrugged my shoulders and let him have his way.

'Will you shelter the Countess, Ramon? And keep her man?'

'That is easy enough, my lord. God forgive me, but I am known as a smuggler, and no one hereabouts is astonished if we sit down to breakfast one morning four souls instead of two.

'Then that is settled,' said I. 'And now can you recommend shelter for us that are left. If it's not too far, we can make it before the dawn.'

As I spoke, I heard hoofs in the street and a moment later someone was kicking the shutters which kept the mouth of the forge.

'Troopers,' breathed George. 'Who else would knock up a smith?'

Without a word Ramon left us to seek the door of the house, while George slunk close to the shutters to hear what was said.

Before we had recovered our wits, he was asking in broken German to have a horse shod and swearing that he would pay double if the smith would do it at once.

'You must wait until daylight,' said Ramon. 'I cannot yet see.'

'Nor I,' said the other roughly. 'You must do it by candle-light. I tell you, I'll pay you double–'

'At dawn,' said Ramon shortly and shut the door.

As he re-entered the forge–

'Who on earth is that?' said George. 'And what is he doing here?'

'He is out of the circus,' said Ramon. 'I heard it was here. They passed through Elsa last night and are going to a pitch beyond Vardar, to give their show. But they must have been delayed by the way, for they ought to be there by now and taking their rest.'

'And so we should,' said the voice we had heard before, 'if we hadn't been stopped for three hours by the – police. There's something the matter with this country. Never again. And now come on and open.'

Not to be denied, the fellow had entered the house and stood in the little passage that led from the kitchen to the forge.

As Ramon began to protest, I heard the ring of a hoof and a frightened snort.

The next minute all was Bedlam.

By the mercy of God the Countess was gone upstairs, for the kitchen was full of two horses, and one of them cast.

I suppose, being circus horses, they were more bold than most, for they had clearly followed their master in.

Since the street-door led out of the kitchen, they had no hall to cross, and once they were in, no doubt the door had swung to, for when I got there it was shut, and the horse that was still on its feet was essaying the stairs.

As luck would have it, George and Bell and I were well used to horses. But for this chance, I do not know what would have happened, for the kitchen was very small and the poor beasts were mad with fright. Add to this that the one that was cast at once kicked over the table on which stood the candlesticks so that only the fire remained to illumine the scene. Had the smith and the stranger been alone, one or the other would, I believe, have been killed, for it took the five of us all our knowledge and strength to save the horses and get them into the street.

When the flurry was over, their master wiped his face. 'I've a lot to thank you for,' he said, peering. 'Those horses are worth five hundred pounds apiece. Stroke o' luck your being here.' He hesitated. 'Not out of a job are you? My shoeing-smith's down with typhoid, and two of my grooms were stopped at the frontier-post. Their passports were out of order. To tell you the truth, I don't know how to get on.'

He spoke in English. No doubt in the confusion we had given ourselves away.

'Yes,' said I suddenly. 'We're all three out of a job.' I turned to Ramon. 'Let him into the forge,' I said.

Once in the forge, the circus-master looked round.

'I ask no questions,' he said. 'I'm too damned glad to have you. I'll give you three shillings a day and find your food.'

There was a moment's silence.

'Where is your train?' said George.

'By the side of the road,' said the other. 'Five miles the wrong side of Vardar. Why do you ask?'

'Because,' said George, 'we'd better be getting on. You don't want us here, and I guess you've plenty of horses that need to be watered and fed.'

'So,' said the other quietly. 'Well, I daresay you're right. All cats are grey in the dark, aren't they?'

'Exactly,' said George.

The circus-master laughed.

'Seems I fetched up at a very convenient time. What do they want you for?'

'A girl was in trouble,' said George. 'We had the nerve to help her out of this cursed land.'

'Good enough,' said the other shortly.

Then he told us how to get to the circus, and, when we were there, to report to a man called Bach.

'Pitch him some yarn or other. He's very

87

dense. And then get on with the feeding as quick as you can. Watch out for a mare called Ada; she's got ill wind.'

'In two minutes' time,' said George. 'We must have a word with the smith.'

Ramon was with his wife, who was doing her best, poor woman, to put her kitchen to rights. The Countess it seemed had slept through the hullabaloo.

Hurriedly we told him our plan.

'We should be safe,' said I, 'for, as you heard, the police have been through his vans and I don't think it's very likely they'll trouble to do it again. When the Countess awakes, tell her, and say that as soon as it's safe we'll come again. They can't guard the frontier for ever. And once the stir has died down, we'll cross by night. Till then, will you keep her safe?'

'I will, my lord,' said Ramon.

Against his will I gave him what money I had.

'That's for expenses. Carol must be clad as a peasant, and I think it would be as well if her ladyship changed her clothes. And now we must go. If you want us, you know where to find us. If we don't come before then, send us word the moment the troops are withdrawn.'

Then we spoke to Carol and told him to serve his mistress as best he could and that as Ramon said he must do in every particular.

Thirty seconds later we were out of the house.

It was broad daylight before we reached the train, and I shall ever remember the feeling of thankfulness with which we stepped in among the horses and asked for Bach.

The latter seemed dazed – I imagine, for want of sleep, and I doubt if he heard the story we tried to tell; in any event, he was past caring who we were or whence we came, so we were to help him in a labour which Hercules might have shirked. He had but two stableboys that were fast asleep, and more than thirty horses were in his charge, all of them good to look at and most of them cross.

We told him what Reubens had said – for that, we learned was the circus-master's name – and hearing the song of a brook behind a hedge, asked him to give us buckets and fell to work.

By the time that Reubens was back, all the horses had been properly watered and fed; five minutes later the circus was under way.

From then till the show was over, no one, so far as I saw, either rested or ate; myself, I have never worked harder in all my life, and had we not broken our fast before we started, we could not, I think, have endured such gruelling toil. That everyone was too busy and, later too much exhausted to trouble about new faces was very clear, and

I think that half the circus were strangers to one another and that life was too hard for the members of that unhappy fellowship to take any interest in any affairs but their own.

Indeed, if only the police did not repeat their visit, we seemed to be safe, for our time was spent in the horse-lines, from which the public was barred, and Reubens did not suggest that we should enter the ring.

Before the evening performance we had a short rest and were able to eat some rations which Bach produced. Whilst we were eating, Reubens came down the lines, tricked out in a ring-master's dress, to say that the tents would be struck at eleven o'clock and that we should leave at midnight for Janes, twelve miles away.

There was nothing to be said: but Janes was twelve miles from Vigil, from which we were now twenty-four.

When the Jew was gone, we sought to consider our plight.

We could not get out of the country: therefore, we must lie hid. So long as we stayed with the circus, we were comparatively safe. That the circus was moving westward was most unfortunate: for one thing, we were leaving the Countess: for another, each step that we took would have to be later retraced.

We bitterly repented that we had not thought to tell Ramon where we had left the Rolls and bade him take out the Countess

90

the instant the troops were withdrawn. This would have been common sense, but the stress of the moment had played the deuce with our wits, and now, like all the others, that chance was gone.

There was nothing to be done.

After a little we lay down and slept like the dead – for less than an hour.

At eleven o'clock that night we assisted to strike the tents, and shortly after midnight we shambled on to the road.

From Janes we went to Vigil.

Our pitch lay west of the city, some two miles out. Our feelings may be imagined, yet what could we do?

We saw no papers, heard nothing of what was happening, feared to inquire. We could not communicate with Madame Dresden, still less with Leonie. Lest we be recognized, we dared not leave the horse-lines, much less dared leave the circus, for without some means of transport we could not even reach Gola during the night.

But for the Countess, our way would have been plain enough. After five more days the circus would leave Riechtenburg, crossing the western frontier on Thursday night. Here the country was flat, and the river which made the border was, I knew, used by barges and could not, therefore, be dangerous to men that could swim. Even if the troops were still out – and this seemed unlikely – we ought to be able to evade them without any fuss. But that was a dream. The moment we dared, we must return to Gola. Reason suggested that we should return very soon. What frightened me most of all was that Leonie, hearing no news, might act for herself.

One good thing we had of Vigil, and that was a full night's rest. But when I awoke the next morning, I then and there made up my mind to leave the circus that night.

When I told George, he nodded.

'I wondered,' he said, 'how long you'd be able to stand it. I would have left at Vardar, but I thought that if you could stick it, why, so could I.' He took a deep breath. 'Marching the wrong way is bad for my heart. So is suspense. For all we know, Marya Dresden was taken two hours after we left.'

'God forbid,' said I.

'Amen,' says George. 'Never mind. Do we tell Fred Karno, or no?'

'I think so,' said I. 'I'm not mad about his style, but we don't want to let the man down.'

'I've no compunction,' said George, 'about walking out. The man hasn't helped us he's used us. We've taken no money and far more than earned our keep. No one would work as we have for this food and three shillings a day.'

'I know,' said I. 'All the same, he's been

very convenient.'

'So've we,' said George. 'Very. Never mind. You're usually right.'

Half an hour later Reubens came down the lines.

'This afternoon,' he said, blinking. 'I'll want one of you in the ring. Ada kicked up a fuss last night, and these – boys are afraid. What's more, the mare knows it. She'll play them up to glory, and so I must have one of you.'

George shot me a glance. Then–

'I'm sorry,' he said. 'but we can't show up like that.'

The Jew looked down his nose.

'The police won't be there,' he said, softly.

'Perhaps not,' said George. 'But, frankly, we mustn't be seen.'

Reubens tapped his teeth with the knob of his riding whip.

'This is damned awkward,' he said. 'Strikes me I'm guilty of harbouring.'

'I don't see that,' said George. 'You were short-handed, and we came and asked for a job.'

'And got it in one,' said the other. 'No questions asked. You know as well as I do, I'm taking a hell of a risk.'

'I fail to see it,' said George. 'We've given you no cause for suspicion.'

The Jew looked at him curiously.

'That's true,' he said. 'No cause for suspicion – to date. At least, no cause they can prove.' He hesitated. 'Well, don't give me one – that's all. If you do – well, I don't want to hurt you, but I've got to look after myself.'

There was a little silence.

'Do you mean,' said George, 'that you want us to enter the ring?'

'No,' said the other. 'I guess I can climb that fence. But don't show me one that I can't. You know that we move at midnight?'

'I'd heard so,' said George.

'Well, don't forget,' said Reubens.

With that, he was gone.

'There you are,' said George. 'What did I say? That's what they call "the straight tip." "Leave me, and I go to the police." It's just as well we didn't tell him.'

I shrugged my shoulders.

'Business,' I said. 'Reubens is a business man.'

'He's a dirty dog,' said George violently.

'There's just one thing,' said I, thinking and speaking my thoughts. 'Why should he come and say this? Why should he think we were thinking of clearing out?'

George looked at me.

'You're right,' he said. 'He'd some reason. What does he know?'

The question remained unanswered till near midday.

A boy had come round with papers about ten o'clock, and, while he was drawing the rations, we looked at the one Bach had bought.

The manoeuvres which the 4th Brigade was suddenly called upon to perform came to an end last night. In a General Order the G.O.C. expresses his satisfaction with the energy and keenness displayed by all ranks and especially with the alacrity with which they responded to the alarm, the intention to raise which had been kept secret even from the Commanding Officers.

We determined to go that night, moving with the circus and leaving it in the first half which was called upon the road.

The afternoon performance was nearly done, and the mischievous Ada was kicking her way through her tricks when Bell whipped up to my side.

'Look, sir,' says he. 'There's Carol. He's trying to catch your eye.'

It was true.

Clad in white linen, as a peasant, the butler was alternately watching and clapping his chin to his shoulder to see if he was observed. He had come, of course, to tell us the troops were gone.

As I have said, the public was not allowed to approach the lines, but, the show being on, I suppose there had been no one to stop him and Bach and the stable-boys were busy at the mouth of the tent.

I was by the man's side in an instant.

'Quick,' said I. 'We mustn't be seen. Is the Countess safe?'

Carol nodded and gave me a little note.

Richard,
Do everything Carol says, and do it at once.
Marya.

As George came hastening, I gave it into his hand.

'What are we to do, Carol?'

The butler pointed north.

'On the road over there, sir,' he said, 'there is waiting a car. It has just brought me and is ready to take us all back.'

A car … in waiting…

I could hardly believe my ears.

'Now?' said George stupidly. 'Now?'

'At once, sir. It is very important that you should lose no time.'

'Go on,' said George. 'We'll be there as soon as you.'

As he turned, came the burst of applause which always followed Ada's endeavours to dance.

In another instant Bach would be back in the lines. And a hundred yards distant, this side of the gateway which gave from the road to the pitch, sat a couple of mounted police.

Only waiting to take up our coats, George and Bell and I slipped through a gap in the hedge against which the lines had been pitched. Under cover of this we ran the length of the field and then slid down a high bank and into a lane. This ran north and south... A moment later we padded into the road. There was but one car to be seen, for those that were waiting to take people back from the circus were parked to the east. As we hastened towards it, Carol emerged from the field and stood to its door.

The bonnet was facing away, and we could not see who was driving or whether he sat alone, but, as we drew near, the car seemed faintly familiar, as though I had noticed its like a short time before.

As we came up, I heard the engine running...

Then we were all inside, and the door was shut.

Instantly the car moved eastward.

It was a cabriolet, and its hood was up. In front sat two men, wearing dustcoats and peaked blue caps.

'And now,' said George, 'what has happened? How on earth has Madame contrived to get hold of this car?'

'Sir,' said Carol, 'I am simply obeying orders. I know no more than do you what Madame has done.'

Both of us stared at the man.

'You know more than we do,' said I. 'Have you come straight from the forge?'

'No, sir. I've come from Bariche, where Madame is now.'

'Bariche?' screeched George. *'Bariche?* Oh, give me strength. D'you mean she's over the border?'

'That's right, sir. We're going there now.'

'But how on earth–'

'Sir,' said Carol, 'I am as bewildered as you. Less than an hour ago Madame gave me that note to give you and told me to enter the car.'

'At Bariche?'

'At Bariche, sir. At the sign of *The Broken Egg.*'

'When did she leave Gola?'

'Yesterday, sir. A little before midday.'

'But why? How came she to leave?'

'I do not know, sir. I was at work in the fields, and when I came back she was gone. Last night this car came to fetch me, but I have not spoken with Madame except to receive her orders to come and fetch you.'

Try as we would, we could wring no more out of the man.

The car went wide of Vigil and joined the Austrian road four miles from the town. I think it was the sight of a corner which I shall never forget that flickered that page of my memory which I had not been able to turn.

'My God!' I cried all of a sudden. *'This is*

Grieg's car.'

For a moment there was dead silence.

Then—

'That's right,' said George quietly. 'And those two chauffeurs are police.' He sat back and closed his eyes. 'After this nothing will surprise me. I don't know what Marya's done, but I take my hat right off and put it under the seat. I mean, this is more than artistic. Grieg's car at our disposal to take us out. *Grieg's.* I suppose Prince Paul will be at Elsa with a bunch of sweet peas.'

At the mention of Elsa, Carol moistened his lips.

'When you came to the frontier, sir, I was to tell you to be careful to sit out of sight.'

For a moment we stared at the man.

Then—

'I give it up,' said George weakly. 'I thought she'd been pulling wires, but it seems I was wrong. Marya has done it on them. Marya. Marya Dresden has done it on Grieg.'

I confess that I sat confounded.

That Marya Dresden unaided should have brought off this dazzling coup was inconceivable. We had left her shaken and exhausted, with the fear of arrest upon her, thankful to hide her head. Now by some extraordinary means, she was not only up and doing, but had herself escaped and was bringing us to safety upon our arch-enemy's back. The thing had the smack of an exploit

99

out of a page of Dumas – of arras and wine and a ring which those who were shown were bound to obey.

Presently we came to Elsa, and George and I sat back, while the others kneeled down on the floor.

The precaution seemed to be needless, for the car and its police were plainly known to the sentries, and those of both countries merely nodded their heads.

Even at this distance of time I find it hard to express the relief we felt at regaining Austrian soil. For four full days we have lived and moved in a nightmare of apprehension, helplessly stumbling upon ground which we knew very well might any moment give way. Riechtenburg was a cage into which we had been decoyed: its keepers were men from whom, if we were taken we could expect no mercy because both we and they were without the law. No unhappy wretch stepping out of the jurisdiction of the Court of Star Chamber ever breathed more freely than we.

Twenty minutes later the car slid into Bariche and up to the door of an inn.

Carol was out in a flash.

'Madame is on the first floor, sir. Will you please to go up?'

We needed no bidding, and George ran before me into the humble house.

At the head of the stairs was a servant, with a tray in her hands.

'The Countess Dresden,' cried George. 'Which are her rooms?'

The woman stared.

'The Countess Dresden?' she said.

'The lady,' I cried. 'The lady that came here today – yesterday. The one that has rooms on this floor.'

Before the woman could answer–

'Excuse me, sir,' said Bell's voice.

I turned to see him standing with a note in his hand.

'What is this?' said I, for the envelope bore no address.

'I've no idea, sir. Carol put it into my hands and asked me to give it to you.'

With a cry, George snatched the letter and ripped its envelope off.

My dears,

I am to have a pardon, but I could not get one for you. You must never, never enter this country again. One condition of my pardon is that I do not leave Riechtenburg, and another that no communication whatever shall pass between you and me. I am sure you will respect this for my sake. Goodbye.

Marya.

George let fall the letter and clapped his hands to his face.

As he did so, I heard the sound of gears being hastily changed...

I took the stairs at one bound, but George was first in the street.

The car, which had gone about, was thirty yards from the inn and was gathering speed. Carol was standing on the step, holding fast to the screen.

'Stop!' yelled George Hanbury. '*Stop!*'

His cries were disregarded, and twenty seconds later the car swung round a bend and we saw it no more.

Passers by had stopped and were staring, but George stood still in the road, with his eyes on the cloud of dust.

After a little, I went up and took his arm.

He turned at that, as though I had aroused him from a stupor, and I cannot forget the tragedy in his face.

'She's bought us off,' he said thickly. 'Marya's bought us off. She's not done a deal with the Prince, or our being seen by the sentries wouldn't have mattered a damn. Grieg's car. Grieg's men. She's done a deal with Grieg … and she's bought us off.'

Sitting in a tiny room at *The Broken Egg,* we sought to piece together what fragments of truth we had.

Marya had made some arrangement to which she knew very well that we should never consent. Carol had, therefore, been taken into her confidence and had been charged to betray us into playing her game.

Everything was pointing to some private arrangement with Grieg, who was without any doubt double-crossing the Prince. Her statement that she was to be pardoned was, therefore, no more than surmise: only the Prince could pardon, and the Prince so far knew nothing of what had been done. As for the 'conditions' of her pardon, these she had clearly invented to keep us out of the country and prevent us from asking questions to which she could make no satisfactory reply.

Of the nature of her bargain with Grieg we dared not think. The man was harsh and brutal and knew no law. More. He had good reason to hate us with all his might. The price he had set upon our freedom must have been very high...

Before twenty minutes were past, our plans were made.

I made them, and George approved them. What Marya meant to him, I had not guessed. But now there was no mistaking the frantic look in his eyes.

I think we both shrank from using the bridle-path. That way was too slow and was now most likely suspected as one which lawbreakers took. Besides, we could not take it except by night, and that would mean wasting time, for darkness was three hours off. What was more, that path would bring us into the danger zone. If we were to come to Vigil – and that, of course, was our aim –

we must not attempt to traverse the region through which we had fled. Now Riechtenburg is only a little country, some half the size of Ireland, or thereabouts. By using the Rolls, therefore, in a very few hours we could reach the western frontier without leaving Austrian soil. As I have said, that border would be easy to cross, and since it was the furthest from Littai, it was not likely that, if we were still to be sought for, we should be sought for there. That it lay far from Vigil could not be helped. At least, we were sure we could cross it, while of the southern border we knew nothing at all.

I have said we were bound for Vigil. Our one idea was to get into touch with the Countess and so with Grieg. Now that she had struck some bargain, the fellow was likely to allow her to go to her house. The bargain, whatever it was, must depend on the Countess' health, and this had been put in peril by what she had undergone. And so he would send her home. The Prince might rave about treason, but Grieg would not care for that. The man knew too much. If he wished to preserve the Countess, the Countess would be preserved.

Here I may say that, so far as appearance was concerned, we were much more fit for our venture than we had been five days before. Our linen was foul, we had not shaved for four days, and our heavy work with the horses had gone far to ruin our clothes. I do not pretend that we could have borne inspection, but it was perfectly clear that we could pass in a crowd.

The first thing, then, to be done was to reach the Rolls. To this end we hired a car and were driven up to the farm.

Rowley's relief to see us was overwhelming. Between fear for us and inaction, the poor man was at his wit's end. Three nights running he had gone up the bridle-path and had actually tracked us to the side of the rushing stream, only to return more troubled than he had set out and more than ever uncertain what he should do. He had had no razor and stood as unkempt as we, for, to pass the time, he had been tending swine and setting to rights a byre which was very foul.

His state decided me to take him with us and to send Bell back to Littai, to give Leonie our news. This, when we had been brought to the river we meant to cross, for events had shown that to keep a car in waiting was an unprofitable precaution and that though, as luck would have it, we now were glad of the Rolls, this was a chance in a thousand which would not occur again.

When I saw Rowley so moved, the concern I had felt for Leonie's peace of mind rose into a wave of apprehension which would not be stilled. If her spirit was high,

105

my wife was of Riechtenburg and so knew far better than Rowley the danger in which we should stand if ever the Prince came to know that we were within his gates. The five full days of silence must have passed very slowly at Littai and the shocking fear that, unable to bear such suspense, she had herself started to find us kept laying hold of my heart. I would, indeed, have given the world to see her, but for me to visit Littai would have meant a delay of eight hours, and, since any waste of time was not to be thought of, I sought to console myself by insisting that Bell would be with his mistress before another day broke.

When we left the farm, it was not yet eight o'clock, and, the way being easy to find, we went very fast, first of all driving due south and then very nearly due west and skirting the Riechtenburg frontier all the way.

We had covered some ninety miles, when I, who was keeping the map, gave George some wrong direction, and, since it was now very dark, a quarter of an hour went by before we discovered my mistake. This we did by running into some suburbs much too substantial to be ignored by the map, yet not marked upon the road which we had intended to take. What was worse, when George had slowed down, I could not perceive my mistake, for, to judge by the map, there was no town for thirty miles round, save only one called Sallust, and that stood in Riechtenburg.

It seemed dreadfully clear that we were miles out in our reckoning, and that at a time when we had not a moment to lose.

Bitterly reproaching myself, I called to a passing soldier and asked him the name of the place. He said at once that it was Sallust.

'Sallust?' I cried. 'But Sallust is in Riechtenburg.'

'Ay,' said the man, 'the old town. But this is the new. They are all one really, but the river divides them in two. If you want to go in' – he pointed – 'that is the way to the river, and so to the bridge. The Customs are there.'

With that, he was gone, and George and I studied the map. This gave no sign of any such state of affairs, but it showed that Sallust stood forty miles from Vigil, while the point for which we had been making lay sixty-five.

'This is the place,' said George. 'With a dual population restrictions are bound to be slack.'

As he spoke, he let in the clutch...

He took the Rolls down to the river and berthed her under some limes. Then we alighted and strolled along the bridge.

This was busy. Maybe because it was Sunday, all sorts and conditions were crossing, and nearly everyone was going to Riechtenburg. In the midst of the bridge a movable bar or turnpike prevented all wheeled traffic and forced the people afoot to go by in single file. Here the rule of the road was strictly observed, and whichever way a man passed he kept the bar on his left. Those going to Riechtenburg went without let or hindrance, but those coming out were inspected by three of that country's police. Leaning on the bar were four sentries, engaged in talk and glancing now and again at such as approached the police.

All this we could see very well without being seen, for on either parapet, directly in line with the bar, was a huge wrought-iron lantern, dispensing electric light.

I cannot pretend that I liked it, but this seemed to be our chance. For all the attention paid them, those that were going our way might have been leaving the gates of a football ground, and, indeed, they gave the impression of going home after some entertainment from which they had been lately dismissed. If this were so and we were indeed to join them, it was clearly unwise to delay, for any moment their number would begin to diminish and this would increase such risk as we were to run. Without more ado, I therefore, gave Bell his instructions and bade him get back to the car.

We watched his retreating figure, and when the Rolls had stolen into the shadows, we turned to the bridge.

By one consent we parted, and casually mingled with such as were going our way…

As I was leaving the road, I saw George nearing the bar in the midst of the bridge, and though I could not see Rowley, I knew that he was between us, for I had watched him go on.

It was well we had wasted no time, for already those crossing were fewer than when we had first arrived, but, the passage by the bar being narrow, the press there was still thick enough to offer a fair protection to a man that stuck close to the wall.

Now as I came up to the bar, I found myself next to a peasant who had drunk more than his fill. He was not reeling, but he was very unsteady, and he cursed and muttered as though he was sick of life. He was bearing upon his shoulder a basket of good-looking figs, which threatened every moment to leave their perch, and I could not help thinking that if they came safe to market, their porter would be lucky indeed. I think the press annoyed him, for he was in that condition which needs more than ordinary room, and, when he stumbled against me, he cursed me loudly as though the fault had been mine.

This conduct attracted so much notice that I could have broken his neck, but, since I could not withdraw, there was nothing to be done but go forward and hope for the best.

We were full in the light of the lamps when

he stumbled and cursed me again.

'Order, there. Order,' cried a sentry – and brought the sweat out on my face.

But worse was to come.

As I made to pass by the turnpike, the drunkard thrust for the gap. Then he struck my shoulder with his basket and sent its burden flying all over the flags.

I suppose it was natural that he should hold me to blame.

Had he not seized me, I could have gone on my way: but his outcry was such that the people ahead turned back to see what the matter might be and before I could shake him off a ring had been formed.

Afraid that my speech would betray me, I let the man rave. Then I shrugged my shoulders and began to pick up the fruit.

As I straightened my back–

'Whence do you come?' said a voice.

Two of the police were looking me up and down.

'From Switzerland,' I replied. 'I am making a walking tour.'

'Your passport, please,' said one, and put out his hand.

'I'm afraid I've lost it,' said I. 'I am going to the consul at Vigil as soon as I can.'

'Without a passport we cannot allow you to pass.' He turned to his fellow. 'It cannot be one of them. He is going the opposite way.'

The other shrugged his shoulders.

'He answers the description,' he said. 'You say you are walking. Where did you sleep last night?'

He could not have asked a wrong question. I had no idea of the country which, had I come from the west, I must have passed through.

'I slept at a farm,' I said. 'I do not know the name of the place.'

'What was the last town you passed?'

Frantically I cudgelled my brains. I had read some names on the map, but, because they did not concern us, they had not stayed in my mind.

'I cannot remember.'

There was a moment's silence.

Then—

'He must come to the station,' said the one that had spoken last.

'Yes,' said the other softly, with the queerest look in his eyes, which were fast on my coat.

The next instant he fell upon me, shouting some words of *patois* which I could not understand.

To struggle was hopeless, and so I stood perfectly still. Then a hand went into my pocket and brought my pistol out.

CHAPTER 4

The Common Enemy

Now as is sometimes the way, the blow having fallen, I instantly felt more at ease and was able to think more clearly and measure what chances I had.

The discovery of my pistol plainly convinced my captors that I was one of the culprits whose arrest was so earnestly desired, for they could not hide their excitement and they held one to each of my arms as though I had mastered the trick of slipping out of my skin. I, therefore, took care to continue to stand very still, and, after arranging with the sentries to bear their fellow a hand, they turned me about, and we started towards the old town.

I cannot blame them for fearing that I should try to escape, for I fully intended to do so before they could lodge me in jail. Unless I was much mistaken, the streets would be poorly lit, and while I am as strong as most men, George and Rowley would certainly shadow my progress and the instant I made my effort would come to my aid.

For the moment I could do nothing

because of the throng, but I said in my heart that, once we had passed off the bridge, the crowd would quickly diminish and leave me a clear enough field.

Here I was sorely mistaken.

I can only suppose that the vigilance shown by the police for the last three days had aroused such an interest as Sallust had seldom known and that, now that an arrest had been made, everyone that was not abed came running to see the victim and prove the achievement true. What was far worse, they were not content to stand and watch me go by, but must move the way I was going and so form a curious escort through which no prisoner could break.

Indeed, I soon saw that it was hopeless, for George and Rowley could never have won to my side, and when, by the light of some lamp, I caught sight of the former's face, I made haste to shake my head as though to forbid an endeavour which could not succeed.

We passed up a long, steep alley and turned to the left, the crowd all the time increasing and seeming to bear us along, and plainly proposing to see me into the jail. No Barabbas was more duly attended, and, though I was shown no ill will, the progress had the air of a triumph, as many marching in front as were marching behind.

Again we turned, to enter a very old street,

where the houses seemed to be topless and the yellow-burning lamps to shed more shadows than light. For a crime or a rescue it was a likely place, and I could have stamped to behold the very venue I had wished for, yet now could not use. Then a large, hollow, metal body fell suddenly out of the air and into the press of people directly ahead.

I cannot describe the confusion the incident caused.

The street being dark, no one had seen the ponderous missile in flight, but the noise which it made on the cobbles and the yells of pain and dismay from such as had embarrassed its fall declared some misadventure of an unusual sort. Eager to sift the mystery, those behind pressed forward and those in front turned back, while those that were hurt and their neighbours fought and clamoured to leave the danger point.

It follows that my captors and I were very soon jammed in the press, for although they demanded way, they might as well have addressed the waves of the sea.

Now had they contrived to emerge, my rescue would have been done, for, except for George and Rowley, they would clearly have had all the rest of the street to themselves: but though they tried, they could not, and when I tried, they withstood me, because, I suppose, they thought I was trying to escape.

So we heaved and swayed and shouted, while two good minutes went by. Then I saw the flash of a torch approaching the scene and three more police came bustling to seal my doom.

They had come, of course, to see what the outcry might be, but as soon as they learned what manner of prisoner I was, they made a way for their fellows and the five of them carried me off.

The station stood in a square a little way off, and before five more minutes had passed, I was hauled up a flight of broad steps and into a low-pitched hall, where two or three police were standing about a small fire of logs. From there I was led to a room in which an inspector sat, and to him the police that had seized me told their tale. Then I was questioned, but stuck to what I had said, and after two jailers had searched me they thrust me into a cell.

I was presently given some supper of which I was very glad, for though we had eaten at Bariche, that meal had been hasty and broken and our drive through the cool, night air had served to sharpen a hunger that had been but half appeased; and when my supper was done I made bold to smoke, for, though they had turned out my pockets, the jailers had taken nothing but only the map.

I cannot think why I assumed that I should be kept at Sallust until the next day, but I was about to make the best of my pallet, when I heard the sound of an engine whose throttle is thrown wide open and suddenly closed. I listened carefully. Then came steps in the hall, and some door was opened and shut.

I could tell from the engine's note that the car was not that of Grieg, but I guessed it had come from Vigil and had brought two or more detectives to carry me back.

I sat down on my stool and waited, but not for long.

Almost at once the jailers came to fetch me, and thirty seconds later I was back in the inspector's room.

The scene stands out of my memory, clean and sharp.

As I had expected, there stood two plain-clothes men, one of whom I judged a sergeant, both of whom looked civil, but very grave. A little apart stood the police that had made my arrest. Two more uniformed police were standing against the wall, and behind a rude, deal table the inspector sat back in his chair. One of the whitewashed walls was bright with steel: handcuffs and chains and even a pair of fetters hung from their several nails. Over all one unshaded lamp was throwing a brilliant light.

At a gesture from the inspector the jailers turned on their heels and left the room.

There was a moment's silence: some

excitement that I could not interpret was in the air: the local police were gazing at the detectives, and the latter were speaking together below their breath.

The inspector leaned suddenly forward.

'We are right?' he said. 'It – it is he?'

The detective-sergeant nodded.

'Yes,' he said. 'It is he.'

An audible sigh of relief ran round the room, and the stir that always follows the lifting of some suspense made itself heard.

A moment later the inspector was repeating the report which my captors had made.

Before he had got very far, the detective-sergeant frowned.

'"Coming into the country?"' he said. 'You mean "going out".'

At once the police that had found me insisted that I had come in, to the plain contempt of the detectives, who flatly refused to allow that I had not been in the act of leaving the land. Such confident disbelief was most provoking, and I was not surprised when my captors began to bridle and give back scorn for scorn. An argument so conducted could have but one end, and before a minute was out the four had lost their tempers and were doing their utmost to shout each other down.

Now whilst they disputed, I thought – and that very hard.

Our suspicion of Grieg's misconduct was

fully confirmed. No one but he and his chauffeurs had any idea that we had been driven to Bariche six hours before. From Prince to constable, the executive of the country had been betrayed.

It occurred to me that I held one very good card, and since I had had my fill of losing chances, I decided to wait no longer, but play it forthwith.

A lull in the altercation gave me the opening I wished.

'Gentlemen,' said I, looking round, 'I have a statement to make. I think it will be of interest to everyone here. But before I do so, be good enough to give me a chair. I am something tired of standing, and I think I have a right to sit down.'

There was an electric silence.

From behind his table the sturdy inspector stared.

'What right?' he said, frowning.

'This,' said I. 'I am Richard Chandos, husband of the Grand Duchess Leonie.'

The inspector laughed.

'Aha,' said he. 'I have been waiting for that. We were told you would probably dare to take that name.'

I shrugged my shoulders.

'So I was christened,' I said. 'But we will not argue the point. His Royal Highness may well deny me. If the Baron Sully were here–'

The man started out of his seat, and his

four subordinates gazed at me open-mouthed. Only the two detectives showed no surprise.

At length–

'Is this true?' said the inspector weakly.

'Yes,' said the senior detective. 'It is perfectly true.'

The inspector took a deep breath.

'I should have been told,' he said shakily.

'How could I know?' He turned on the gaping constables. 'Fetch his lordship a chair, you fools. You heard what he said.'

A chair was hurriedly brought, and I sat myself down.

'And now,' said I, 'for my statement. The officers that took me are perfectly right. I was not leaving the country. I had that instant come in. I had come by car from Bariche as fast as I could.'

'From Bariche?' cried a detective.

'From Bariche,' said I.

'But, sir, you were two miles from Vigil at half-past five.'

'So Reubens told you,' said I. 'Well, Reubens told you the truth. I was within his horse-lines at half-past five. And at half-past six I was at Bariche, at the sign of *The Broken Egg*. I crossed the border at Elsa, *and I travelled in Major Grieg's car.*' There was a gasp of amazement, and I heard the detective-sergeant smother an oath. 'He put me out of the country to serve some end of his

119

own; but I don't much like his assistance, and so I came back.'

With that, I described Grieg's chauffeurs and the inside of his car; and I bade them ring up Elsa and ask if this had not passed twice between six and seven o'clock.

They heard me out in a silence big with wrath, and seemed to be very willing to believe what I said.

When I had done—

'Tell me one thing, sir,' said one of the plain-clothes police. 'Between Vigil and Elsa are they anywhere mending the road?'

'Yes,' said I. 'Some two miles this side of Elsa we passed a roller at work.'

'That's right,' said his fellow. 'They started this afternoon.'

'I can beat that,' said I, and showed them the bill for the food we had had at *The Broken Egg*. This was dated and bore the name of the house.

In silence the paper was passed from hand to hand.

'So you see,' said I. 'I shouldn't report to Grieg. I mean, he's let you down once.'

A sound like a snarl of approval came from the uniformed police, but trouble looked out of the two detectives' eyes.

'It is done, sir,' said the sergeant. 'He must have learned that you were taken almost as soon as we.'

'Where is he?'

'At the seat of the Baron Sabre, who is away just now, whose cousin he is.'

'Baron Sabre.' His was the spreading estate upon which we had lost our bearings four days before. If she was not at Vigil, the Countess...

I wrenched my thoughts away and fingered my chin.

'Grieg's appointment is very recent. To whom would you have answered a fortnight ago?'

'To the Chief of Police, sir. But this is a special job.'

'I can well believe that,' said I. 'Never mind. The point is this. I've shown you that Grieg is a blackguard and–'

'You have that, my lord,' mouthed the inspector. 'A price of five hundred pounds had been set on your lordship's head.'

With his words, the scales fell from my eyes. By making my disclosure, I had done better than I knew. Grieg might be a traitor, but he was also a thief. By putting me out of the country, he had wilfully taken the bread out of his subordinates' mouths. That I had restored it so handsomely was beside the point. Every man in that room was thirsting to bring Grieg down.

I pressed my advantage home.

'And on those of my friends?'

'Two hundred and fifty, my lord.'

'Well, that's gone,' said I. 'They went with

121

me to Bariche and you'll never see them again.' The inspector choked. 'And now, as I was saying, the point is this. The moment Grieg learns that I'm here, his one idea and object will be to – to shut my mouth. He will, therefore, come here to get me and take me away *alone*. Well, I don't mind standing my trial, but I've no desire to be murdered – you know what he is.'

There was a pregnant silence.

At last a detective spoke.

'Will you write out a statement, sir, of all you have said?'

'With pleasure,' said I, rising.

'That we can take, with the bill from *The Broken Egg,* and show to the Chief of Police. And on those he will surely act.'

'Too late,' said I.

'If you write it at once, sir, we will return to Vigil and go to his private house. Then he will give us an order which Major Grieg dare not defy.'

'And if he comes while you are gone?'

'He will not, sir,' said the sergeant. 'He will not come before day.'

I took my seat at the table and started to write.

My statement must have read very ill, for I am no German scholar, and though I can speak well enough that unattractive tongue, I could not write down correctly one half of the words I use. Besides, I wasted no time, for I knew I had spoken the truth and that Grieg, full ripe for murder, was on his way.

One lie only I told, and that was that George had set me down at Sallust and then gone with Bell to Littai, to comfort my wife.

Then I subscribed my name, and pinned to the sheet the bill of *The Broken Egg*.

As I got to my feet–

'I think,' I said grimly, 'I think that should fix Major Grieg.'

'Sir,' said the sergeant, 'you have just signed his death warrant.'

With his words came the squeal of brakes, and then the heavy slam of the door of a car.

In a flash I had slipped the statement under a blotting-pad.

'What did I tell you?' I said.

As I spoke, I saw my pistol, lying there on the table six inches away.

'By your leave,' said I, and whipped it into my pocket before they could think. That no one present protested argues, I think, that they liked me better than Grieg.

Then I stood back from the table and turned to the door.

The next instant this was opened, and Grieg flounced into the room.

Swiftly he looked about him.

'What does this mean?' he rasped. 'Why isn't this man in a cell?'

'I've been making a statement,' said I. 'I was just going to write it down.'

Grieg's eyes narrowed.

'You can write it at Vigil,' he said.

'Don't you want to hear it?' said I. 'It's a very extraordinary tale.'

I heard the man suck in his breath.

'If you think it worth repeating, you can tell it to me as we go.'

I raised my eyebrows.

'I see,' said I. 'Where are we going this time?'

I thought the fellow would strike me, for he started forward and thrust his face up to mine.

'"This time"?' he snarled. '"This time"? What – lie is this?'

I gave him back look for look.

'I dined at Bariche,' I said. 'And I've got the receipted bill. And it's dated, Grieg ... dated.'

Twice he essayed to answer, and twice he failed.

At last–

'You – you rave,' he said thickly. He turned to the table and struck the wood with his hand. 'Make out a receipt for this prisoner. He goes with me.'

'Alone?' said I.

'Alone.'

I addressed the boggling inspector.

'You will please record my protest. For reasons which I have given, I prefer not to travel alone with Major Grieg.'

The latter stamped his foot.

'Make out the receipt,' he roared.

With a shaking hand, the inspector picked up a volume and sought for a pen...

Grieg addressed the detectives.

'Handcuff this man and take him out to my car.'

In a deadly silence the sergeant pointed to the gyves, and one of the uniformed police took a pair from the wall.

As the detectives approached, I put my wrists together and held them out...

When the handcuffs were on, they laid their hands on my shoulders and turned to the door.

A moment later we were crossing the hall.

'I am very sorry, sir,' said the sergeant. 'But what can we do?'

'You can post to Vigil,' said I, 'and show the Chief my statement as soon as ever you can.'

'Depend on it, sir: we shall leave the instant you've gone.'

We passed to the head of the steps and stood waiting for Grieg...

The man came treading with the violence he always used. He thrust from the doorway and down to the waiting car.

With his hand on its door, he paused. Then he turned back to the steps and spoke to the police.

'Where is the car you came in?'

The sergeant pointed to lights on the opposite side of the way.

'Your work is done here,' said Grieg. He stepped up and seized my arm. 'Get back to the jail at Vigil and say that I'm coming on.'

The sergeant stared.

'To the jail?'

'To the jail,' said Grieg fiercely. 'At once. Tell them to have a cell ready and warn the guard.'

The sergeant spoke with his fellow and turned to the hall.

'Where are you going?' barked Grieg.

'To fetch our hats. They are in the inspector's room.'

With that, he was gone, while his fellow ran for their car.

I confess that here my heart sank down to my boots. Grieg's order could have but one meaning – that he did not want the detectives *behind* him upon the road. Such provision was ominous.

I knew, of course, that the sergeant would pick up my statement and take it to Vigil with him. But Grieg's disgrace and ruin seemed suddenly trifling gains to set against the loss of my life. I certainly had my pistol, but, now that I was handcuffed, I could not reach it without such an awkward movement as even a child must remark. I began to wonder dully how Grieg would go to work... As for Madame Dresden, I must acknowledge with shame that she and her fortunes never came into my head.

Here the car drew out, and the sergeant emerged from the hall. Hat in hand, he was plainly about to speak.

'Get on,' said Grieg roughly.

The other pursed his lips and went down without a word.

Then a door slammed, and the car began to storm up the street...

As its snarl faded, Grieg thrust me down the steps and up to the cabriolet.

'To Vigil,' he snapped. 'Headquarters.'

The chauffeur inclined his head.

Without releasing my arm, Grieg opened the door and stepped in. I followed as best I could, and the door was shut.

We jolted out of Sallust and on to a country road. As the car gathered speed, Grieg picked up the speaking-tube.

'Half-speed,' he said. 'Don't go more than twenty until I say.'

As the car slowed down, I saw him glance at his wrist.

'No point in overtaking them,' he said softly. 'And now, my friend, I'll trouble you for that bill.'

The sudden, natural demand took me aback. I should, of course, have foreseen it and been ready with some excuse, but, as I have said, I was thinking of other things. Had the police been further ahead, I would have cheerfully answered that they had both bill and statement for, though his rage would have been shocking, he would at once have seen that he would have nothing to gain by taking my life, but something to lose, for if he delivered me safe, that would be a rebutter to my statement which might be mistrusted, but could not well be ignored. As things were, however, I dared not tell them the truth, for his was the faster car and could have outrun the detectives' before that had gone halfway.

'Come on,' said Grieg roughly.

I took a deep breath.

'Today to you,' said I, and made a movement to put my hand into the pocket furthest from him.

Grieg laughed – and let go my arm.

'Today,' he said, 'and tomorrow, and the day after that.'

As he put out his hand for the paper, I jammed the mouth of my pistol against his ribs.

'Not even today,' I said thickly.

Grieg sat like a thing of stone, not seeming to breathe.

'Raise your hands,' said I, 'and take hold of the lapels of your coat. I advise you to move very gently, for the safety catch is up, and you know how these things go off.'

Very slowly he did as I said.

I could not take his pistol, for the man was

left-handed and carried his arms on his left: and, since I sat on his right, because of my handcuffs I could not reach so far. There was nothing for it, therefore, but to stay as I was, for I knew that the man was fearless and was waiting to turn the tables if I gave him the ghost of a chance.

As though he could read my thoughts–
'Stalemate,' said Grieg quietly.

'Don't you believe it,' said I. 'If I have to kill you, I shall – as you would have killed me. You know as well as I do, you meant to shut my mouth. "Shot whilst attempting to escape."… And now I'll tell you something. This pistol was taken from me when I was caught: but when I had told my story and they heard your voice in the hall, they knew you were out for murder and let me take it back.'

The fellow shifted a little, but spoke no word.

'And I'll tell you another thing. I'd put my statement in writing, before you came. It was on the inspector's table under the blotting-pad. The bill from Bariche was with it – I pinned it on myself. And when the detective-sergeant went back for his hat–'

I felt him repress a start.

'That's right,' said I. 'He got it. He'd promised to take it straight to the Chief of Police. Not tomorrow morning – tonight. The instant he got to Vigil. And then you very kindly sent him ahead.'

There was a long silence.

Suddenly–

'This won't help you,' said Grieg.

'It'll help the Countess,' said I.

'I see,' said Grieg. 'Did you read the letter she wrote?'

'I did,' said I. 'But I don't come in on deals of that sort.'

The man said nothing.

The car proceeded slowly, and I sat watching his hands and racking my brain.

We were bound for 'Headquarters, Vigil'. Unless I could make some move before we arrived, my race was as good as run. That Grieg's race was undoubtedly run afforded me great satisfaction, but it was galling to reflect that, having got so far, I could not go one step further and save myself.

I could, of course, have bade him order the chauffeur to drive elsewhere; but, had I done so, I should have wasted my breath. The fellow would have laughed in my face. He knew that I would kill him if he moved or cried out: and so he did neither. But force his hand I could not – he was not that kind of man.

But for my handcuffs, I could have taken the trick. As it was, I could not disarm him; and, so long as he had his pistol, I dared not lose sight of his hands for one moment of time. If I was to keep him covered, I could not even open the door. In a word, I was a one-armed man. As such, it seemed painfully clear that I had shot my bolt.

Suddenly the brakes were applied, and the car came to rest.

Not daring to turn my head, I strained my ears.

I heard a door open and one of the police descend. He shut the door behind him and walked ahead…

The next moment a windlass creaked.

We had come to a level crossing, and, since there was no keeper, the man was raising the bars.

The creaking stopped, and I heard the man walk on to the further bar.

I had expected to hear the further windlass, but, though my ears were pricked, I could hear no sound but the steady mutter of the engine and the hurried slam of my heart.

So for perhaps two minutes. Then the second policeman alighted and followed the first.

As I heard his footfalls retreating, I knew that this was my chance to leave the car, but the moment I moved I saw Grieg's left hand quiver and, inwardly raging, I held my pistol still.

'Stalemate,' said Grieg. 'I told you. You're – well stuck.'

Then the second windlass creaked, and almost at once the returning driver's footfalls made themselves heard.

My chance had passed.

The driver resumed his seat and drove the car over the rails.

I had expected that, once across, we should wait till the bars were let down, but, whilst we were moving, the second man stepped aboard, and a moment later we were again under way.

As though to crown my discomfiture, it became immediately clear that the check had put Grieg's injunction out of the driver's mind, for, instead of proceeding slowly, we now began to go like the wind, and the chance of overtaking the detectives once more lifted its head.

Grieg was laughing softly, and the blood came into my face.

I could, of course, have shot him, and that would have left me free to deal with his men; but, though I knew that he would have done it to me, I could not bring myself to take the man's life in cold blood.

So I sat, pressed against him, staring at the white of his hands and wondering what I had done that Fortune should have me in such manifest derision.

We had covered another ten miles, or so I judged, when again the car slowed down and came to rest.

This was natural, for, as I have often observed, where a road follows a railway, they cross again and again.

Dully I waited for one of the police to descend.

Then both of the doors were opened – the doors, I mean, that served the back of the car – and a torch blazed over my shoulder to light Grieg's face.

George Hanbury was speaking.

'Don't move a muscle, Grieg. I've got you cold.'

Though we did not then waste time by telling one another our tales, I think it will here be convenient to show how George came to be there and to strike, like a man in a play, when my need was most sore. And since his style is far more lively than mine, I will do my best to recapture his very words.

'When Rowley told me you were taken, that sinking feeling I'd heard of became an accomplished fact. The illusion of stomachic subsidence was quite startling. I actually felt myself to make sure there was no protrusion which hadn't been there before. Then we joined the crowd to see what we could do. This wasn't much, until you came off the bridge. We were up on some steps by then, and we saw you go by.

'Well, we clung to the side of the crowd and hoped against hope. But the further you went, as you know, the bigger it grew. It was then that I thought of a distraction. The crowd must be distracted. The trouble was that it mustn't be attracted to me. Whilst I was flogging my brains, I fouled a dustbin … I think the pain gave me strength. I emptied it out, of course. Even void, it was heavy enough. I was sorry about the victims of the prospective outrage, but I daresay they deserved it, and anyway the rain falls "on the just and on the unjust". The only fear I had was of hitting you. When it was over and I saw you standing still *behind* the worry, I could have yelled with delight. The distraction was a hard fact: the vultures had a new carcase – to judge from the squeals, two or three. Once you were clear of the press… Then the police reinforcements arrived and tore my dream.

'Act Two. We followed you to the station and watched you in. For a long time I considered a frontal attack: and I'm not sure now that we mightn't have brought it off. Two strong men armed, you know. What frightened me off was the thought that you might be locked up in a cell. If you were, we were done – obviously. Shock tactics are all right, but you mustn't meet any wire. I, therefore, withdrew in good order and tried very hard to foresee what the night would bring forth. The exercise was fruitful. I perceived at once that Sallust would telephone to Vigil and that Vigil would send detectives to bring you in. Very well. Your transfer from

Sallust to Vigil would give us our chance. All Rowley and I had to do was to find a suitable place at which we could hold up the car.

'The Sallust police favour the cycle. What's more they keep their scooters in a rack by the side of the jail... The thing was too easy. Before choosing a mount, I asked the way to Vigil. Five minutes later we were pounding along the road. I suppose we'd done twelve miles, when a car which was coming from Vigil went by all out. The detectives, of course. Well, that was all right. We were between them and Vigil. All we had to do now was to pick a suitable place, shove some obstruction in the road and sit down and wait. We rode on peering. Of course no place presented itself. And no obstruction, except the trunk of a tree which weighed about twenty tons. I began to get uneasy. Then, three miles on we came to a bullock-cart. This was empty and standing to the side of the way...

What it cost us to get that wagon across the road won't go into any words that I know. You might as well try and adapt Rabelais to a Children's Service in Lent. At first, I thought the brakes must be on. Then I found it was weight – sheer, dead weight. I imagine it was left where it was because the bullocks were whacked... Well, we got it into position, staggered to the side of the road and lay down to die. It didn't seem possible that the body could survive such a hideous output of strength. After about one minute we heard another car coming, *going the same way as the first.*

'If you can gauge our emotions, you must have an expansive brain. I haven't got them right yet. Instinctively we knew – I believe the correct word is "sensed" – that this was the car that mattered and that the one which was gone was of no account. Well, there you are. If we left the wagon where it was, a thousand to one the police would fail to move it and have to turn back. If they were able to move it, what do you think they would say when, *on returning,* they found it, not where they had left it, but once again in their way? Exactly. Something would tell them that it hadn't moved on its own. I mean, there was no wind.

'Well, we got it out of the way. As we collapsed, Grieg's car went by a blue streak. As soon as I recovered consciousness, I perceived the miracle. How was it we had been able to move the wagon in time? There was only one explanation. Between the time when we had first heard Grieg's car and the moment at which it went by, that car must have stopped on the road. *Must.*

We mounted and rode on slowly. I didn't care if I never saw the wagon again. Two minutes later we found the level crossing…

After that it was easy enough. We let the

detectives go by and waited for Grieg. At first I was afraid of his headlights. Then I saw there was a kink in the road, and that when the car was stopped it would be so much on the skew that the windlass would be out of the beam. There was a sack all ready by the side of the gate. We made it into a sandbag, and then, one after the other, we knocked the chauffeurs out. I'd no idea what a nice, clean job you can do with a couple of pounds of grit. Rowley seemed to know all about it. You've only got to find your length.'

I stood before Grieg, who was sitting by the side of the road.

'Up to now they've looked for three men: very soon they will be looking for four. I think that's indisputable. Nobody – not even a Prince – likes being double-crossed. I imagine, therefore, that, if you could have your way, you'd put yourself over the border as quick as you could. Very well. Help us to what we want, and we'll do our best to get you out with us.'

Grieg laughed an unpleasant laugh.

'What's the alternative?' he said.

'We see that you don't get out. No leaving you here.'

For a moment Grieg said nothing, but sat with his eyes on the road and his underlip caught in his teeth. Then–

'I suppose I can trust you,' he said.

'I suppose so,' said I.

'All right,' said Grieg. 'Carry on.'

'Where's Madame Dresden?' said I.

'At the Lessing Strasse,' said Grieg.

'Why d'you say that?'

'I took her there myself at eight o'clock.'

'Is she under arrest?' said George.

'No.'

'But confined to her house?'

'No. The police are withdrawn.'

'Why?'

Grieg shrugged his shoulders.

'She told you she was to be pardoned. It was perfectly true. And the moment that she was pardoned the police were withdrawn.'

'Why was she pardoned?'

Grieg laughed again.

'It's very simple,' he said. 'I found her on Saturday morning, a day and a half ago. I had authority to offer her a free pardon if she would say where you were. At first she didn't see her way to – to disclosure: but after twenty-four hours we came to terms. She said you were with the circus, and when the police saw Reubens they found she had spoken the truth. By the time they got there, of course, the birds had flown. But that wasn't my lady's fault. She'd done her half of the bargain, and so her pardon holds.'

This calm avowal of as dirty a piece of work as ever was done made my gorge rise.

I felt that I wanted water to rinse my mouth.

'Yes, I wonder where Dante would put you,' said George thickly. 'You've deliberately represented that, in order to save herself, the Countess betrayed her friends.'

'Naturally,' said Grieg, yawning.

'When all the time the truth is that, in order to save her friends, she betrayed herself.'

Grieg raised his eyebrows.

'Of course,' he said, 'you can put it however you please.'

I heard George draw in his breath. When he spoke again his voice was a little unsteady – a very rare thing.

'You said that you "came to terms." What were those filthy terms?'

'Oh, go to hell,' said Grieg shortly. 'You asked where she was, and I've told you and given chapter and verse for all that I've said. If you want to get out of the country, I shouldn't stand slobbering there.'

George Hanbury stood very still.

'The temptation to kill you,' he said, 'is almost too strong. I know we've passed our word, but I shouldn't try us too far. We're only human, you know, and I've known a rope that was warranted snap in two.'

Grieg laughed again, and since the man's demeanour was not to be borne, I laid hold of George's arm and we turned away...

We found no tools in the car with which

my wrists could be freed, but there was a hank of cord with which to bind those of Grieg.

The fellow protested, of course, and when we proposed to gag him, he fought like a beast. This, I confess, to our liking, for we had been itching for an excuse for violence and took a grim delight in subduing his energy.

When it was done–

'It isn't that we don't trust you,' said George, 'but from what we know of you, we think that you might forget. You see, if you were the means of getting us caught in Vigil, they might write off your shortcomings; and that wouldn't suit our book. And now will you enter the carriage? Or shall we kick you in?'

A moment later we were once more aboard the car, which Rowley was fairly lifting over the crest of a hill.

George sat in front with Rowley, and because of my handcuffs I sat within, with Grieg.

We went so fast that though we did not pass the detectives, by the time we came to Vigil we must have been close on their heels, and as we turned into the peaceful Lessing Strasse, I heard some clock striking one.

The street was dimly lighted, for though there were lamps enough, the pleasant burden of the lime trees, obscured their light, and though the place seemed to be empty, it might have been hiding a regiment ready to spring to life.

I found myself praying that Marya was not abed.

If she were, we must take Grieg with us and enter the house. To sit without, waiting while she dressed – for all we knew, the loadstone of fifty eyes, was more than I felt that I could face. Besides, a patrol might come by and stop to have a word with Grieg's chauffeur – only a word...

As the car came to rest before Madame Dresden's house, *three men stepped out of the shadows and touched their hats.*

For the tenth of a second I think my heart stood still.

The Grieg flung himself forward, making a rattling noise.

I had him by the throat in an instant and must near have broken his back, for I forced his head into the corner from which he had sprung and threw myself on his body to keep him from using his feet.

I heard George whispering hoarsely.

'Governor's asleep,' he said. 'I believe he's come for the Countess.'

'The Countess?' said one of the police. 'Why should the Countess be here?'

'Let her go, Rowley,' says George, as cool as you please.

He spoke in English, for Rowley knew no

German: but the change of front was so obvious that nothing was left, I fancy, for speech to betray. Still, if it was obvious, it was swift...

As the car leapt forward, one of the police gave a cry, but, if he had smelt the truth, he had smelt it too late, and the chance was gone before his suspicion had set.

We swept up the street like a squall, and if they took an action, I do not know what it was. Indeed, the whole matter was like an 'in-and-out' jump, and had it been midnight instead of one o'clock, the clock which we had heard striking as we came into the street might well have been still striking as we went out.

When we had swung round a corner, I let Grieg go. Then I put my head out of the window and spoke to George.

'All's well that ends well,' said I. 'And now for Baron Sabre's. We might have known she'd be there.'

'I don't see how we could have,' said George. 'It was more than likely, of course: but we should have been insane if we hadn't drawn Vigil first. And what about Satan's delight? Is he yet alive?'

'Yes,' said I. 'But I should value his room.'

'When we're clear of the town,' said George. 'Just as well we didn't get out.'

That was a true saying. Had only George alighted, there on that shadowy pavement our venture would have come to an end.

Had he been seized, we could not have gone and left him; because my hands were useless, Rowley must have gone to his help; and, though I might have taken the driver's seat, had I been interfered with I could never have got us away when the moment came.

I cast no stone at Grieg for leading us into the trap. All is fair in war, and he was a desperate man. He played the right cards. That these were dirty was because his hands were unclean.

Five miles beyond the city, we put him out of the car.

We took the gag from his mouth and lashed him back to a gatepost by the side of the Austrian road. There he would be found in the morning and, we supposed, set free by some passer-by, too late to save his bacon, with nothing to do but go into instant hiding in the hope of leaving the country before his arrest was made.

We had not spoken in his hearing of Baron Sabre's house, and I have no doubt that he thought his secret safe.

To fortify this conclusion—

'You've lied to us once,' said George, with his foot on the step. 'Would you like to do it again?'

The black eyes lighted with malice.

'You'll never find Madame Dresden.'

Not till long after did I see the truth of his words.'

Two heart-breaking hours went by before we found the mansion to which we had come so close four days before. God knows that was long enough, but I sometimes think we were lucky to find it at all, for our precious map was at Sallust, and we had to go round by Vardar and pick our way back from there. And this was the devil, for the night was dark as pitch, and we could not see enough of the roads to enable us to determine whether we had used them before. Twice we knocked up farmers to ask our way, but though they were civil enough, the one declared that the house we sought was not on this side of Vigil, while the other had not slept off his liquor and could not be persuaded that we did not desire to be directed to the tavern from which this had come. We were, indeed, growing desperate when somehow or other we blundered into a park through which a thin white road went curling into the night.

There could now be no doubt that at last we had stumbled upon the Sabre estate, for I was quite sure that no other private house had been shown hereabouts upon the map. The road, therefore, seemed certain to take us straight to the mansion which we had been seeking so long, and I cried to George to tell Rowley to let the car go.

For a while the drive was level, but after five minutes the ground began to rise. Then we must have passed over some ridge, for all of a sudden we saw a light stabbing the darkness against the mass of a house.

The road ran straight to the doorway above which the lantern hung: there it swelled into a sweep, and Rowley, who needed no telling, brought the car round and up to the broad, low steps.

No light came from any window, and when the engine was stopped, we heard no sound.

We descended furtively.

As George put a hand to the door, this was silently opened, and there was an old serving-man with a lamp in his hand.

He asked no questions, but only set the door wide and held it until we were in. Then he shut it slowly, and shot the ponderous bolts.

As he turned.

'Take me to the lady,' said George. 'I bear an urgent message from Major Grieg.'

The old man turned to me and lifted his lamp.

'Why, I thought that was he,' he said, peering.

'That,' said George, 'is his prisoner,' and touched my gyves.

'Lord, lord,' said the other, staring. 'But what a grim present to send. I think a posy of flowers would have been more to her taste.'

'That's as may be,' said George. 'I take it

the Major knows best. And now lead on, my friend. It's late, and we're not through yet.'

We followed him up a great staircase, George leading and Rowley behind...

Arrived at some tall double doors the old fellow went very close and inclined his head. Then he knocked very gently, and, after waiting a little, made bold to open a leaf...

It was a handsome chamber, too broad for the two candelabra whose candles had burned very low. Great curtains masked the windows, and tapestry hung upon the walls. The furniture was massive and stilted and seemed more fit to be looked at than put to use, and I remember thinking that only the brave sunshine could truly furnish an apartment so big with dignity. The fireplace was presenting a mouth through which a small car could have passed, and the ashes of a dead wood fire lay in the monstrous grate.

At first the room seemed empty. Then I saw the Countess sitting stiff in a high-backed chair.

Her face was white and drawn, and her hands were holding fast to the edge of the tapestry seat. Her eyes were wide, and she was looking before her at the huddle of cold, grey ash.

As I closed the door behind me–

'Marya,' breathed George. 'Marya.'

For a moment she stared upon us, as though we were risen from the grave. Then her eyes fell to my handcuffs and she started up to her feet.

'My God!' she breathed. 'My God! Carol told me–'

She stopped there, shaking terribly, with both her hands to her mouth and her eyes so like those of a madman that my hair seemed to rise upon my head.

It was shocking to see her so moved, and I was truly thankful when George's arms went about her and he caught her hands to his breast.

'Marya, darling, we're safe. We've come to take you away.'

She continued to tremble, like a man sick of the palsy, and making George seem to tremble because she was in his arms.

'Away?' she whispered. 'You can't.'

George nodded cheerfully.

'The car's waiting, sweet. There's no one to stop us now.'

'No one?' She looked round fearfully and again her eyes fell upon my gyves. 'Why is Richard wearing those things? Carol swore–'

'Did you think we would leave you, Marya? When we found that you weren't at Bariche, of course we came back: and Bill got caught on the way, but they lost their grip. And now get a coat, my beauty, we mustn't waste time.'

Marya stopped shaking, disengaged her hands and put them up to her eyes. When she spoke again, though she seemed to speak with an effort, her voice was calm.

'You must go without me,' she said. 'Where – where is Grieg?'

'Without you?' cried George. 'Without you? But we came back to get you, Marya. We–'

'George, dear, don't make it worse. I say you must go without me, and I mean what I say.' With a sudden movement she turned and took his face in her hands. 'Do you love me, George?' she whispered, and seeing, I suppose, his answer in the light of his eyes, she drew his head down to hers and kissed his lips.

For a moment they clung together. Then very gently Marya put him aside.

'I can't come,' she said quietly. 'I've passed my word.'

'To Grieg?'

She nodded.

'Grieg is disgraced – broken. If he's found, he'll be arrested. His only chance is to leave the country at once.'

Marya stood very still.

'In that case,' she said, 'it's to my interest to stay. You see, Grieg is my husband. We were married here in the chapel at eight o'clock.'

CHAPTER 5

Cold Blood

I remember thinking that George would never move.

He stood like a man that has seen some Gorgon's head and has in the act of vision been turned to stone. His lips were parted, and one of his hands was half way up to his head, and the dust with which his features were powdered gave him the look of a being that was not of flesh and blood.

Then I saw his chin go up, and I turned to the door.

A moment later I was descending the stairs.

One thing had to be done, and done at once.

Marya's ship was afire. It was no good her winning her action if she was to be consumed. The fire must be put out at once – *before it could spread.*

So I went out to do murder, if you can call it such.

George, of course, could do nothing. For if he was to play the hangman, he could hardly expect to marry the widow that he had made. Any woman must have recoiled from so grisly a bed.

Now I was so bent upon my purpose that I forgot my handcuffs until I slipped on the stairs and sought to stretch out a hand to lay hold of the banisters. At once my embarrassment hit me between the eyes. Unless I was to kill Grieg as one kills a pig, before I did anything else I must free my wrists.

What the old servant imagined I cannot tell; but I think the events of that night had disordered his failing wits. When I told him to draw the bolts and open the door, he only gaped at my gyves, and when Rowley had done the business and I bade the poor man make fast and open again to no one without first advising George, he began to speak of his sister, recalling the day of her wedding and the flowers she had worn in her hair.

The next moment I was seated by Rowley, and the car was flying along the thin, white road.

I am not given to imagining vain things, but fancies crowded about me during that drive. The hour was ghostly: neither day nor night could have claimed it, and the sleeping world was abused by its treacherous light. Nature herself seemed aware of my dreadful errand. The country I knew for handsome was a stage of tricksy shadows and looming shapes: when we stopped by a bridge for an instant, the suck of a neighbouring sluice sounded so monstrous that I was glad to be gone: and more than once I could have sworn to the beat of wings upon the air. The seats behind were empty, yet I had a horrid feeling that we were not alone, but that something was riding with us and sitting where Grieg had sat. All the time Grieg danced before me in a hundred postures of death. Now he was flat upon his back, with his black eyes wide and empty, regarding the sky: now his bulk was huddled, like that of some friendless wretch that is cold in his sleep: and once he lay as I have seen a dead man, sprawling against a bank like any puppet, with his head fallen sideways and a puzzled stare upon his face.

As I have said, I could not play the butcher, so Rowley drove me to Gola, and, whilst he was going about, Ramon the smith came down and set me free. Though he begged me to let him do it, I would not wait for him to cut off the cuffs themselves, but when he had severed the chain that held the two together, I shook his hand and left him, with a bracelet on either wrist.

The dawn was near now: colour was creeping into the woods and meadows, and distance beginning to take her lawful form. In a little while we should have no need of our headlights, and in less than an hour the sun would be over the mountains and making the valleys glad. But not for Grieg. He would not see the dayspring for which he

151

was wishing so hard.

I was driving now and I think that I frightened Rowley, so high was our speed. My one idea was to have done with the business, for Grieg was haunting me now as I was very sure his ghost would never haunt me when once he was dead.

At last we flashed through the village a mile or so from which we had left him lashed to the post, and, since I could not be sure of his exact position, I slackened speed.

'Not yet, sir,' said Rowley, peering.

'It was dark,' said I. 'I can't be sure to a mile.'

'I shall know it, sir,' said Rowley. 'It's a furlong beyond some crossroads and round a bend.'

'Watch for the crossroads,' said I.

It seemed an age before I heard him cry out.

As I set my foot on the brake, I saw the crossroads ahead.

I overran them slowly and brought the car to rest.

'Are you sure you're right?' I said.

'Yes, sir,' he stretched out an arm. 'It's round that bend we left him. There's a pile of stones by the gate.'

I stepped down into the road.

'Stay here,' I said. 'Turn the car and stay here. If you hear a shot, don't worry. I shan't be long.'

For a moment the man did not answer. Then–

'Very good, sir,' he said quietly.

Before I had taken ten paces I heard him turning the car.

As I went, I tried to determine the course I should take.

I must free the man, of course. That went without saying. And when the man was free, I must give him some law. If he did not run, I must stand back the width of the road. If...

Here I perceived with a shock that I could do nothing of the kind. For Marya's sake the man *had* to be destroyed. That he deserved to die was beside the point. A millstone had been hanged about the Countess' neck, and nothing but Grieg's decease could take it away. That it was he that had hanged it there made his death just: but had he made her marry a swineherd, *the clown would have had to die.* I was not there to punish Grieg. I was there to free the Countess from her most dreadful plight.

It seemed that after all I must play the butcher, and, as once before that morning, my stomach turned at the thought.

I could see the stones now – a low barrow of metalling, ready to mend the road. It occurred to me that that was his gravestone. A ditch lay behind the barrow. There I must lay the body and cover it thick with stones from the pile to hand.

I went on with dragging feet and my eyes on the ground.

I decided to tell him the truth and give him two minutes in which to prepare for death. After that I would shoot him through the head. After all, there was no cause for compunction. The man was worthy of death.

I raised my eyes to see an empty gate-post, some twenty paces ahead.

For an instant relief came flooding. Then I perceived that Rowley had made a mistake. A hundred yards further on was another bend in the road, and just at the turning another grey barrow of stone.

As I moved forward, I trod on a piece of cord.

I picked it up, staring...

More cord was dangling by the gatepost, caught by the latch of the gate. I found there were three short lengths, the edges of which were clean cut.

I do not think I should have been human, if I had not been honestly thankful to find that my prey was gone. But even while I stood frowning, twisting the cord in my hands and blessing the early riser that had put such a spoke in my wheel, I heard the sound of a car being hastily started from rest.

In a flash I had leaped to the bend, to see the car reach the crossroads and fling up the broad, black road down which we had come.

And two hundred yards away lay a figure

154

in a white dust-coat half on and half off the grass.

The sun was up before Rowley opened his eyes.

I had carried him over a meadow and down to a little brook, and but for the fresh, cold water I think that he would have lain senseless another hour.

I do not know which was the stouter, his heart or his head, for, though on the back of the latter there was an ugly swelling the size of a pocket-watch, he had hardly recovered his senses, before he was up on his feet.

'Lie down,' said I. 'Lie down. You're not fit to move. You won't be fit for ten minutes. Perhaps not then.'

Wildly he stared about him.

'But the car, sir. What's happened? I was—'

'You were laid out,' said I. 'Laid out by Grieg. It wasn't your fault. Somebody must have undone him, for when I got there he was gone.'

The man's hand flew to his side.

'He's taken my pistol, sir.'

'I know,' said I. 'What's more, he's taken the car. He's off to Baron Sabre's – where we left Mr Hanbury, you know. I only hope that when Mr Hanbury hears him, he doesn't assume that it's us.'

'Oh, my God, sir,' says Rowley. 'What have I done?'

'Don't blame yourself,' said I. 'If it's anyone's fault, it's mine. Besides, when he sees Mr Hanbury, he'll get the shock of his life. And now lie down for ten minutes, and let me think.'

I was in a queer state of mind and nearer, I believe, to submission than ever before or since. There had been so many fences and I had been heavily thrown so many times. The last twelve hours had imposed a continuous strain, and the horrid duty which I had set out to perform had played the deuce with my nerves. Because of that, I suppose, this fresh disaster set up no answering action in my weary mind. I looked on it, saw that it was bad, deplored it and – considered the lilies of the field. I found the lush grass absorbing, the babble of the brook a chapter, the piping of the birds most rare. But of our enterprise I was tired. It was clear that in our haste we had bitten off more than we could chew: and now I was sick of chewing and cared not what was the end.

So I sat idle and listless, now watching the bustle of the water and now the birds about their business, and sometimes glancing at Rowley, face downward upon the turf.

Suddenly I remembered Leonie.

The thought of her roused me as an electric shock. My apathy died there and then. Our case was critical. I must do more than fold my hands if I was ever to see my wife again.

I knelt to the brook and made a rude enough toilet that did me a world of good. Then I looked round, to meet Rowley's questioning eyes.

'What is it?' said I, smiling.

'You had meant to kill him, sir, hadn't you?'

'I had,' said I. 'For my sins.'

'Ah, sir,' says he with a sigh, 'you should have left it to me. It wouldn't have spoiled my breakfast.'

'Wouldn't it now?' said I, and got to my feet. 'Well, come on and do it, Rowley, before it's too late.'

It was eight o'clock that morning before we re-entered the park, and half past eight before we sighted the house.

I had already decided that we must stay in the background until we had learned, so to speak, the state of the game: for if this was going against us, to blunder upon the scene would be the act of a fool and I had no desire to play for the second time clean into the enemy's hands. Directly, therefore, I saw the chimney-pots, we laid ourselves down in the bracken and started to crawl, and, very soon making the ridge which I had remarked from the car the night before, perceived the mansion before us two furlongs away.

To stay so far off was useless, but a moment's survey sufficed to show us how to approach.

Except at this point the home park was heavily timbered. We had, therefore, but to go back and bear to the right or left. In this way, if we went with care, we should be able to come to within a stone's throw of the house and then, still keeping cover, to go about it and view it from every side. The mansion was neighboured, however, by a girdle of naked turf.

Ten minutes later we lay upon the edge of this sash.

It was a grey, old place, for the most part two stories high, and had, I judged, been added to more than once, for its various portions did not agree together, some being very humble and some ornate. It seemed as though the main entrance had formerly stood to the west, for though now nothing but windows looked out that way, an apron of cobbled pavement had made good standing for coaches in days gone by, and a road ran away from that side and out of the shallow basin in which the mansion stood. This was, of course, the drive which led to Vigil, which Grieg had used that morning, which, had we but had our map, we should have sought and taken the night before.

Here I should say that Grieg's car was not to be seen: indeed, a curl of smoke from a chimney and two or three open windows were all the signs of life that we could descry, and, since a great deal may happen in four or five hours, it came to me that we might be wasting our time upon a stable from which the horses were gone. My better judgment, however, insisted that we should lie close, and, since from where we were hidden we could watch the south and west sides, I bade Rowley stay where he was and started to make my way round, to view the rest of the house.

Now I could not do this without crossing the second drive. I, therefore, fell back until I was out of the hollow and over the ridge, for I guessed that if Grieg was watching, his eyes would be bent upon the road that led towards Vigil, for that was the way down which his fortune would come.

I had crossed the road on my stomach, just out of sight of the house, and was hastening back into the hollow through a parcel of whispering firs, when I saw the sparkle of nickel, and there was Grieg's car.

It was empty and its engine was cold.

For a little I could not conceive why the car should be there. Then it flashed into my mind that Grieg had thus bestowed it against his arrest. Had he left it at the door of the mansion or even within some yard, he could scarcely have reached it, much less have driven it off, except by consent of those who had come to make his arrest, but by leaving it hidden *beyond* the girdle of turf, he had only himself to gain cover, make his way round to its lair and then drive quietly away while those who had come to take him were searching the house. To support this conclusion, the car had been backed into hiding and so stood all ready for a precipitate flight.

After a moment's reflection, I opened the bonnet and took the contact-breaker away. I slid this into my pocket and shut the bonnet again. The car was now at my service, but at that of nobody else, yet showed no sign of having been disabled or even of having been touched. When I glanced at the petrol-gauge this showed that the tank was half full. I then recovered Grieg's pistol which Rowley had put in a locker behind the back seat, and so licked clean the platter which luck had thrust under my nose.

We were once more both of us armed and we had control of the car. This was conveniently hidden and ready for use. Lastly, though he did not know it, Grieg's means of escape was gone.

I went on my way cheerfully...

To the north of the house stood stabling about a yard, but I heard no sound of horses and saw no movement at all. What I found to the east, however, repaid me for making the round.

This face of the house rose from a row of arches which gave to an empty cloister, flagged with stone. Above ran one row of windows, and these very tall, suggesting a gallery or banqueting room: and right at the end stood the chapel with, rising above it, a belfry in which hung a poor-looking bell.

Now, as I have shown, we could not come up to the mansion without crossing the girdle of turf, and though Grieg might not see us, he was almost certainly keeping some sort of look-out. I found it unlikely, however, that he would attend to this side, and the cloister, when once we had made it, would afford the finest cover that any man could desire. As like as not, moreover, it served as a porch to some door, and I made up my mind to fetch Rowley without more ado.

It took me some time to make my way back to his side, and when I had told him my news and had given him Grieg's pistol, I turned on my back for a moment, to take some rest.

Before I had lain for two minutes, far in the distance I heard the sound of a car.

Even as I heard it, it faded, only to swell into earshot more clear than before.

Some car was coming from Vigil – at least, from the west.

We waited breathlessly...

Then a closed car flashed from the trees and swept to the house. On the seat by the driver sat one of the uniformed police.

It seemed that Grieg's hour was come.

I was watching the car swing out to sweep to the door, when I heard another car coming, though not so fast as the first.

I returned to the latter to see get out the sergeant who had been so friendly to me the night before. Two other police were with him, one in plain-clothes.

Their mission admitted of no doubt. But since of the four not one took the simple precaution of stepping as far as the corner and looking down the side of the house, I would have laid any money that they were doomed to draw blank. Indeed, it came into my mind that now was the moment for us to repair to Grieg's car, for that there we should be certain to find him and Rowley could do his business and shoot him dead.

The notion was idle, and I dismissed it at once, if only because of the attention which the sound of the shot would attract; but even as I dismissed it, I saw the outstanding value of such a move.

Rowley had Grieg's own pistol. Once he had killed the fellow, he had but to thrust the weapon into its owner's hand and make himself scarce. The police would rush to the scene to find that *the man they were seeking had put an end to their duty by taking his life.*

Their work being, therefore, over, they would see to the bestowal of the body and go their way, little dreaming that we were but waiting for them to take their leave.

As George Hanbury would have said, 'the thing was too easy'.

As I turned to give Rowley his orders, I heard a familiar sigh – the sigh of a well-tuned engine, running very slowly just out of sight.

The second car had just surmounted the ridge and was gliding into the hollow, or standing still. *And I knew whose car it was and why he had come.*

Prince Paul had been shown my statement and had come in all his fury to settle with Grieg.

It was now more important than ever that we should not lose a moment in giving effect to my plan. I, therefore, touched Rowley's shoulder, and, using the greatest caution, began to move back through our cover in order to come to Grieg's car.

So for some fifty paces, and then we were brought up short.

A pleasant ride cut through the wood we were using and lay like a smooth, green river full in our path. Running due north and south, it was at this hour full of sunlight, and, though it was screened from the mansion, anyone standing at the point where it met the drive could have seen a rabbit crossing a furlong away. And there, at that point of vantage, no more than twenty yards distant from where we lay, was resting the royal car.

I could not see the Prince, but I could hear him speaking, though not what he said. A door of the car was open, and two men I

163

had never seen were standing close beside it, looking towards the house. One I had little doubt was the Chief of Police. By the side of the chauffeur sat an officer, wearing field-service dress.

My first idea was to withdraw, with a view to crossing the ride at its farther end: then I saw that to fetch such a compass would take us full twenty minutes if we were to move with care, whereas, if the royal car passed on, we could reach Grieg's car in a moment from where we now lay. Add to this that until the Prince moved, we could not put our plan into action for fifty Griegs, for, let alone the risk of an outcry, a shot fired at quarters so close would have brought his companions about us before we could make ourselves scarce.

So we lay in the undergrowth, peering through a lattice of brambles and straining our ears.

I cannot say how long we waited before we could hear what was said, but the Prince was impatient as ever and kept up a fire of what I took to be grumbling, for those about him said nothing, but only shifted and frowned and continued to stare down the road. They could, of course, see nothing except a slice of the house, but that, I think, was because the very odour of peril offended their master's nose.

At last he flung out of the car and on to the turf.

'–the fools,' he spouted. 'Four of them to collar one rogue, and they can't bring it off. They're funking it, Weber. They're afraid.'

The Chief of Police summoned a crooked smile.

'I don't think so, sir,' he said.

'Then why don't they come?'

The other inclined his head.

'Sir,' said he, 'I can offer a dozen reasons. He may not be there, for one thing. Or if he is there, they may have found him abed.'

'Rot,' said the Prince. 'He's there all right, and they know it. But they'll come back and swear he isn't because of the value they set on their dirty skins. Suppose they'd been placed as I was the other day. Alone in a high-walled garden, with three men trying to kill me – and I without a stick in my hands. Three of them, man. I admit I went up a tree, but that was because I couldn't get into the house. I laid two of them out, anyway. And the third ran like a rabbit to get behind a shutter and shoot me as I came to the steps. And then I had to watch my two chauffeurs give away the game I had won. Dirty white-livered skunks.'

Weber made no reply. I fancy he knew his man.

'The point is this,' said the Prince. 'If Grieg–'

'Here they come, sir,' said Weber's companion.

The Prince stood his ground.

'Have they got him?' he said.

'Yes, sir.'

'Is he handcuffed?'

'Yes, sir.'

The Prince fell to biting his nails. Suddenly he started forward.

'I'll get back in the car,' he said. 'No, I won't.' He stopped in his tracks. 'Candel, get down and come and stand by my side. Have your revolver ready, and if he moves a muscle just shoot him down.'

The officer alighted and stepped to his monarch's side.

To this day I do not know how Grieg came to be caught. Having no one to share his vigilance, he had, I imagine, taken some petty risk. Had he opened a tap, for example, the noise of the running water might well have covered the sound of the oncoming car. And he had the look of a man surprised at his toilet, for he wore no coat or collar, and the sleeves of his shirt were rolled back.

He was between two police, and at a sign from Weber the three marched on to the sward.

His face was like a grim mask, and his lip was curling a little, as though in insolent scorn.

I found myself wondering what cards he was going to play.

He made no sort of reverence, but took his

166

stand firmly and looked the Prince up and down.

The latter's eyes narrowed.

'You're a pretty blackguard, aren't you?' he said.

'No doubt your Royal Highness knows best. You always do.'

'You insolent swine,' cried the Prince. 'This is what I get for taking you back. I exercised the prerogative of mercy–'

'Why?' said Grieg.

'Because it was my pleasure,' said the Prince, with a lift of his chin.

'Because,' said Grieg deliberately, 'you believed me the only man that could lay these scum by the heels.'

The other stamped his foot.

'Don't dare to answer me back. I decided to give you a chance, and you've used it to let me down. You're a filthy traitor, Grieg. You always were. But you've cut your throat this time, and by God, I'm going to put you where you belong.'

Grieg shrugged his shoulders.

'"Put not your trust in Princes",' he said.

The monarch put his hands on his hips and wagged his unpleasant head.

'Nothing doing this time,' he sneered. 'How much did they pay you, Grieg?'

'We are not upon those terms,' said Grieg shortly. 'They know me too well.'

'I see,' said the Prince softly. 'Well, I'm

sorry to say they've split. They've given you away with both hands. The price isn't mentioned, but how d'you explain how they know the inside of your car?'

Again Grieg shrugged his shoulders.

'I can only attribute that to the use of their eyes.'

'The inside, Grieg. Not the outside.'

'Same answer,' said Grieg insolently.

The other's smile changed to a glare.

'Are you trying to bluff?' he demanded. 'Because if you are—'

'I am not in the habit,' snapped Grieg, 'of wasting my time. You've made up your mind I'm a traitor – "a filthy traitor" I think were the royal words. As is your way, you've therefore had me arrested out of hand. No doubt you will deal with me as you think I deserve.'

'By God, I will,' said the Prince.

'And with the English swine you commanded me to capture – by hook or by crook.'

The Prince's eyes burned in his head.

'To capture, Grieg, to capture,' he raved. 'Not to succour, you hound. Not to put out of the country – out of my reach. Did they have a good meal at Bariche? Whose health do you think they drank at *The Broken Egg?* Don't you think they laughed as they went by the guards at Elsa? Don't you think she's laughing at Littai? Hooting with laughter to think that I've been befooled? And where's

168

Chandos? You had him last night alone, with cuffs on his wrists. Where is he now? He was in your charge, and I demand him. You gave a receipt for his body. You signed the book. He was safe under lock and key, and you used the power I gave you to take him out. Perhaps you lent him your car to go to Littai...'

Grieg threw back his head and laughed.

'Listen,' he said. 'You suddenly restore me to favour and give me orders which I promise to execute. Before my work is over, without a word of explanation I am put under arrest. That by the very men of whom half an hour ago I was in command. D'you think that conduct's conducive to getting your way?' He flung out his manacled wrists. 'How the devil can I produce Chandos or anyone else? More. Why the devil should I produce them in the face of treatment like this? Why should I answer your questions? Why open my mouth? I signed the receipt for his body. You've cancelled that receipt by having me put in irons. You gave and you have taken way. That is the prerogative of princes. I have been, somewhat brusquely, relieved of my authority. You will no doubt replace me by someone whom you can trust. It does not amuse me to teach my successor to gather the fruit of my work.'

There was an uneasy silence.

I saw the Prince glance at the others and

his hand go up to his mouth. Then he took out his case and lighted a cigarette.

'I'll see you,' he blurted suddenly. 'Explain your conduct – if you can. I'll hear what you've got to say.'

Grieg eyed the youth with supreme contempt.

'Your Royal Highness is rather dense this morning. I have been at some pains to point out that I am dismissed your service.' He bowed elaborately. 'I have, therefore, nothing to report.'

'Oh, go to hell,' said the Prince. 'I've every – reason to think that you've let me down. So's Weber. So's everyone. You put those swine out of the country. God knows why one came back. But he did, and was pinched at Sallust. And you – you took him away... Say where he is – produce him, and you can go free.'

'You asked for the three,' said Grieg. 'You gave me a free hand, and you asked for the three. If you had cared to trust me, you would have had them tonight.'

'Yes, that's easy,' sneered the Prince. 'If you think–'

'I don't,' said Grieg. 'I know you. When I took the job on, I knew it would end like this. But against these men I had a personal grudge. And so, against my judgment, I took it on.' He flung out a bitter laugh. 'If I had gone round searching farms and visiting frontier-posts, I shouldn't be handcuffed now; but because I play the scum at their devil's own game I am immediately suspect – presumed "a filthy traitor", and that out of Chandos' mouth.' He expired violently. 'He tells you I sent him to Bariche. Maybe he produces a bill from *The Broken Egg*. Does he say whom he met at Bariche? Or what he arranged with them? Does he say that he *and his fellows* were back here by ten o'clock – according to plan, *my plan?* That again I gave them my car, to try and find the Countess and take her away? Does he tell you the path that they're going to take tonight? The secret smugglers' path which nobody knows? Does he say who's going to be there … waiting by the side of the water … with only one servant with her … and the night too dark to distinguish any man's face?'

'My God,' cried the Prince hoarsely. 'How do you know?'

'It's very simple,' said Grieg. 'Everyone here has been looking from Vigil to the border and back, till they've got St Vitus's dance. I've been watching Littai.'

He stopped there, as though to regard the sensation his words had caused. This was manifest. His audience did not seem to be breathing. Only Weber fingered his chin, with a distant look in his eyes.

'What happens at Littai tells me what's happening here. The Grand Duchess moved to Bariche three days ago. That meant they were going to communicate. Very well. Their only way of getting a message to Bariche was to go to Bariche themselves. And as I wanted to know what that message was going to be, I took the trouble to send them to Bariche myself. They were bound to come back to get the Countess... Of course the police at Sallust meant well, but they very nearly ruined–'

'But not quite,' cried the Prince excitedly. 'Not quite. Where's the path you speak of? I'll send–'

'That, sir,' said Grieg, 'is my secret. Had I not been arrested, I should have been there tonight – to gather the fruit. But I have already declined to teach any man alive to win my game.'

There was an electric silence.

Then the Prince's forgotten cigarette burned its way to his fingers and he flung it down with an oath.

'It's all damned fine,' he said fiercely. 'You say "Put me back, and I'll deliver the goods", but–'

'Pardon me, sir,' said Grieg. 'I have said nothing of the kind. I'm through with this job of work. If you went down on your knees, I wouldn't touch it again. I've told you as much as I have, to show you what you've missed – to show you the catch I'd have landed, if you hadn't let me down. And now I'm sick of talking. Where do I go?'

This master-stroke of bluff had its reward.

Before two minutes were gone, Grieg was free of his handcuffs and had somewhat stiffly accepted one of his Royal Highness' cigarettes.

To round the picture, I heard him arrange with the Prince for three closed cars to be waiting from nine o'clock on, to bring in the prisoners which he was certain to take. These cars were to wait at Vigil until his orders came, and the surly deliberation with which he appointed the hour would, I think, have deceived a far shrewder mind.

I could not help wondering how long the cars would wait and whether Grieg would be at Salzburg before his royal victim discovered that he had been bluffed. What was so strange was the closeness with which his fiction approached the truth. He had plainly been taught the bypass the smugglers used when taking the bridle-path, and had guessed or learned that we had come by that way. And on that he had built his story – his fairy-tale. He could not possibly know that we were in fact proposing that night to do as he said. The thing was absurd. I did not know it myself. As for his mention of Leonie…

With a shock I found myself asking whether indeed it was a chance that had brought him so close to the truth, whether he had truly been bluffing – from beginning to end.

My hair rose at the thought.

Had Grieg some information which gave him just cause to think that that very night we should take the bridle-path? And that Leonie would be waiting on the farther side of the fall?

After a little I dismissed this fantastic notion and turned my attention again to the matter in hand.

To the end of the curious scene I cannot speak, for, fearing that any moment Grieg would return to the house, I determined to try to enter before he came out of the wood. I, therefore, whispered to Rowley to say where he was and crawled as fast as I could the way we had come.

Once out of earshot, I ventured to take to my feet, but I had to fetch a wide compass because of the police with the car, and I fancy ten minutes had passed before I was facing the cloister which, now that I meant to prove it, looked very dark and grim.

As I gathered myself together to sprint across the girdle of turf, I heard the police car move forward...

An instant later I was standing upon the flagstones straining my ears.

The car which had been moving had come to rest, but its engine was none too silent and its stammer was all I could hear. I, therefore, made bold to look round the edge of the house, to see Grieg speaking with the detectives some forty or fifty yards off.

What he was saying, of course, I could not tell, but the men were listening so intently that I there and then decided that, come what might, we must find some other way out of Riechtenburg. The bridle-path was suspect. As such, from being a pass, the place had become a trap. Tonight the trap would be set – so much I had heard with my ears. But I had not the slightest doubt that now it would be set every night, so long as we were at large.

Now since the front door of the mansion was full in their view, my chance of using that entrance was plainly dead, but, as I went by, I had seen a door in the cloister and, hoping that this might be open, I hastened back.

The door was open and led me into a passage, which served three doors. On the walls were glass cases in which hung harness and bits, and two fine old 'watchman's' chairs were standing at either end.

Leaning against the wall between two of the doors was a handsome peasant-girl – at least, so her habit declared her, but her face was fine and gentle and her figure was slight, and both of them argued some sire that had never set hand to a plough. Her brown legs and feet were bare, and her dress was of fair, white linen such as they wear in those parts. A sleeveless scarlet jacket suited her very well.

Finger to lip, she regarded me.

Something touched my knee, and I looked down to see the wolf-hound that had been the Prince's dog.

As I gave him my hand to lick–

'You must be Chandos,' said the girl, with a pleasant smile.

'Yes,' said I. 'That's my name.'

'Ah,' says she. 'I was to tell you that those you seek have gone on. Tonight they will take the road that is under water. They trust you will join them there.'

I stared at her dumbly.

'The road that is under water' could mean but one thing – the way beneath the fall which Ramon the smith had shown us five days ago.

'Where are they?' I said at length. 'Which way did they go?'

The girl shook her lovely head.

'I do not know. I met them down in the greenwood a mile away. I was bringing a telegram. I am waiting now for the tip which they always give me.'

'"Always"?' said I. 'Do they have many telegrams here?'

'Two a day lately,' she said. 'I have waited for nearly an hour.'

I took out a fifty-crown note.

'There is your tip.'

The girl's eyes widened.

'Oh, sir, this is fifty crowns.'

'For your pretty face,' said I, and opened the door. 'I'll tell Major Grieg I paid you. And please tell no one of having seen me or my friends.'

She shot me a curious look.

'Is that why you gave me the money?'

'No,' said I. 'I told you I gave you that for your pretty face. Did the telegram come from Littai?'

'Yes,' said the girl lightly. 'They all come from there.' With a foot on the threshold she paused. 'Will it please you to kiss me?' she said.

As a man in a dream, I kissed her, and watched her move like a deer across the sward.

Half way over she turned to wave a bare arm.

I waved back dazedly.

CHAPTER 6

I Keep Fair Company

For some moments I stood in the passage, staring at a case full of harness which many museums would have been glad to display. Then I pulled myself together and stepped to the door on my left.

As I had half expected, this opened into the hall we had entered the night before. There was the grand staircase and there the front door of the house, as well as three other doors, admitting no doubt, to rooms: and, though it was just possible that Grieg would not enter from the drive, the place was so much of a junction that anyone using the house would be certain sooner or later to come by this way.

I, therefore, took up a position beneath the spring of the staircase, by the side of a tall oak press, and made up my mind to attack, the instant Grieg showed his face.

Whilst I was waiting, I sought to consult with myself, but, though I did not feel tired, I think that my brain was weary, for I could not digest the matter which I had learned, and my thoughts kept returning to Littai and the horrid peril to which my wife was to come.

At last I beat out some conclusions, and I think they were more or less just.

In order to obtain his freedom, Grieg had taken conjecture and dressed it up as a fact. He had reason to think we should take the bridle-path, and take it as soon as we could. If he was well served at Littai, he might have reason to think that my wife was going to move. He had drawn a bow at a venture in all that he said: and tonight he would picket the path, to see whether in fact his shaft would bring anything down: and if it did not, he would himself leave the country by the bypass the smugglers used.

Now with Grieg's death – and that I hoped would occur at any moment – the danger would not disappear, for I could not forget the intentness with which the police had been listening to what he said and I had no doubt whatever that, though Grieg himself might fail them, from this night on an ambush was to be laid between the waterfall and the mouth of the bridle-path.

When, therefore, he was dead, we must somehow find George and the Countess and stay their attempt, and when that was done, I must contrive to cross the water in case by some shocking chance Leonie verily meant to attempt to come in that way.

Now when ten minutes had passed, but Grieg had not come, I began to wonder what he was doing, for I was almost certain that when the girl was crossing the sward, I heard the sound of a car. If I was right in this, the police had been gone very nearly a quarter of an hour. Yet Grieg had not come.

It occurred to me suddenly that something might have impelled him to visit his car.

At once I saw that this explanation was good.

Grieg had gone to his car, to bring it up to the house, and was trying to start the engine and wasting his time.

The conclusion did me a world of good, for if it was sound – and of that I had little doubt – Grieg would be playing clean into Rowley's hands. Any moment now the latter would take Grieg's life, and I should be spared a business which as like as not I should bungle – although I must confess I did not dread it as I had when I thought the man helpless as any sheep.

I began to strain my ears for the sound of the shot…

I have always found inaction the hardest of all things to endure, and when ten minutes more had gone by, my impatience began to obtain the upper hand.

If Grieg was not coming, I was wasting valuable time. I could hardly believe that he did not mean to return, but since no shot had been fired, his absence began to argue that he was taking some action of which I should know. I was out of touch with Rowley, who would not dare come to fetch me because I had bade him stay. By leaving the house I should not be yielding ground, for I could always return by the cloister door.

With suchlike rubbish I cheated my common sense and so committed a folly for which I have no excuse.

I stole to the door which had brought me into the hall and let myself into the passage from which I had come. Thence I passed into the cloister and, after glancing about me, across the girdle of turf.

As I did so, my heart smote me, for I knew very well that I ought to have stayed in the hall. Rowley was there to watch the outside of the house and would, if he could, stalk Grieg and shoot him down; but if, before he could do so, Grieg should withdraw to the house, he would count upon my being there to deal with the man.

On the edge of the wood I paused, uncertain whether or no to retrace my steps. And whilst I was hesitating, a shot rang out.

I listened to the echoes fading with a hammering heart.

Rowley had done the business and saved my face.

Now if I had stopped to think, I should have made straight for the point at which the shot had been fired, for now there was no longer any reason for avoiding the girdle of turf; but because I had grown so accustomed to keeping myself out of view, without thinking I held to the woods, alternately running and walking as fast as I could.

It was therefore ten minutes or so before between the trees I made out the shape of Grieg's car.

'Rowley, where are you?' I cried, something out of breath.

A screech answered me.

'Down for your life, sir!'

With the words came the roar of a pistol

and a bullet went by my ear.

No dead man ever fell flat so quickly as I, or ever lay more still. Indeed, I frankly confess that I feigned myself dead, for for all I knew I was fully exposed to Grieg's eye, and all my hope of safety was in convincing the man that his shot had gone home. Since Grieg was no simpleton, this hope was excessively thin, and I should have made ready to die had I not been absorbed in remarking the beauty of life.

I was now in a kind of danger which I had never known.

It was not so much that I was helpless, as that I dared not run the risk of helping myself. Grieg might be unable to see me: I might be in a position to bring him down. But because I had no means of knowing whether or no I was exposed, my hands and my eyes and my wits were as useless to me as the buttons upon my coat. I knew that the wood was not open, that here and there were patches of undergrowth: and though these were thin and straggling and would have been rejected as cover by any patrol, if I had fallen behind one it would have served my need. But whether I was behind one I did not know: and in case I was not behind one I dared not look.

That is an account of my condition. My state of mind began and ended with fear.

The impression that Grieg could see me was painfully strong, and I am ashamed to say that I solemnly debated my chances of hearing the fatal shot.

Two things I knew. The first was that Rowley was a little way off to my right, and the second that Grieg must be somewhere directly ahead, quite close to the car. So much my ears had told me. Whether they were standing or lying I had not the faintest idea.

I, then, lay as I had fallen, flat on my chest, with my right cheek pressed tight against the earth and my left eye upon a small spider that seemed very much concerned.

I shall never forget the silence which now prevailed.

It was not the silence of the night, for now and then a bird piped or fluttered, and the steady hum of insects was lading the soft, warm air; but the imminence of havoc lent it the air of a prelude the end of which might at any instant arrive. As such it was charged with a suspense which had I not borne it, I would have said could not be borne, and to this day I cannot pass without a shudder through any spinney which remembers that deadly scene.

I afterwards learned that Grieg was lying behind a wheel of the car and Rowley behind a tree-stump, with ten feet of ground around him as bare as his hand.

As I had expected, Grieg had come for the car, and Rowley had followed him softly, to take his life. To make quite sure of his prey, he had rightly taken his time. By the time he was in position, Grieg had grown sick of trying to start the engine and had opened the bonnet and was cursing and peering within. When he looked up from his business, there was Rowley on the opposite side of the car, pistol in hand. Before he could move, Rowley had fired at his forehead, but to his horror the pistol had failed to go off. To stand still, fumbling, was fatal, and Rowley had leaped for cover with all his might. Had Grieg stood his ground, he could hardly have missed his man: as it was, he fired under the car and the bullet went wide.

The result was a deadlock.

Grieg lay behind his wheel, and, twenty feet distant Rowley behind his stump, each of them waiting and watching for the other to move. And I lay a little apart, waiting and watching my spider and wondering dismally whether my hour was come.

We might, I suppose, have stayed where we were until dark. Indeed, I think we must have done so, had not a strange thing happened to cut our Gordian knot.

I became aware of some sound which was faintly disturbing the silence I found so hard to endure. It was half a rustle and half a medley of thuds, and, after a little, swelled into the movement of bodies and the patter of many feet. The next instant my nose declared the approach of a flock of goats.

Now goats are fearless and curious and like to inspect anything which they find unusual, in the hope I suppose, of its proving fit to be eaten or containing some food: moreover, a wise goatherd will let them go much as they please, for if he allows them some licence, they will generally do his bidding without any fuss. I, therefore, hoped very hard that the way they were going would take them close to the car, for if once they espied its coachwork, I was sure they would not be content to pass it by. Since they were approaching from behind me, any such movement would be likely to screen me from Grieg and so would give me a chance of taking the cover of which my need was so sore.

So it fell out.

The smell grew stronger, and the sound of their coming more loud. Then a goat walked stiffly past me and another stopped to pluck at the edge of my cuff. An instant later the flock was thrusting like a wedge between me and the car.

In a flash I was up and darting between the trees...

I swung myself round a chestnut, to see Rowley running, bent double, for a bramble-bush on his right.

As he took up his new position, I swung myself on to a branch and so to a fork which made a natural embrasure commanding the car.

The first thing I saw was the goatherd, who was staring open-mouthed upon a tussock of grass. After a little he addressed it though I could not hear what he said. For a moment I thought him an idiot: then it dawned upon me that Grieg was behind the tussock and that the clown was asking him what he did there. An instant later Grieg lifted a furious head.

Comedy and tragedy sometimes go cheek by jowl.

I have never seen anything more ludicrous than Grieg's rabid rejection of the goatherd's ill-timed advances, unless it be the goatherd's indignation at his repulse. So far from withdrawing, the latter protested with vigour against what no doubt he considered a breach of good taste, wagging his forefinger, as though reproving some urchin, and of course advertising Grieg's presence with all his might. When his victim moved to a bush, he actually followed him up to conclude his harangue, till at last Grieg sprang to his feet, sent his tormentor sprawling, took to his heels and was instantly lost to view.

As I slid down from my perch, Rowley leaped up in pursuit, but caught his foot in a trailer which brought him down. By this time the goatherd was roaring like any bull, so that the sound of Grieg's passage was utterly lost, and since to follow him blindly in such a place would have been worse than foolish, I shook my head at Rowley and turned the opposite way.

An instant later we crossed the drive that led to Vigil and entered the coppice beyond.

Now it was in my mind to make for the house. Then I saw that if Grieg did not follow, we should be as good as beleaguered until night fell. And so long we could not wait, because, whatever happened, we had to find the Countess and George. I, therefore, led the way to the point from which we had first that morning surveyed the house, for this made an excellent covert which we could leave unobserved whenever we pleased.

There Rowley told me his tale and displayed an affecting relief to find me alive and unhurt. Hearing me fall, he had made up his mind that I was dead, and the fact that I made no movement confirmed this belief. He inclined to the view that while I was on the ground I was out of Grieg's sight, 'for, sir,' said he, 'he's not a man to take chances and, as for killing the wounded, why, he'd use them like stepping-stones if it saved his feet getting wet.'

'He didn't kill the goatherd,' said I.

'Because he wasn't wasting a shot, sir.

He's only got three rounds left.'

As like as not he was right. Grieg was a hard man.

Here I should say that I dared not fire upon the fellow whilst I was up in the tree, as well for fear of hitting the goatherd as because of the hue and cry which the clown would have certainly raised if I had killed my man.

The time was now eleven o'clock, and we were both hungry and thirsty and very tired: so I bade Rowley sleep for an hour, whilst I kept watch, 'and then,' said I, 'I'll sleep for another hour. Unless we can lay Grieg's ghost, we shall have to let the car go. And that means we must leg it – perhaps to the bridle-path.'

'Very good, sir,' said Rowley cheerfully.

Two minutes later he was sleeping like the dead.

I seemed to have slept for two minutes when Rowley laid a hand on my arm, but when he showed me my watch, it was one o'clock.

He had nothing at all to report, and, after a little discussion, we crawled out of sight of the mansion and started across the park. We bore south-east, for this was the line which the peasant-girl had taken and so, presumably, that of the Countess and George; but my hope of finding them was extremely faint and I was not at all sure that we should not do better to try to make certain of Grieg. I had, however, no stomach for scouring the wood, and such watch as we could keep on the mansion was simple enough to elude. Indeed, for all we knew, the man was already on his way to the bridle-path.

It is hard to say, looking back, that we made a mistake. Subsequent events proved nothing. And I often think that whichever way I had chosen would have brought us to the same conjuncture, for that, had we but known it, the matter was now out of our hands and we were but playing out the parts which Destiny itself had approved.

We had gone perhaps half a mile when I thought that I saw some movement a little way off. At once we crouched in the bracken, to which we had kept; but the movement was not repeated, and I was beginning to think that my eyes were too ready to see, when the Prince's dog came gambolling out of a dip in the ground and an instant later the scarlet coat of his mistress rose into view.

I bade Rowley rise and we went to meet her at once, for I had no doubt she was bearing a telegram and I meant, if I could, to contrive to see what it said.

As we came near—

'I was hoping to see you,' she said, 'because I have found your friends. If you please, I will lead you to them, when I have taken this telegram up to the house.'

She plucked a folded paper out of her fair, white shirt.

'May I see it?' said I.

She gave it into my hand.

It was addressed to 'Baron Sabre', and when I turned it about, I found it was carefully sealed.

'Are they all so addressed?' said I.

'Yes,' she said. 'They are opened by Major Grieg.'

'My servant will take it,' said I. 'And you shall turn back and take me to find my friends.' I turned to Rowley and gave him the telegram. 'That wire is for Major Grieg. I have told her that you will take it up to the house. Make as if you were going to, and as soon as you're out of our sight, turn round and follow us. Whatever you do, don't lose us. She's going to take me to where Mr Hanbury is.'

'Very good, sir,' said Rowley; and, with that, he touched his hat and turned back the way we had come.

'Good,' said the girl softly.

She whistled the dog and set her face to the south.

I was not proud of my deceit, but, if I was to see the message, unless I had involved its bearer, I do not know what I could have done. There and then I determined that my pretty friend must not suffer for her credulity. To that end I asked her name.

'I am Lelia,' she said. 'I live with my uncle at Merring. Now that he has married again, I have little to do. Why do you keep a servant, yet go unshaved?'

'Because I am in hiding,' I said. 'I am a stranger here and I have broken some law. I hope to get out of the country before very long.'

Lelia regarded me straitly with fearless eyes.

'You do not look a malefactor,' she said.

'They would make me out one,' said I.

Lelia lifted her head.

'Perhaps they are envious,' she said. 'You are very tall and strong. And your friends are in hiding, too?'

I nodded.

'That is why this morning I asked you to hold your tongue.'

'I have done so,' she said. 'But not because of your money.' She stopped there and flushed. Then a hand went into her bosom and pulled out my fifty-crown note. 'I would like you to take this again. I do not want money from you for what I have done.'

'I want to make you a present, Lelia; and I have nothing else.'

'I do not care,' she said. 'Take it back – for your pretty face.'

I had to laugh, but though she was smiling, she set her chin in the air.

As I put out a hand for the money, the cuff

of my coat slipped back and showed the steel on my wrist.

In a flash she had hold of my arm.

'Who has done this?' she breathed. 'Who has dared to put handcuffs upon you?'

All her kindness of heart looked out of her fine, brown eyes.

'I told you I had enemies,' I said. 'But see. I have been set free. The link has been cut.'

'It is shameful,' she said hotly. 'I will beg a file from the blacksmith and cut them through. See where this one has chafed you.'

The rub was nothing, but she would not leave the matter until I had let her pull down the sleeves of my shirt and slip the steelrings within the silk double-cuffs. This, much against my will, for though Bell has washed my shirt in a canvas bucket at Vigil, beside her spotless linen it seemed very foul.

'I am very dirty,' I said. 'I have not changed for a week, and I have slept in my clothes.'

Lelia drew in her breath.

'When I come with a file, I will bring a sweet shirt,' she said. 'And a pair of my stockings if you will put them on. I do not always go barefoot.'

I shook my head.

'No,' said I. 'You must keep your small hand out of this. You are very sweet and kind, but if they found out that you had helped me, they would come down upon you.'

'I am not afraid,' said Lelia. 'But why does

not this Major Grieg help you? I thought he was head of the police.'

'Between you and me, I don't trust him. That's why I am leaving this house.'

Leila nodded.

'I think you do well,' she said. 'He is a brute of a man. How is it that my dog knows you? Your friends were sure that he would, but they would not say why.'

'He did me a service,' said I, 'a few days ago. He was set on to me, but, instead, he licked my hand. And so, to save him a beating, I took him away and lost him here in this park.'

'And here I found him,' said Lelia. She turned a radiant face. 'There is your present, you see the present you wanted to give me. And I never knew.'

'I could not wish him a better mistress,' said I.

'I think he is happy,' she said. 'And I have never had such a present: all his ways are so handsome, and he will not eat except at my hand.' She whistled again, and the dog was by her side in a flash. As she caressed him—'He is very obedient, you see,' she added artlessly.

'There is more than obedience,' I said, and so there was.

All this time we were making our way through the park, sometimes passing through bracken and sometimes beneath the trees, but I saw no sign of buildings, and if we were treading some path, it was such that I could not see.

'I do not understand,' said the girl, 'your having to do with Grieg. You are not of his kidney. How could you think that he would give you shelter and play the friend?'

'It's a long, dull story,' said I. 'Don't trouble your pretty head.'

Lelia stooped to gather a flower.

'I do not think it is long, or dull either. And – and I should like to know.' She rose, set the flower in her shirt and looked into my face. 'Of course, if you do not trust me...'

I would like to be shown the man that could have faced those eyes.

'Lelia,' said I, 'I have played you a rotten trick. Grieg is my enemy. That telegram you were taking – I did not send it to him. I told my servant to keep it, and when you were gone to give it to me to read.'

For a moment she regarded me steadily. Then, to my infinite distress, I saw her eyes fill with tears.

'I would have given it you,' she said shakily.

Then she put up her bare, brown arm, hid her face in its crook and began to weep.

I have never felt such a brute: and when I remembered that, thanks to my positive orders, Rowley's eyes were upon us, I have never felt such a fool. Indeed, to this day he must think me utterly shameless and bold as brass, for I set my arm about her and put her hand to my lips.

'You did not trust me,' she sobbed. 'You speak to me fair, but you think–'

'I deceived you,' said I, 'for your sake – not for my own. I knew that if I asked you, you would give me the telegram. But I did not want to involve you. If there was trouble to come, I wanted you to be able to say you had been deceived.'

'No, no. You did not trust me.'

'I did, indeed,' I protested. 'This morning I felt the better for having seen your face. I have told you the truth, Lelia – by no means to your advantage, still less to mine; but I am a poor liar, and your pretty eyes are to blame. And if you care to hear it, I will tell you my tale.'

She lifted her tear-stained face and looked into my eyes.

'I will believe you,' she said, 'but please do not do it again.'

With my mind very much upon Rowley, I let her go; but I think she would have liked me to kiss her, and since God knows I had hurt her enough for one day, I sought to explain my indifference as best I could.

'I have a wife, Lelia, with whom I am deeply in love.'

'Where is she, then?' said the girl.

'She is in my heart, Lelia.'

'Hers should be leaping,' said she. With a little sigh, she set her head in the air. 'Will you tell her I'm hard to please, but I liked her man?'

'I shall tell her you were very good to him,' said I.

Then she called to the dog, and we went on our way.

As we went, I told her our story, but mentioned no names. I had no desire to dishonour the Prince in her eyes. And of course I said nothing of the Countess' marriage to Grieg.

She listened greedily.

When I had done—

'You must wait awhile,' she said. 'You cannot escape just now. This Grieg is full of some dirty work for the Prince. They are looking for someone, you know. They had the troops out for three days. And until they are caught, I think you had better lie close, or the net they have spread for another will fall upon you. They say that the Grand Duchess' husband is here in Riechtenburg – the Grand Duchess Leonie. She is a darling. She was to have married the Prince, but when he came to the throne, she said she could bear him no more. And if the Prince could take him...' She broke off and shrugged her shoulders. 'I think it is true,' she added, 'for Leonie lives at Littai, and that is where the telegrams come from twice in the day. Why did you want to see the last one I brought?'

'Oh, Lelia,' said I, laughing, 'must I tell you the truth?'

'Why not?' says she, with her big eyes full of surprise.

'Well, then, I have a message for Leonie – a message from you.'

'From me?' cried the girl, staring.

I nodded.

'You gave it to me just now. I was to tell her that though you were hard to please, you liked her man.'

She started violently. Then–

'For heavens sake!' she breathed. 'And I never guessed. Oh, my lord–'

'I am no lord. I am plain Richard Chandos.'

Lelia lowered her eyes, and the blood came into her face.

'I am very sorry,' she said humbly, 'and very much ashamed. I – I have made very bold.'

'You have been very sweet and natural.' I took her hand and kissed it. 'If I did not respect you, I should not do that.'

'You must tell her Highness,' said Lelia. 'She would be very scornful.'

'Not she,' said I. 'She will write you a letter of thanks for being so good to "her man".'

Lelia stared at the sky.

'She is very lovely,' she said irrelevantly. 'I do not wonder that you have eyes for nobody else. She never goes barefoot, I suppose.'

'No,' said I, smiling.

Lelia sighed.

'I do not always,' she said. 'I told you. I look much better in stockings and bright leather shoes.'

'Never wear them for me,' said I. 'If Leonie lived as you do, she would never put on a stocking from one year's end to the next. Besides, I – I like your bare legs.'

Lelia smiled.

'I am glad if they please you,' she said.

Since now she knew who I was, I told her the rest of our tale, only suppressing Marya's marriage to Grieg. At once she declared, as had Ramon, that the Prince was afraid for his throne, for that all the country loved Leonie and would be only too glad to have her to reign in his stead.

'Be that as it may,' said I, 'I'm afraid she's leaving Littai. I cannot believe she will come by the smugglers' way, but Grieg may have information which I have not. But he cannot have known that we were to take that path and take it tonight. That was pure–'

Lelia let out a cry and clapped her hands to her face. In her eyes there was plain horror.

'Oh, my lord, *I told him.* I never gave it a thought. When I took the first telegram. I could not find old Andrew and so I went into the hall. Grieg was there – on the stairs, in his shirt-sleeves, with a towel in his hands. He asked me if I had seen anyone by the way. And I said I had met your friends and was looking for you. And he said he would give you the message, if I would give it to him. And so I did – *I betrayed you.* Mother of God, forgive me! I meant no ill.'

As well as I could, I brushed her reproaches aside.

'How could you know, Lelia? Besides, if you did any ill, you have made it good. I feared that my friends would walk clean into a trap, but now it is you that have saved them by showing me where they are.'

For all my logic, she would not be comforted, till I said she should help to hide us until we could make our escape some other way.

'Will I not?' she cried. 'You shall lie in the Great Bear barn. I will watch the livelong night, and you shall sleep like a child.'

'Not tonight, Lelia. Tonight I must take the path in case Leonie comes.'

'But they will take you,' she cried and caught at my arm.

'Not they,' said I. 'Forewarned is forearmed. I shall be there before them, and the odds are on him who comes first to a place like that.'

'I cannot recall it,' said Lelia, knitting her brows. 'I know the path, but I cannot remember the fall.'

I told her again of the bypass and how easy it was to find it for such as had ears to hear the water come down.

'But you will return?' says she. 'Even if her Highness is there, you will come back.'

'Oh, yes,' said I. 'I must return for the Countess. If Leonie comes, I shall send her back to Bariche. But I do not think that she will.'

'And then you will let me help you and watch while you sleep?'

'Indeed, I will, Lelia. I shall be very tired.'

She sighed contentedly.

'Then that is settled,' she said. 'I am very glad. And please tell me more of her Highness. Does she have a great many dresses? And is there always a servant behind her chair?'

If her talk was downright, she was as naïve and eager as the first breath of spring upon the year; Eve herself cannot have been more natural, and I have seen many women that bore big names, yet had not a ghost of her charm nor a tenth of her dignity. About her fancy for me she said no more, but was so frank and friendly that all my embarrassment fled and I felt an ease and comfort that I had not known since I left Littai six days before. Why she liked me so well I shall never know, for she was as fresh and charming as I was haggard and foul; indeed, I have seen many tramps by the side of the road that cut a nobler figure than I did that day. But I think the truth is that I had the look of a hunted man and that, as Desdemona the Moor, she pities me.

She would, I believe, have questioned me till bed-time, but ten minutes later we came to a sudden valley with a falling stream at the bottom and, brown and white in the sunshine, a little old mill. Its water-wheel was silent, and the place seemed derelict; ivy was scrambling up its chimney-pots and tall grass leaned over the path which led to its door; but it was by no means a ruin, and the bulwarks of foliage about it made it so lovely a bower that I think that, once he had seen it, a painter would never have rested until he had done what he could to capture the scene.

'They are there,' said Lelia, pointing a slim, brown arm. 'I left them in the old parlour that looks out upon the pond. I will not go with you now, because I must go to the village to get the file, but I shall be back in an hour. If you would bathe, I think you may do so safely, for nobody comes this way. But you will please be careful to bathe below the mill. I do not want to be tiresome, but–'

'You are very sweet,' said I. 'I will not bathe in the pond. And now listen. If you should be asked, you took the telegram to the house and, seeing no one, you left it on the mat in the passage for Grieg or Andrew to find.'

She nodded intelligently ... with her eyes fast upon the mill.

Then–

'Good-bye,' she said softly, speaking half to herself.

'"Good-bye"?' said I. 'But you are coming back, Lelia?'

'Oh, yes, I am coming back to you – and your friends.'

With that she was gone.

When she was out of sight, I went down to the mill, and when I reached its doorway, I turned and looked back. Instantly Rowley appeared at the head of the dell...

As I might have expected, the telegram made me a message I could not read.

Palette two tubes vermilion two indigo noon.

One thing only it told me. That was that Grieg's spy was playing the part of an artist to cover his dirty work. Their arrangement was simple. A list of painting materials had been turned into a code which if he had not before him, the most skilful of cipherers could not interpret one word of the messages sent. I regretted bitterly that when Grieg had been in our power we had not searched his pockets for any such document.

I handed it back to Rowley.

'Burn this to ashes,' said I. 'And pick a place here from which you can keep a lookout. The river side is all right, but under the sound of the water a man could enter the building before we knew he was there.'

'That's right, sir,' said Rowley.

'And look out for – for Miss Lelia. She's a heart of gold, and she's coming back in an hour.'

With that, I stepped over the threshold and into the mill.

I found myself in a hall but a few feet square. A broken staircase faced me, and an open door on the left gave directly into the room where the grinders lay. If the parlour looked on to the pond, I knew it must lead from this room, and there, sure enough, was a door on the farther wall.

I was just about to approach it, when it was softly opened and Marya Dresden appeared.

Her manner was so striking that I stood still where I was, with no thought to spy upon her, but because I was taken aback by what I saw.

Her air was furtive, her movement that of a thief, and had her world been shattered, she could not have looked more listless or more forlorn. Her eyes that seemed always alight had lost their lustre, her body seemed heavy-laden, and she was plainly absorbed in the contemplation of grief.

She closed the door behind her and stood for a moment with one hand up to her lips.

As she took a step forward, I spoke her name, but she did not hear my voice for the constant rush of the mill-race a few feet away.

Suddenly she saw me and started against the wall.

'What is it, Marya?' said I, and made to come to her side.

'No, no,' she cried, shrinking. 'Stand back.'

I stared at her, saucer-eyed.

'What on earth's the matter?' I said. 'What–'

Marya cut me short.

'By what right?' she flamed. 'By what shadow of right have you dared to do this thing?'

Looking upon her, I made sure she had lost her wits.

'What thing?' I said at last.

'Murder,' says she. 'Murder.'

I shook my head.

'I have done no murder,' said I.

'Liar,' she rapped, recoiling. 'There's blood on your hands.'

'Come, Marya,' said I. 'I give you my solemn word that no blood has been shed.'

'George said–'

'I daresay he did,' said I. 'But the bird has flown.'

She drew in her breath.

'You went out to do murder,' she said.

'I don't put it like that,' said I. 'I went out

to settle with Grieg.'

'By what right?' she cried, leaning forward with blazing eyes. 'Isn't that my affair? Isn't it for me to say whether I want him killed? and you – you take it upon you–' She clapped her hands to her face. 'Oh, God, why was I born?'

I stepped to her side.

'I'm sorry, Marya,' I said. 'But I never thought twice. And anyway I've failed. He – is alive and well.'

'You went out to kill him,' she said, 'without telling me.'

'I know. I suppose I was wrong, but–'

'"Suppose"? The man's my husband.'

'I know,' said I. 'But that doesn't make him my friend.'

'It gives me the right to be told before my friends put him to death.'

'So be it,' said I shortly. 'And here and now I tell you that the very next time I see him I'm going to try again.'

'And I forbid you,' she cried. 'I have the right.'

'The point is this,' said I. 'I've only one life. And as Grieg is out to get it – well, I've got to look after myself.'

'Do you blame him?' said Marya. 'He knows you're trying to kill him. Do you blame him for self-defence?'

'I don't, said I. 'But that doesn't alter the facts. He's taken to shooting at sight.'

'Then keep out of his way.'

'Unhappily his way is my way. Tonight he's going to meet someone. She doesn't know it, of course; but mercifully it's come to my ears. Perhaps you can guess who I mean.'

Marya put a hand to her throat, and although she did not speak, I saw her lips frame the word which she would have used.

'Who?'

'Yes,' I said. 'You're quite right. He's going to meet Leonie.'

I had expected that my news would, so to speak, silence her guns. I was never more mistaken. It merely unmasked a battery of which I had never dreamed.

Marya shut fast her eyes, put her hands behind her and leaned back against the wall.

The queer, old-time surroundings, her artless pose, her slight, short-skirted figure and tumbled golden hair argued absurdly that she and I were two children quarrelling over some by-law of hide-and-seek.

As though to attest this conceit, Marya tilted her chin, pushed back her hair with a little, petulant gesture and opened her eyes.

'I will stop him,' she said. 'I am going back to my husband, and I will make him see reason to hold his hand.'

A moment or two went by before I could find my tongue.

Then–

'You're going back?' I said.

Marya nodded.

'That's right. I must, of course. I've married the man. Unless and until he gives me cause to leave him–'

'"Cause"?' I almost shouted.

'Hush,' says she. 'George is asleep in there. I – I don't want him waked.'

'But for his sake,' I cried. 'He loves you. He's risked his life to–'

'I know,' said Marya. 'I know. It's a dreadful mess. I sold myself to save him, and now we're both down on the deal. Don't you want something to eat?' She jerked her head at the doorway through which she had come. 'There's bread and wine in there.'

'They can wait,' said I. 'We've got to settle this first.'

'There's nothing to settle,' says she. 'I've shot my bolt. I shot it last night in the chapel, and when I fled this morning I wasn't myself.'

'But if you love George–'

'"If"?' She clasped her hands and put them up to her throat. 'When I came out of that chapel I felt that my heart was dead. I was mentally paralysed. My mind wouldn't work. Only my body went on. When he said "Sit down", my body did as he said. When he said "Drink", my hand and my mouth obeyed. When I signed the register, he had to spell out my name, and I wrote it down by letters just as he said. After dinner he was sent for… Waiting for him to come back was the worst of all. My fingers were stiff – he'd kissed them. It seemed as though now he'd turned my body to stone… And then George came to me, Richard, and raised the dead. You couldn't have done it; nor even Leonie. I was out of the reach of medicine. George's love never did it. It was the touch – not of the man that loved me, but of the man I loved.'

'Then why break his heart?' said I.

Marya raised her eyebrows.

'D'you think,' she answered, 'that Clytæmnestra could sleep?'

'Clytæmnestra subscribed to her husband's death. If I kill Grieg in fair fight, it's nothing to do with you.'

'Of course it is. I've got to try and save him – try to prevent the duel. Can't you see my position, Richard? You went out last night to kill him, because by my consent he had made me his wife. The marriage register was your warrant – your executioner's warrant for what you were going to do. By the grace of God you failed and saved me from a reproach which no woman could ever bear. But can't you see that, just because he is my husband, he simply must not die at the hand of one of my friends?'

'No, I'm damned if I can,' said I.

'I'm in love with George. Doesn't that make it any clearer?'

I shook my head.

'I admit,' said I, 'that the business smacks of the Stone Age: but that's Grieg's fault. Three hours ago I heard what he said to the Prince. "Against those men I had a personal grudge, and so I took the job on". So, you see, the quarrel was there before ever we dragged you in. I also heard him allege that he had no compunction in sending us out of the country *because he knew we'd come back.*'

'He was bluffing,' said Marya swiftly.

'At that moment,' said I, 'he happened to be speaking the truth. "They were bound to come back to get the Countess" was what he said. And so we were. To put it brutally, he sold you a pup. When he stood by your side in the chapel, he must have laughed in his sleeve. But, Marya, that's what comes of a lamb lying down with a lion.'

'But he couldn't have known, Richard. You might have believed my letter, and, besides, he did his part. In getting you out of the country he took a tremendous risk.'

'He never dreamed he was taking a risk at all. Provided he shut his men's mouths, who was to know? If we hadn't come back, the Prince would have thought we'd escaped. But he knew that we would come back. And if I hadn't been arrested in the very act of entry, and if I hadn't kept our bill from *The Broken Egg...*'

Marya shook her fair head.

'There's nothing doing Richard. I know he's ruthless and I'm sure he hasn't a scruple of any kind. But he did his part of the bargain he made with me. As a result, he's an outlaw – unless you've overheard something which shows that he'd bluffed the Prince.'

'And you've done your part,' said I. 'The deal is over and done with; and if you can't see that, *he can*. Two hours and a half ago I walked clean into his arms. He had his pistol out. I never suspected his presence, and he never gave me a chance. He fired without warning, point-blank – and the bullet went by my ear. Don't think I'm complaining – I'm not; I'm stating facts. You say you can't marry George, if Grieg dies by my hand. Can you love and cherish Grieg, if I die by his?'

Marya stared upon the floor.

'I've got to stop it,' she said. 'I'm the only person who can, and it's plainly my job. I've a foot in each camp.'

'Don't you believe it,' said I. 'Grieg's no respecter of persons. Not even the Prince has any standing with him.'

Marya averted her eyes.

'If I – I kept him at home tonight...'

'You'd sit down four,' I said grimly. 'And get up three.'

There was a little silence.

All of a sudden Marya began to laugh.

'I throw in my hand,' she said. 'I retire. I

give up. I can't compete with the Stone Age. I'm out of my depth. A week ago I was shopping – choosing gramophone records and matching silk. And now…' She broke off and shrugged her shoulders. 'So far as I can see, I've messed everything up. I was made the decoy to get you here; I made you stay in my garden and so fall foul of the Prince; I've gone and married the man who's trying his best to kill you; and, like a fool, I've let George see that I love him – if I'd had any sense last night, I'd have ordered him out of the house. And now, as I say, I retire. I think I've done enough damage. And I feel I don't care what happens.' She put a hand to her eyes. 'Oh, I'm so sick of it all. D'you think we shall ever see Littai? And sit on the little terrace under the limes?'

'The day after tomorrow,' said I, 'if you do as I say.'

'All right. I'm beaten, Richard. You've a compelling way. Don't you want something to eat?'

'In ten minutes' time,' said I. 'But first I must have a bathe.'

'And Rowley?' says she.

'He's keeping watch outside. You never heard me come in, and it might have been – somebody else.'

'Where is he? I'll take him some food.'

Together we went, to find him flat on the

211

tiles of a little outhouse, so sheltered by the slope and the ivy that had he not spoken, we should have sought him in vain.

As she turned back to the doorway–

'D'you think it's safe to bathe, Richard? I mean, if they came upon you, what would you do? Without any shoes, you couldn't so much as run.'

I pointed down stream, where trees overhung the banks and the water flowed into hiding beneath the spread of their leaves.

'Safe enough there,' I said. 'If the enemy came, he'd only have eyes for the mill. Besides, he won't. Lelia says that nobody comes this way.'

Marya opened her eyes.

'Who ever is Lelia?'

'You knew her before I did,' said I.

'Oh, I know. The peasant-girl. Isn't she sweet?'

'She is indeed,' said I. 'What's more, she's out to help us with all her heart.'

'How much have you told her?'

'Everything else,' said I. 'All she asks is to be trusted.'

Marya nodded thoughtfully.

'"For beauty lives with kindness",' she said.

With that, she went into the mill, and I made my way to the willows and stripped in their shade.

The water was warm, and since I had in my pocket a small piece of soap, I made a better toilet than I had known for a week. Indeed, to leave the sweet water and put on my dirty clothes was so distasteful a step that I shirked it again and again, and twenty minutes went by before I got back to the mill.

From his perch on the tiles of the outhouse Rowley regarded my wet and rumpled hair with an envious eye.

'Your turn next,' I said smiling. 'But you mustn't bathe directly after a meal.'

'I haven't had a meal, sir,' was the dismal reply.

'But the Countess was going to bring you something to eat.'

'She hasn't yet, sir.'

A sudden fear seized my heart.

'She hasn't gone out, has she?'

'Oh, no, sir. She's still inside.'

I entered the mill, frowning.

The room where we had argued was empty, and I crossed to the door in its wall.

I opened this very gently, to see George fast asleep on an armful of fern. To one side lay some small loaves of bread and two flasks of wine. Of Marya Dresden there was no sign at all.

When I looked round, I noticed a second door. This was made in two halves, the upper of which was ajar and was laying a ribbon of sunlight upon the floor.

In a flash I had pulled it wide open.

It gave to a little footbridge which spanned

the foaming race and led to a patch of green-sward. To this the woods came down, so that anyone going that way would be out of sight of the mill in ten seconds of time.

I do not doubt that far shrewder men than I have been fooled by a girl, but I think that only a fool would have been gammoned as I was, and when I remembered Marya's sudden submission and her desire to be shown where Rowley was keeping his watch, I was ready to stamp for vexation with my simplicity.

Marya was gone back to Grieg – of that I had no shadow of doubt. And she had twenty minutes start...

Ruefully I stared at the woods.

"I've got to stop it. I'm the only person who can, and it's plainly my job".

Brave beyond all compare, loyal to her high estate, scrupulous to a hair, Marya Grieg was gone to cast her pearls before swine. I wondered dully whether her backguard husband would rend her or no.

Then another sentence of hers stole into my mind.

"If I – I kept him at home tonight"...

For a moment my heart stood still.

Then I vaulted over the half-door and on to the bridge.

As I landed, the timbers gave way as though they had been but match-sticks fastened together with glue; for a fraction of a second the mill-race roared in my ears, and then I was fast under water with a shocking pain in my head.

CHAPTER 7

The Way of a Maid

Had the wheel been running, I must, of course, have been killed: but though I never looked, I fancy its spindle had bent until the fans or paddles were resting on the bed of the race.

As I sank, I was seized by the current, and before I could think, the savage rush of the water had hurled me against a fan which was wholly submerged and was holding me there, as a puppet that has floated down stream may be held against the bars of some sluice.

When I sought instinctively to rise, the fan next above prevented me, and such was the weight of the water that I could not get clear.

The uproar, the darkness, the merciless thrash of the mill-race upon my body and limbs, the strain of holding my breath and the horrid sense of being held down to be drowned – these things, I think, were for my salvation, for such a load of torture inspired me with the passion of a madman to save my life.

After my head had struck the fan, the water had laid me sideways against the wheel, but the channel was not very wide, and with my hand I was able to touch the wall. At once I forced my left arm as far as I could through the flood, keeping my hand to the wall in the hope of encountering something which I could clutch. So, by God's mercy, my fingers came to a niche which I knew was above the water, for I felt the air on my hand. This afforded me handhold, and by dint of bending my arm, I hauled myself just far enough to clear the fan above me and draw in one blessed breath, before again giving way to the weight of the head of water which held me down.

After resting a moment, I hauled myself clear again, as much to take breath as to see what next I could do, but such was the welter that I could see nothing at all and, after a frantic moment, was forced to yield to the pressure and sink back beneath the fan which, like some merciless ceiling was holding me down.

I was now near as desperate as ever, for to fight such a fight for more than another few moments was not in any man's power, and unless I could make some progress, I was as good as dead.

I decided to take one more breath and then make a great endeavour to find the niche with my right hand, instead of my left. In that way, when I was clear, I should have my face to the fan, instead of my back, and if I could only contrive to fling my left arm above it, the water would hold me against it like a rag which a stiff wind holds to a clothes-line without any peg.

I did not at all like letting go my niche, for heaven only knew if in all the welter I ever should find it again; but if there were other ways, I could not see them, and I think I was lucky to be granted even this use of my wits.

How I managed to turn under water I cannot tell, nor yet how I found the niche with my other hand, but I know that my lungs were bursting when I hauled my head into the air and that when at last I had my arm over the fan that had held me down, I hung like a wretch on a cart's tail, more dead than alive.

And that was as much as I could do.

As though enraged at my presumption, the waters seemed to conspire to war me down, roaring like fiends, leaping like hangmen upon my neck and shoulders, bruising my chest against the edge of the fan and holding my legs from beneath me with a drag before which I was as helpless as a straw in a gale of wind.

By now I was shouting for help with all my might. This with scarce any hope, for Rowley was out of earshot and George was asleep and the roar of the water went far to drown my voice. Indeed, it seemed that I had but postponed my end, for while I could do nothing more to help myself, it was very plain that I could not hold out for long before such punishment.

Still, I shouted desperately, now thinking of Marya Dresden, and now of Grieg, and now of Littai and Leonie and a little way she had of holding her precious hands.

If Lelia had not returned before her time, I must have been dead.

As it was, my strength was fast failing, when I heard a shriek from behind me and then, a moment later, a cry from George.

'Rowley,' I yelled. 'Get Rowley and open the hatch.'

As I spoke, I nodded my head at the little hatch or window that gave to the wheel. This was some two feet square and was used, I think, by the miller to clean the fans.

I afterwards learned that George could not hear what I said, but that Lelia read my gesture and dragged him off to the hatch.

Whilst she was fetching Rowley, he flung the shutter open and clambered on to the wheel, but though I could see him above me, he could not reach so far. Then Rowley came and caught hold of George's legs, and a moment later his hands went under my arms.

By now I was so much exhausted that I could give him no help, until I had taken some rest, and since, though he could support me, he had not the strength to drag me clear of the fan, we stayed as we were for two minutes with our faces four inches apart, like a couple of acrobats.

'The Brothers Bung,' said George, grinning. 'In their daring confidence trick. Real water. And you needn't tell me what happened, because I can see for myself what's left of the bridge. Damned dangerous things, they are. And now if you've had a breather, shall we try and go home?'

He must have suffered torture, but he never complained, and, whilst he held me, I dragged myself up his body as though it were the trunk of some tree.

Then Rowley's hand grasped my wrist, and George began to go back, and two minutes later they pulled me out of danger and through the hatch.

As I reached the floor, Lelia's arm went about me and she put a phial to my lips...

'And now where's Marya?' said George.

As well as I could, I told him my wretched news, while Lelia fussed about me, now taking off my coat and now my shirt and rubbing my chest and shoulders with handfuls of fern.

Poor George clapped his hands to his face. 'Gone back?' he said shakily. 'Gone back to the butcher's yard?'

'You must take Rowley,' I said, 'and follow at once. For God's sake be careful. Myself, I think it likely that Grieg may have gone. What's at least equally likely is that Marya will lose her bearings and then her way. So don't rush in. And come back here when you can. We can't get out to-night – Rowley will tell you why. And he'll tell you why I must go to the bridle-path. The line to take with Marya is that it's my life or Grieg's. And if you can, turn Lelia on to argue the point with her. She's very downright; but when you're dealing with Grieg, you can't wear gloves.'

'By God, you're right,' said George.

Then they were gone, poor Rowley with a flask in his hand and munching bread as he went, and I was insisting to Lelia that if I was to strip any more she must first go out of the mill.

For sheer, vexatious misfortune, I think the collapse of the foot-bridge is hard to beat. It added a quarter of an hour to Marya's start, and it put me out of action for three good hours, two of which I passed asleep in the sunshine while Lelia watched.

When she had withdrawn, I stripped and rubbed myself down with fern. Then I wrung out my trousers and put them on. She had brought me a beautiful shirt like that which she was wearing, and as it was full for her, it did for me very well. I fear that I burst the sleeves which were but four inches long, but the pleasure of putting on clean linen far more outweighed a tightness under the arms. She had also brought me silk stockings, but these I would not use: for they would have been too small and my socks had been well enough washed and would soon be dry.

Of her gentle care of me I do not know how to speak. It made a world of difference, for I had been badly shaken by my fight with the race and since when I fell, I was needing both food and rest, the misadventure had brought me to the end of my tether and left me with scarce strength enough to lift up my head. Indeed, if I had had to shift for myself I do not know how I should have fared, for with none to wake me I should not have dared to sleep, yet not only was slumber the physic my state required, but my state would, I think, have insisted upon its rights.

My ears were singing when I limped out of the mill and I must have gone down on my knees if Lelia had not sprung forward to hold me up. She led me into the sunshine and made me sit down upon the turf: then she fed me with bread and wine, and when I had eaten, she helped me to dry my pistol and never plagued me to leave it as so many women would have done. Then she took my faithful wrist-watch which even the rage of the water had failed to disturb, and, passing her word to wake me at five o'clock, sat down on the green beside me, like any slave, with a frond of fern in her hand to rout the flies.

As I settled myself, I looked up.

'You are very good to me, Lelia.'

'But of course,' says she. 'I – I like you. Would her Highness do this for you?'

'Yes,' said I steadily. 'But she could do no more.'

Lelia lifted her head.

'I have always heard say,' she said, 'that she is beyond compare.'

'So she is,' said I quietly. 'But I did not know there were two women who could be so sweet.'

I am glad to remember she bent a glowing face...

I had hoped against hope that George would come back with Marya whilst I slept, for I was most uneasy about his mission, and the sinister neighbourhood to which he and Rowley had gone was for me the abode of misfortune as well as the 'haunt of the arrow that flieth by day'. But when I awoke, there was no one but Lelia there, and she was lamenting that she had kept her word.

'You were sleeping so fast,' she said, 'so fast and well. It went to my heart to wake you, and you so tired. Please sleep again. I will wake you in half an hour.'

I dared not let her beguile me, though I

think I could have slept for a week, and when I had got to my feet, I found to my great relief that my strength had come back. I was something stiff and felt as though I had been beaten from head to heel, but otherwise no worse for my adventure, and the pain in my head was gone.

The hunger which had left me had now returned, so when I had stretched my legs, I sat down beside my nurse and began to eat.

The spot was peaceful, and looked more fair than ever now that the shadows were long. It had all the grace which belongs to a fairy-tale, so green was the turf, and the water so clear and bright, while the great bank of woodland, rising beyond the mill, might have been set as a bulwark against the workaday world. Indeed, when I looked at Lelia, sitting with her small feet crossed and her hands in her lap, for one instant the fancy struck me that I was dead, that I had, after all, been drowned in the foaming race, and had passed to some simple existence in which strife and battle and murder would have no part.

This absurd imagination was almost at once displaced by the astounding reflection that but twenty-four hours ago I was actually with the Circus, moving within the horse-lines, tending the sprightly Ada and reporting to Bach. These things seemed already so distant that I could hardly believe they belonged to yesterday's date, and had some wise man appeared to declare that the sun had been lately proceeding at a fifth of his usual pace, I should have accepted his statement without a thought.

'I suppose you are set,' said Lelia, 'on taking this bridle-path.'

'I must,' said I, and threw a piece of bread for the wolf-hound, who had been dozing, but had risen at the sound of my munching and had come and sat down at my feet with a meaning look. 'I'm going to start at six.'

'You will fall by the way,' says she. 'And, so far from saving her Highness, you will not be able to save yourself.'

'There will be no to-do, so long as I manage to get there before the police. I have only to cross the water and wait on the farther side: and then, if Leonie comes, I can send her back.'

It sounded simple, but I did not deceive myself. If Grieg in truth believed that Leonie was to arrive, he would himself cross the water and lie in wait. And then, if she came, there would be the deuce of a fight. But whether she came or no, in view of what I had learned I did not see how I could let the man go his way for if his spy could be active at Littai itself, Grieg would not lose his sting because he stood on Austrian soil.

Lelia said nothing, but when I had finished my meal, she took my right hand

and set it upon her knee. Then she stuffed a little cushion between my wrist and the ring and when she had it to her liking, she took a file from beside her and fell to work.

I was astonished to see her use such method, for that is less the way of a woman than of a man, and I know no man that would ever have thought of a cushion, unless it were Bell.

'Who taught you to free prisoners?' I said.

'Do not laugh at me,' she answered. 'I know–'

'Laugh? I can think of no man that would do it so well.'

'But I am not a man,' Lelia said softly.

After a little I asked what story she had told the smith.

'I used Grieg's name,' she said. 'I said that he had told me to ask the smith for a file.'

It occurred to me that Lelia had little to learn.

Now filing through a steel band is very slow work, and before she had worked for ten minutes Lelia began to fret.

'I am doing so badly,' she wailed. 'I had thought to free you in no time, and look at that stupid scratch.'

'Believe me or not,' said I, 'no smith could go any faster. The steel is too hard.'

'Oh, my dear,' says she, 'I shall never have done by six.'

'You'll have freed this hand,' said I. 'And

the other can wait.'

'Till when?' says she. 'Till tomorrow? Till this day week?'

'You know,' I said, 'that I hope to return at dawn.'

'I know,' said she, 'that you have no seven-league boots.'

I looked at her sharply, but, though I think she knew it, she never looked up from her work.

Her thrust was cogent.

From where we sat to the fall was thirteen miles – at the least. If I did nothing else, to walk there and back would take me at least nine hours. Such a march in my present state was beyond my power. I simply could not do it. What was far worse, by leaving at six I never should make the water before it was dark: and unless I was there before Grieg... My own words came into my mind– 'The odds are on him who comes first to a place like that'.

To this day I cannot account for my making so bad a mistake. But for Lelia's observation, I believe that I should have set out on surely as wanton a journey as ever an idiot made, and I can only suppose that the blow on my head was to blame for my oversight.

Be that as it may, I now saw that unless I used Grieg's car, I might as well stay where I was. The thing stood out. Even if I could do it – and, looking the distance in the face,

I was not at all sure that I could – I must arrive late and jaded, unfit to keep any tryst, much less frustrate the ambition of such an enemy. There was nothing for it. I had the key to the car, and I must be thankful for that; but the thought of returning to the spinney and going alone about my business to get the car under way made me sit very silent, and when Lelia began to chatter, I scarcely heard what she said.

'You are not listening to me.'

'I know,' I said. 'I'm sorry. What did you say?'

'What were you thinking about?'

'That I am more dull than usual this afternoon. Of course I cannot walk to the path.'

Lelia nodded.

'Your reason is returning,' she said. 'Do you think you can do as you have, and keep a clear brain? When the wheel stopped running, old Agen, the miller, drowned himself in that race. It took six men to get his body out, and the water had broken his neck and both of his legs.'

'God forgive me,' said I. 'I am very lucky.'

'You are very strong,' said she. 'If I told them the truth in the village they would laugh me to scorn. I am glad you see that you cannot–'

'I am going by car,' I said. 'And I want you to teach me the way.'

It will be remembered that Grieg had so

bestowed the car as to be able to drive away without being seen from the house or its curtilage. But the car was beside the drive which led to Vigil, while the drive which led to Vardar was now my way. Since I could not gain the latter without driving up to the house, I had no choice but to make towards Vigil until I was out of the park and then turn south and east as soon as I could. But remembering how we had floundered the night before, I was very shy of the country and fearful of losing my way; so I asked her to tell me how to fetch the compass which would bring me around the park to some road that I knew.

Here I confess that, though we both tried our best, Lelia and I were soon speaking different tongues. Corners and cross roads meant nothing at all to her. She had no eyes for the highway, but only for the lie of the land and the look of the neighbouring farms. Hog's back and bluff and pasture – she knew them all: but I could not absorb such direction, and when I brought her back to the road, she could not tell me its turnings or how it ran.

'Never mind. I shall get there somehow,' I said at last. 'The first farm you spoke of, Bremmas – is that on my right or left?'

'I do not know,' said Lelia, 'which side of the road it stands. But you will see the roof of the homestead rising like a grey haystack amid the green of the trees. And if it is on your left, you must go straight on.'

'And if it is on my right?'

'Then you must bear to your right, till you see the gap I spoke of with the sugar-loaf hill beyond.'

I suppose my manner betrayed me, for after a little silence she spoke again.

'You cannot learn your lesson, and I am not surprised. I will come with you, instead, to show you the way.'

'Indeed, you will not,' said I.

Lelia regarded the heaven.

'You are very wilful,' she said, 'this afternoon.'

Then she bent again to her filing and left me to chew the cud...

It was past a quarter to six before the steel ring parted and fell away.

'Let me cut the other,' said Lelia. 'You need not leave so early, now that you are taking your car.'

'Tomorrow,' said I. 'You have done enough for today. And thank you very much, Lelia. Be sure I shall never forget.'

She looked at me sharply.

'That is how people speak that are going away.'

I swallowed.

'I am not going tonight,' I said. 'But you know I am going tomorrow – if I possibly can.'

'I know that, but for your friends, you would go tonight.'

'But not without telling you, Lelia.'

'And thanking me for what I have done.' She leapt to her feet and stood, breathing fast and hard, with her eyes on my face. 'Am I some farmer's grandmother that you should use me so? I know you are high and mighty, and I am a barelegged peasant of no degree, but what I have done I have done because I love you, and then you – you thank me, and throw my love in my face.'

'You do not love me, Lelia,' I cried. 'We have a lot in common, and we found it out very soon. And perhaps you like tall men, and I think you were sorry for me. But that is not love.'

'Why do you think I gave you back your money? I have never had fifty crowns in all my life.'

'Friends don't give each other money,' I said. 'You gave me back the money when you made me your friend.'

'And brought you a shirt and cried when you did not trust me?'

'I cannot help it,' I said doggedly. 'I know that this is not love.'

'How do you know? Has her Highness taught you the workings of women's hearts?'

'But you are a child,' I cried. 'You–'

'I am twenty-two,' said Lelia. 'I do not think you are much older. But what of that?

230

Your friend is better-looking than you, and I cannot bear foul linen, and yours was foul, and you are unshaven and – and not at all at your best. And yet when I saw you, none of these things mattered, and I – I felt just a little faint.'

'Lelia, for God's sake!' I cried, and got up to my feet.

'Then do not withstand me,' she said. 'If I like to love you, that is my own affair. I do not seek to make it yours. I do not ask you to love me – I should not like you if you did. But I have shown you my heart–'

'Why?' I cried. 'Why did you do it, Lelia?'

'Because I am like that,' she said. 'I wanted you to know. It is a little honour – even a peasant-girl's love.'

'It is a very high honour, Lelia. But I am not worth it, my dear.'

'Her Highness does not think so.'

'Oh, Lord,' said I, miserably. 'Was ever a man so placed?'

'Well, then, I have shown you my heart. It is not kind of you to bruise it.'

'I would not hurt you,' said I, 'for anything in the world. I cannot say I love you because I love Leonie. But you – you are a great beauty, and I – I am very glad of you, Lelia – because you are so sweet.'

'Will you promise not to thank me again for what I may do?'

'I promise,' I said.

Lelia looked at me with a measuring eye. Then she smiled and came forward and set her bare arm in mine.

'You are almost too good to be true,' she said.

I did not know what she meant, and said as much.

'Her Highness will tell you,' she said. 'And now, where is this car?'

'I cannot take you,' I said.

'Why, please? I have never been in a car, and I should like to go.'

I tried to argue, but I fear that I was as wax in her hands, and in the end I promised that I would take her, provided that she did as I said.

So often as I think of my weakness I am ashamed. But the drubbing which I had suffered had shaken my faith in myself, and I moved in a sea of apprehension of what the next hour would bring forth. And so I gave way, but, as was to be expected, found no relief in promising Lelia to let her run into the danger which governed my use of Grieg's car. Indeed, as soon as I had done it, a host of new qualms began to hem me in, so that I felt bewildered as well as beset and at times when I looked at the beautiful maid by my side she seemed to be a great way off.

I think she divined my condition, for after looking into my eyes, she made me sit down again and drink what was left of the cordial which she had administered when I came out of the race, and when I had done so, she sat very still beside me and let me be.

Now what was the stuff in her phial I do not know, but within a very few minutes I felt a great deal better in body and soul. Though I still felt weary, my slackness seemed to have gone, and my mind became clear and steady, and the mists of dread and uncertainty rolled away. At first I feared that this was the way of some sudden stimulant and that after a while my state would be worse than before, but I need not have been afraid, for from the moment of drinking I never looked back.

Here I should say that the simples brewed in those parts are highly esteemed. Their secrets are jealously kept, being handed from mother to daughter by word of mouth, and all attempts to procure them have always failed; but, if Sully may be believed, their curious, potent virtue is an established fact. That of such was Lelia's cordial I have no doubt. Apart from the help it gave me that evening when I sat on the grass, I cannot forget how I did when I came up out of the race. So far from lying speechless, I had my wits about me and was able to make George free of my counsel without delay and then to get up and strip and rub myself down. These things no man could have done for sheer exhaustion, but for some agent to lift his system up. And the first thing that I remember was Lelia's arm about me and her flask at my lips.

The cool of the day was at hand, as we made our way back through the park. The sun was low and was shedding a golden light, the clear, sweet air was radiant, and the haze that had hung about the mountains had disappeared. All around, there was now a grandeur which had not been there at noon, and the peace upon the face of the landscape was rare and notable.

Presently Lelia pointed away to the left.

'There is the drive to Vardar. Do you see? The road goes curling between those oaks. The house is half a mile distant from where we stand.'

'Very good,' said I. 'Now you will go off and leave me to get the car. Cross the drive where we see it and bear due west and do not turn north until you have gone a mile.'

'Very well,' said Lelia obediently.

I stood and watched her until she was over the road and out of my sight. Then I followed the line she had taken, crossed the drive to Vardar and bore north-west. Ten minutes later I sighted the western drive...

The car was as we had left it, with one half of its bonnet open and one of its doors ajar. So much I saw by peeping, and, though the sight reassured me, I must confess that I dreaded taking possession and getting her out of the wood.

For me the place was haunted. The spot belonged to Murder and all his dreadful train. Here was no peace, nor grandeur, but only a sinister silence, ready to usher havoc and, when the echoes had faded, to steal back into its seat. Grieg might or might not be there. But whether he was or was not I should not know till one of two things happened – the shocking roar of his pistol, or the flick of the road beneath me and the evening air upon my face.

I took a deep breath and glided towards the bonnet with my heart in my mouth…

For my purpose the wrong half was open, and I had, of course, to close it, before I could open its fellow and put back the contact-breaker which I had taken away. I closed it gingerly. Then I passed the front of the car, opened the other half and bent to my task. As I did so, a movement behind me made me leap almost out of my skin, but, though I swung about, trembling, the movement was not repeated and I could see or hear nothing which argued that Grieg was there. This was cold comfort, for the spinney was offering cover for fifty men, and, peering into its depths, I might have been trying to fathom the secret some arras hid. As I stood with my back to the engine, the thought came into my mind that Grieg was there in the shadows, but meant to hold his hand until I had made the adjustment we both required...

No words can tell what it cost me to turn my back on the covert and bend again to my work, and I took twice as long about it as the trifling business deserved.

When it was done I left the bonnet open, in the hope that if Grieg was there, he would think that I had not finished and let me be: then I turned the switch and set the spark and throttle and stepped to the front of the car. I dared not use the self-starter because of the noise it made, but the engine started the first time I swung the shaft.

Though I think it was fairly silent, it seemed to me to make an unearthly din, and I whipped to the steering-wheel with the sweat running down my face. For an instant I shrank from taking the driver's seat, for once I was there, I was trapped, and if Grieg rose out of the bushes, I had no chance. Still, to wait was futile, and a moment later I had my foot on the clutch...

The gears were storming, and the car was rocking like a ship ... behind me the door slammed to, and the clap took a week from my life ... my hands were slipping on the wheel ... and then I was out on the road, and the blessed sunshine was streaming into my eyes and a flood of soft, cool air was sliding over the windscreen and falling upon my face...

So I recovered the car. I am not proud of the memory, but I have set out the truth, to show what a fool his nerves may make of a man; and I have no defence to offer except that the place was a covert and I have but two eyes.

Now I was very anxious to quit the road I was using as soon as I could, for Grieg might have telephoned to Vigil and told the police to call for him with their car, and I had no wish to meet them in such a way. But until I had taken up Lelia, I dared not go very fast, for I had no means of knowing where she would strike the road and I might have set her a longer walk than I thought. Indeed, as the moments went by, but I did not see her, I began to fear that I must have passed her by: then the drive bent round to the left, and there was her white and scarlet a furlong ahead.

She was very much disappointed because I would not allow her to sit with me, but I would not hear her protests, and ushered her and her wolf-hound into the car. Then I let down the window behind the driver's seat, 'for so,' said I, 'I shall hear all you have to say: and you are to sit well back and on no account lean forward whatever befalls. If I should stop or be stopped, you are to crouch on the floor and stay quite still, and if the worst should happen, you must swear that you do not know me, but found the car standing empty and entered it out of mischief and then were afraid to alight.'

Lelia crossed her ankles and threw me a dazzling smile.

'Is this how her Highness sits? Or does she crouch on the floor?'

'She does as I tell her,' I said.

With that, I shut the door and hoped for the best. Then I put down the half of the bonnet which I had left raised, and a moment later we were flying along the road.

Five minutes later we were clear of the Sabre estate.

Now if I had used my wits, I should have known that Lelia, to whom roads mean nothing, would have to see about her if she was to tell me the way. Cooped in the car, she could not get her bearings, and four times I had to stop and let her run to some shoulder or even stand still in the roadway and look around.

It was a sight to see her pick up her line in this way, for the country was blind as could be, but I think she could read the tokens which speak to the birds and beasts, for after a moment she would come back quite confident to say that we stood in some parish of which I had never heard.

Once we ran through a village and we brushed against several farms, but the peasants we passed showed no undue excitement and only stared or cursed me, as peasants will.

At last we dropped down a hill and into a sunken road that seemed familiar, and then in a moment I knew I was close to Vardar and was taking the way I had taken when Rowley and I made for Gola the night before.

The spot seeming lonely, I brought the car to rest.

'Lelia,' I said, looking round, 'I know that I am not to thank you, but you have done the trick. I used this road this morning, and I know where I am. Vardar lies over that ridge, a mile away.'

'That is quite right,' says she; 'but you will not go through the town.'

'Oh, no. I shall go very wide. I have plenty of time. But I must not take you further. As it is, you will not be home till long after dark. It must be six miles to Merring from where we stand.'

With that, I alighted and opened the door of the car.

The dog leaped out, delighted, but Lelia followed slowly, finger to lip.

Before I could shut the door, she had set a hand on my arm.

'Take me with you,' she said.

'No, my dear,' said I. 'It's not to be thought of. For one thing only, this is a one-man show.'

Lelia shrugged her shoulders and turned away.

'I think it is a one-woman show.'

'What do you mean?'

'That you do not want me tonight. That you do not want me to see her. You think you will have to present me and that I am not fit to–'

'Lelia, Lelia, how can you say such things? When Leonie hears about you she will not rest till she has seen you and taken your hands in hers.'

She was round in a flash, and her hands were upon my shoulders, and her face three inches from mine.

'Then take me with you,' she breathed.

'Listen,' I lied. 'I would not even take Rowley if he were here. I am not going to fight; I am going to stop my wife from walking into a trap. Everything depends upon my not being seen, and one can escape notice where two cannot.'

Lelia glanced at the sky.

'It will be a dark night,' she said.

'So much the better,' said I. 'And now you must go to your home. Soon after dawn tomorrow I shall be back at the mill.'

'If you are alive,' said Lelia. 'You cannot answer for that. What shall I do with myself if you do not come back?'

'You must go about your business,' said I. 'Revisit the mill, if you will, and when the Countess comes, do what you can for her. She is very troubled and I know she would like you with her – as anyone would.'

'Except yourself,' said Lelia. 'And what do you think I am made of that you tell me to go about my business if you do not come back? I will bid you good-bye tomorrow and make up my mind that I never shall see you again. And I will not cry, I promise. But I am not ready to bid you good-bye today.'

'Why should you?' said I. 'If I do not come in the morning, be sure I shall come at dusk.'

'Suppose you are taken,' says she, with her eyes upon mine.

'Suppose it,' said I. 'Then I will come when I am free. I am not ready, either, to bid you good-bye today.'

'You will come, if her Highness can spare you.'

'Leonie and I are one, Lelia.'

'Do you love her so very much?'

I nodded.

'She is in my heart – I told you.'

'But not in your eyes,' she breathed. 'Not now. I am here. I can see myself. Why – why are you not ready to bid me good-bye today?'

'Because you are very charming. Because you have meant a great deal to me today.'

'Yet she has meant more.' She took my face in her hands which were very cool. 'Do you wish that I did not love you?'

'Only for your sake, Lelia.'

'And you do not mind when I touch you? Or try to pretend that it is she?'

'No,' said I, smiling. 'Your ways are as

gentle as hers.'

'And she is beyond the mountains, but I am here.'

'She is here, too, Lelia,' said I.

With her face two inches from mine, Lelia took a deep breath.

'Mother of God,' she said, 'but you are a trusty man.'

'My dear,' said I, 'when you see her, you'll understand.'

Lelia lowered her eyes.

'I do not need to see her,' she said.

The least I could do was to kiss her, and that I did. Then I took my seat in the car and she stood back, smiling, with one hand on the wolf-hound's collar and the other up to her breast.

And that, I think, is how I shall always see her, standing so well and truly, her fine head raised and her beautiful eyes alight, with the setting sun behind her, and the dog looking up to her face.

I picked my way to the farther side of Gola, left the car in a meadow behind a byre and walked into Ramon's forge as the sun went down.

Ten minutes later the smith was climbing the slopes at the back of his forge, and I was following after, two hundred yards behind.

Lest the frontier-guards should see me, I was afraid to make use of the bridle-path.

Therefore, I had sought Ramon and asked him to tell me how I could reach the fall without going by that way. At once he had said he would guide me, and when I demurred, had declared that unless I made him my pilot, I might as well stay where I was, 'for,' said he, 'there is not the ghost of a path, and, going this way, you will not hear the roar of the water until you are almost there.'

If my drive had refreshed me, the evening air of the mountains did me more good than wine; but the thought that, in spite of my troubles, I was yet to forestall the men that were to watch for my wife set the blood running in my veins like some elixir. Now I hoped she would come with all my heart, for I was wild to see her and kiss her lips, and I hoped Grieg would try to take her, for that would both force the issue and seal his doom. So far as I was concerned, the hairs of her head were numbered, and the thought of her suffering violence made me 'see red'.

When I was come to the crest of the nearest hill, I turned to look back at Gola and the landscape beyond. This was now very dim, and lights were fast appearing to hasten the rearguard of day. I could see the lamp of the level-crossing at Vardar and the lights of some train which was crawling away to my left, and far to the north a fire was blazing like a beacon high up on some mountain-side.

As I stood there, I must confess that I wished I was looking my last upon Riechtenburg and I came very near to cursing the day that we had set out; for the Prince could not have confined Marya to the country for ever, and all we had done was to drag her into the pit which had been digged for ourselves. Then I remembered Lelia, and I felt ashamed of wishing that I could go over the border and never come back; for, though she made too much of her fancy, she had used me with a fearless devotion which, had she been repulsive, must have touched any man; but since she was so lovely and charming, I think that I should have been no creature of flesh and blood, if, though I could not love her, I had not had respect to the gentle light in her eyes.

I now came up with the smith, for, once we were among the hill-tops, there seemed to be no reason why we should stay apart, and whilst we went on together, I told him our present plight and heard for the first time how Marya Dresden had come to fall in with Grieg.

'All was well,' said Ramon. 'I had found Carol work in the fields, and my lady was quite recovered and full of hope. By day she stayed within doors, and when it was dark I would take her to walk in the meadows which lie below the village and slope to the brink of the water that comes down from Vogue.

From there we could count the camp-fires along the base of the hills, but I knew that the night would soon come when we saw them no more. So for two days and nights.

'Now we have in the house a puppy my wife had found. He was very small and bold, as puppies will be, and I think he thought my lady a beautiful child. From the moment he woke to find her beneath our roof, she was his mistress, and he was her little dog, and very soon, such is the way of these things, she was as pleased with him as he was with her. She bathed his small body and groomed him with one of the beautiful brushes out of her case, and when we went out of an evening, she must take him with her to let him frisk in the fields.

'On Saturday morning, a little before mid-day I was shoeing a mare, when a car came through the village, travelling fast. As it passed the forge, I heard the shriek of a dog. In that instant the damage was done. The mare was restive, and, guessing that I would release her, she started to kick, and, since I had hold of her leg, I could not let go. As soon as I could get free, I ran to the door. There was my lady, with the dying dog in her arms, and by her side was a big, broad-shouldered man, with his hat in his hand.

'"There's a veterinary surgeon at Vardar", I heard him say.

'In a flash she was in his car which had

245

stopped a few paces away, and then it was gone, and I was left, like a zany, watching its dust.

'That night it returned, with a note from my lady to Carol, bidding him take up her things and leave at once. I think that she sent me no message to save my face.

'That, my lord, is the story; and when I went out that night – for I could not sleep – behold, the camp-fires were gone.'

There was nothing to be said, but I could not help thinking that Fortune had made up her mind to show us but little favour and to make us work out our salvation in the sweat of our brow.

By now night had almost come in, but, though we had gone some way, I could hear no sound of the fall, but only the gush and scuttle of very much lesser fountains on either side. This made me anxious, for I had learned my lesson of arriving too late, and I was about to tell Ramon that we must quicken our steps, when we started to round a buttress which the mountain above us thrust out. In that instant the thunder of the fall began to make itself heard and ere we were clear of the spur, we could not hear ourselves speak.

Had I not proved it, I never would have believed that so mighty a sound could be so completely arrested by a bulwark of rock and soil, and the change from peace to uproar was so abrupt that I think if two men were to stand a fair ten paces apart, the one would not hear the water, and the other would hear nothing else.

A moment later I saw the great sheaf of foam...

I touched the smith's arm, and we turned back the way we had come.

When it was quiet, I took the good man by the hand; but before I could speak–

'My lord,' he said, 'I will stay and watch with you.'

I shook my head.

'No,' I said. 'I am armed and have nothing to fear. See me up to the fall, if you will, and once I have found the ledge, make your way back to Gola the way we have come. I cannot be sure, but I think perhaps I shall ask you to give me some breakfast at break of day.'

'We shall await you, my lord,' said Ramon faithfully.

Then we turned again and went back towards the fall. It was now very dark and promised to grow still darker, as Lelia had foretold; but since the noise was deafening, we had only our eyes to help us, in case we were not alone. This I found most unlikely. Night was but a few moments old, and if the police were at hand, they were almost certainly keeping the bridle-path.

After two or three minutes we reached the side of the cliff.

All speech was now out of the question, so I shook the smith's hand again and hoisted myself to the ledge.

An instant later I was passing beneath the water with my face to the wall.

I have not dwelt upon this passage, because for the whole of that day I sought to put it out of my mind. There was little danger about it, but much to make it more frightful than death itself. Could Ramon have helped me, I would in a moment have begged him to see me across, but there was no room for one man to help another, though two might have aided a third by making him walk between them and holding him up with a rope. Though the ledge was so rough and narrow, I cannot pretend that it was easy to fall, but the penalty of falling was so monstrous that it obsessed the mind, and I seemed to be bearding Nature in her very own lair, and she to be in a passion at my audacity.

Still, if the passage was shocking, it was not long – no more, I should say, than twelve paces from end to end: and of these I had covered half, when my hand encountered something which made me jump as though I had touched a snake. In a word, I touched the arm of another man. What was worse, I knew in a flash to whom it belonged, so long and so thick was the hair which covered the limb, like a close-fitting sleeve.

CHAPTER 8

By Deputy

I cannot describe my horror at meeting such a man in such a place, and even whilst I stood shaking and clinging like any madman to the dripping face of the cliff, the meaning of his presence fell like some blazing thunderbolt into my mind.

This was the man who had betrayed us. No doubt he had been found by the guards before he had recovered from the buffet with which I had laid him low; and no doubt he had told them of the strangers who had used him so ill. The guards had reported the matter, and Grieg had known in an instant that we were the strangers of whom the smuggler spoke. This was the man who had taught him the trick of the bypass, *and now he was in Grieg's service,* only too ready and willing to help to gain his revenge.

Had he cared to take it then, I must have lost my race. Had he known that it was I that had touched him, I have no doubt that in a twinkling his knife would have been in my back. To him our surroundings were nothing, but I could no more have given battle than a fly that is mired.

Hardly knowing what I did, I began to drag myself back the way I had come, but my knees were loose and my steps were so uncertain that no progress was ever so laboured or deadly slow. Every instant I was expecting to feel the man's hand upon me, for since I had retired before him, there was no sort of reason why he should not come on, and when at last I staggered down from the ledge, I felt as though I was emerging from the very closet of Death.

I lay back against the rock, still shaking like any leaf, too thankful for my escape to give any thought to this new development, but after a little I pulled myself together and sought to consider how I should meet this very serious turn.

This new ally of Grieg's was as formidable as Grieg himself. He was violent and ruthless and bore me a bitter grudge; but, what was worse of all, *here and by night a smuggler was cock of the walk.* His eye was trained to pierce the darkness, his foot not to slip or stumble, his body to move like any shadow; and I had little doubt that he knew this neighbourhood as the palm of his hand.

If his presence was disconcerting, the thought that he was now standing on Leonie's side of the water made the hair rise upon my head.

He had plainly retired, as I had, because

he could not tell who I was, but my failure to follow him over must have shown him that I was no friend, and I had no doubt that he was now waiting, as I was, at the other end of the ledge.

If Leonie came, she and Bell would walk clean into his arms. And I could do nothing to stop them, *because he was waiting for me.*

Had I been more familiar with the passage beneath the fall, I would have crept across and made my attack; but, as it was, for me to attempt such a movement would have been to court destruction with my hat in my hand.

I sought to take comfort in reflecting that if Leonie was coming indeed, she would not arrive for at least two hours and a half; but I knew in my heart that if by that time the smuggler had not come across, I must myself go over and take my chance.

And now came a period of waiting which I can only hope that the wretch beyond the water found as distasteful as I, for though by the mercy of heaven I was not plagued by an inclination to sleep, all vigilance was so much embarrassed by the darkness and the roar of the fall as to seem utterly useless and a waste of time. Indeed, I had early perceived that my only chance of becoming aware of some presence was to watch the great sheaf of foam, for that that would act as a screen against which any body that passed between it and my eyes was bound to appear. To this end, I drew back a little against the rock, so that at least no one could leave or approach the ledge without my seeing their movement against the white of the fall.

So for two mortal hours, in a distracting uproar as changeless as silence itself and a darkness so thick and oppressive that the earth seemed wrapped in some garment against the virtue of light.

I had just determined that if five more minutes went by, but my man did not come, I must essay the passage come what might, when I saw a definite movement three paces away.

The next instant a figure was outlined against the foam.

It was not that of the smuggler, for whosoever it was was approaching the ledge, and it seemed less thickset than Grieg's, though I could hardly believe that he had sent one of the police. Still, I cared not whose it was, if only they mounted the ledge, for once they were there, I would instantly follow them up and let them serve as my buffer and meet the smuggler's knife.

To that end, I made ready to move.

Arrived at the base of the cliff, whoever it was seemed uncertain whether or no to go on, and I must confess that they had my sympathy, for to find such a path by hearsay must have been the devil and all. Indeed, I now surmised that when I encountered the smuggler, the latter was crossing the water to keep some appointment with Grieg and that Grieg, grown tired of waiting, had sent to find his ally and learn why he had not come. What I could not understand was why Grieg had sent another, instead of coming himself. Upon further consideration, I decided that the figure was Grieg's. His bulk was not apparent, but nothing was apparent this night, and his figure seemed to be dancing against the rush of the fall. And Grieg would have trusted no one with such an enterprise.

So I stood waiting and watching for him to take the path.

Though now and again he stopped, he did not advance, and the better to observe his outline, I fell on one knee. As I did so, he turned to the ledge, and I saw that he was not alone. Somebody – something was with him. Crouching upon the ground. He had gone on and left it, and it was coming my way.

The next instant Lelia's wolf-hound was licking my face.

I was just in time to catch hold of her slim, bare leg. Even so she did her utmost to shake me off, till I put up my other hand and let her feel the steel ring which still was about my wrist. At once she ceased to struggle, and when I put up my arms she let me lift her down.

As I drew her back to the rock, she set her lips to my ear.

'I came to seek you. Listen. I have over-heard the police by the side of the bridle-path. *Her Highness came in by Elsa an hour ago.*'

Had Lelia been able to hear me, I do not know what I should have said. Her tidings were electric, but for that moment the messenger had my thoughts. She had come alone with her wolf-hound into this mouth of hell, to share my dangerous vigil, because she had liked my face. She had passed the police and had started that nightmare passage, to bring me news of my wife. Here was no sense of duty. Rowley or Bell would have done it, because they would have deemed it 'their job'. But Lelia had done it, because she cared for me. When I thought of her hesitation to mount that ledge which she could not so much as see, and how she had bent to the wolf-hound and what it must have cost her to leave the dog – as like as not to follow and lose his life, I had no words that were equal to the occasion and was thankful for an excuse to hold my peace. But I found her small hand and held it in both of mine and then bent down and kissed it, in the hope and belief that she would know what I meant. After a little, I put my lips to her ear.

'We will go now,' I said, 'but not by the bridle-path. There is another way. It is so dark you must keep your hand in mine.'

Lelia nodded her head...

Now when Ramon and I had arrived, it was not pitch dark, and we had the fall to guide us up to the ledge. But now there was nothing to help me retrace my steps, and I could not see my own hand when I stretched out an arm.

Whilst I stood peering and trying to remember the angle at which we had made for the fall, Lelia started slightly and stooped to the dog. The next moment she drew down my head.

'He is growling,' she said. 'I think there is someone beside us we cannot see.'

I was round in an instant with my eyes on the screen of foam, but I could see no movement and nobody's shape. If the smuggler had crossed the water, by now he was out of my ken. The obvious thing to do was to make ourselves scarce.

I found Lelia's hand again, and we started off.

Now whether we moved in a circle, I cannot tell, but I know that the place seemed bewitched, and I as confounded and helpless as any blind man. Though the spur lay but three minutes' walk, a quarter of an hour went by before I was touching its flank – and then I could not be certain that I had found it at last, until to my great relief the deafening roar of the water began to fade. A moment later the blessed miracle of silence was an accomplished fact.

A step or so further I stumbled upon a tussock, and there, after standing so long, I was glad to sit down.

'And now, my dear,' I whispered, 'please tell me your tale.'

'I was afraid,' breathed Lelia. 'And so, as you would not take me, I walked to the bridle-path. By the time I was there it was dark, and at first I could not find it, though I knew where it was. I went very slowly, because I was afraid of the police. But they are not countrybred, and I presently heard them moving, though they did not hear me. Grieg is there – I saw him. He was giving them some orders, when some other police-man arrived. It was he that brought the news about her Highness. Grieg asked if he had seen her, but he said "No". He said he had been sent from Vigil to bring the news. Grieg was very angry and swore that it was not true, but his way was not the way of a man that believes what he says. At last, "Let her go to the devil", he said. "If she comes, we're ready. If she stays, we'll have the others, sure as fate". He was in a very bad temper and seemed to be waiting for someone who did not come. Then I left them behind, and at once I heard the sound of the fall. After that it was easy. But when you caught hold of my ankle, I thought it was Grieg.'

I told her of my brush with the smuggler and how it was I that had put a spoke in his wheel and had made him break the appointment he had with Grieg.

'Ah,' says she. 'Then it was he that was beside us when the dog growled.'

'I think so.'

'Let us hope that he did not see us,' said Lelia thoughtfully.

'If he did he must have lost us again.'

'For all that,' said she, rising, 'I think we had better get on.'

This was easier said than done.

Had it been daylight, I could have found the way; had there been stars to steer by, I could have brought us to Gola by a circuitous route; but, as I have said, the darkness was like a black fog, and before we had taken ten paces I did not know which way I was facing – and that is the truth.

'Lelia,' said I, 'I am useless. Where is the north?'

'I cannot tell you,' she whispered. 'I have never seen such a night.'

I stifled an oath.

'What brings this cursed darkness?' I said.

'There is cloud above us,' she breathed. 'They come up at night at this season and lie like a pall until dawn. If only the wind would arise…'

There was nothing to do but move forward and take our chance, but almost at once, to my dismay, I heard the sound of the fall. Be sure we recoiled and started the opposite way, and after a dreadful progress I was just beginning to think that Fortune had shown us pity to guide our feet, when to my inexpressible horror I heard it again.

Again we drew back, to meet, I was sure, the same spur which Ramon and I had rounded three hours before. Three hasty steps to the right proved my persuasion sound for I heard the thunder beginning before I had taken the fourth.

I turned back, sick at heart.

'Lelia,' I said wearily, 'we can do nothing but wait. We are back where we started from nearly twenty minutes ago.'

She seemed to put a hand to her head.

'I do not like it,' she murmured. 'If the smuggler saw us, I fear he may go and fetch Grieg.'

Instinctively I lowered my voice.

'He must have lost us,' I said. 'We have doubled upon our tracks a dozen times.'

'These men of the mountains,' she said, 'have eyes like cats. I would to God I could take you the way I came, but the police may have moved and I dare not try to find it on such a night.'

'God knows,' said I, 'you have done your part. It is I that am failing you, Lelia. I said that I knew the way.'

'It is not your fault, my dear. There is no

way tonight. I have never seen such darkness. And – and I am glad to be with you.'

I drew her on to the tussock on which we had rested before.

'I am very glad to have you,' I said.

'Tell me,' she said. 'What is this her Highness has done?'

'I know no more than you, Lelia. But for my sake I do not think she would come in openly unless she held a strong hand.'

'She has always held that,' said Lelia. 'If the Prince were to hurt her finger, the country would rise.'

'I do not think she knows that,' said I. 'And there is the rub. If we could only make Gola, I have the car hidden there, and I would drive you to Vigil and you should tell her yourself.'

'You are very sweet to me,' said Lelia gently. She laid her head against my shoulder. 'I have taken her place tonight. You came to meet her, and then I came in her stead.'

'I am very proud of her deputy,' said I. 'I know no other woman of whom I would say that.'

'Have I been – her deputy – today?'

'Yes, Lelia.'

With a sudden movement she put her arms round my neck.

'I am very happy,' she said. 'And I shall never forget. Please kiss – her deputy.'

I kissed her lips.

Lelia lifted her head and looked to the west.

'The cloud is moving,' she said. 'See? Far in the distance the stars are beginning to show. And the moon is not down yet, and in a little while we shall be able to see.'

With her words, I heard the dog growl.

I was on my feet in an instant, and had my pistol out; but I could see nothing to fire at, and after a little Lelia touched my arm.

She did not speak, but urged me to move with her, and a moment later we had our backs to some rock.

When I would have put her behind me, she would not go, so I slid my left arm about her and held her up to my side.

So we stood, still as death, with all about us that most impressive silence which the steady splash of some waterbrook served to make more profound.

And as we stood there, so still, the world began to grow light.

I raised my eyes to the heaven, to see clear-cut in the wet the edge of the pall of cloud and, beyond it, the radiance of the moon which had not yet sunk into view. I have never seen a more curious spectacle, for the pall stretched like a ceiling from north to south and might have been the sliding lid of some box which had been drawn open a little from west to east, to let the moon sink by.

I lowered my gaze to look around me.

Immediately in front there was something that might or might not have been two men; to the left I was sure there was a figure, for the glow from the west was upon it, as it was upon Lelia and me; but the other mass was in shadow, and I could not see it so well.

What then happened, happened so swiftly as far to outrun my pen.

Lelia gasped and started and flung herself on my breast. As she did so, a tongue of flame leaped out of the mass before me, the roar of a pistol sounded, and Lelia seemed to jerk me against the rock. Then her head fell on to my shoulder, and her body went slack.

Frantically I called upon her.

'Lelia!' I cried. 'Lelia!'

She made no sort of answer, but hung as she had stood in my arms, and I felt her blood running over my pistol hand. And when I made to lay her down on the ground, her lovely head fell sideways, because she was dead.

I laid her down very gently and crossed her hands.

When I got to my feet I saw that the moon was clear.

To my left stood the detective that I had come to know. He had started against the rock and covered his eyes. In front stood Grieg and the smuggler. The latter was standing, staring, with his head on one side, but Grieg was swaying a little, with his right hand up to his head.

The smuggler cleared his throat and spat on the ground. Then he took a step or two forward to peer at Lelia's face.

I raised my pistol and shot the beast through the head.

As he fell, Grieg fired again upon me, but his bullet went wide. I never so much as heard it, and I think the man was shaken with what he had done. Indeed, I now know that he was, for I afterwards learned that he thought, as did all, that Lelia was Leonie, who had, after all, come to meet me where the water came down. And when I had called upon her, so alike were the names that those that heard me made sure I was calling upon my wife.

So, though she lay dead, Lelia served me for the last time.

That must have been Grieg's last round, for as I fired – and missed him – he took to his heels.

I never would have believed that he would run before me, and I never would have believed that he could run so well; but I think that I could have caught him, if he had girdled the earth.

Except where the shadows fell, after that fatal darkness the place seemed as bright as day, and Grieg kept clear of the shadows because, I suppose, he was afraid of stumbling if once he ran into the dark.

He led me back past the fall, and in a moment I saw he was seeking the bridle-path. I, therefore, ran to his right to cut him off from the police, and, though he made a great effort, I gained my end. We reached the path together, but I was nearer its mouth.

I had thought that when he saw this, he would stand and fight, but he instantly turned to the left and began to run up the path into the mountains towards the frontier-post.

I now put up my pistol, for I am a poor marksman and I knew that to fire at him running would be to waste a round, and I did not try to catch him, but only to cling to his heels, for I knew he must come to the chasm from which the bridge would be gone.

The path lay sometimes in shadow and sometimes in the light of the moon, but though I could see him glancing from side to side, he did not try to leave it, because I think he was glad to stick to a line where the going was good.

He was tiring now and I could have caught him, had I wished, without any fuss; but, instead, I spared myself for what was to come.

And after a little, I saw the white walls of the guard-room rising ahead.

It was now manifest that he did not know what was coming, for he made a sudden effort and almost doubled his pace.

I fancy that he had expected that the

guard-room would be open and had purposed to call on the sentry to save his life. Be that as it may, when he saw that the door was shut, he ran straight on.

So he came to the deep ravine and the girders whose floor was gone.

I saw him stop and boggle and glance to either side, but when he turned, I was standing between him and the guard-room ten paces away.

For a moment he stood uncertain. Then he flung up his heavy head.

I could see that his lips were moving, but the water raging below us drowned his voice and because I thought he was bidding me come and take him, I stood my ground.

So for perhaps two minutes. Then he shrugged his shoulders and turned back the way we had come.

I was by his side in an instant, and touching him on the sleeve.

'Not that way,' I shouted.

He drew back and looked me up and down.

'Where, then?' he demanded thickly.

In a flash I had him by the shoulders and had turned him to face the gorge.

'That way,' said I. 'You chose it. And now, by God, you shall take it – and take it alive,' and with that, I hurled him forward with all my might.

He let himself fall and saved himself by a foot, but such scornful usage stung him as nothing else could have done, and he was up in an instant and crouching like any beast. I waited for him to attack me, or seek to go by.

Of the end, my condition of mind allowed no doubt. I seemed to myself so strong that I could have torn him to bits and have flung the murderer piecemeal into the gorge, and, such is the power of confidence that I had for that time a strength before which he could not stand.

Be sure I needed it.

He turned as though to avoid me, and as I leaped to stop him, he changed direction and sprang. I almost lost my balance before the shock, and, quick as a flash, he had my back to the gorge, but I twisted him round again and tore his hand from my throat.

The ease with which I did this must, I think, have shown him his hour was come, for he caught his breath in a sob as a man that has been startled by the touch of some unseen hand. The next instant he was fighting, with no thought, I think, to kill me, but only to save his life.

His game was, of course, to grapple, and I must say he played it well. Twice I fought myself free, but before I could follow my advantage, each time he had closed again. It was as though he had boasted that if he went into the gorge, he would not go alone.

I made up my mind to end it, and let myself go.

The punishment he took was frightful, but his arms were like irons upon me and when I had torn one off, he fastened his teeth in my shoulder and bit me down to some bone. But, though he fought like a madman, he could not outstay the strength which he himself had added to that I had; his effort began to fail before my challenge: I felt his muscles quivering under the strain; and at last I had my way and had turned him round.

We were now both facing the gorge, and I was standing behind him and had him fast by the wrists. If he was thus at my mercy, I showed him none, for all I could see was Lelia and the rare and exquisite light which he had put out.

Inch by inch I forced him towards the brink.

He dared not let himself fall, for so his last chance was gone, and all his hope was in planting his feet and throwing all his weight backward, just as a man that is pulling some tug-of-war. And as such a man is pulled forward by one that is stronger than he, so, little by little, I made my prisoner yield.

We were very close now, and the bellow of the turbulent water, God knows how far below us, was very loud. The sound was awful, and conjured up for me those ancient pictures of The Last Judgment, where the righteous are ascending and the wicked are falling headlong into the power of monsters that hail their prey. If it did so for Grieg I do not know, but I felt his sweat running on my fingers, and I fancy his soul was quaking as he looked on the horrid portal by which he was to go into hell.

I forced him forward six inches and let him gaze. Then I twisted his arm to make him leave his foothold and, when at last he did so, I set my foot in his back and thrust him down.

The effort sent me backward, but as I got to my feet, I saw him swinging from a girder which he must have met as he fell. For a moment I wondered whether, after all, I had failed, but the iron was cold and unfriendly, and ere he could draw himself up, he lost what hold he had and fell like a stone.

Slowly I made my way back to where Lelia lay.

I cannot remember this journey, try as I will. One moment I was by the guard-room, and the next I was looking up at the sheaf of foam. If I had thoughts I do not know what they were, and, except that I was going to Lelia, I had no sort of purpose, and the future cared for itself.

The moon was sinking now, and the darkness was coming back, but as I rounded the spur, I saw three figures standing by where I had laid her down.

I went to them directly and gave the sergeant my pistol without a word. Then I passed to where Lelia was lying and fell on my knees.

So I stayed for a moment, not presuming to commend her spirit, for I think that it needed no prayers, but remembering her youth and her beauty and her natural sweetness of heart and how she had shown me that very nonesuch of love, that she laid down her life for her friend.

Something moved beside me, and when I looked down, the poor dog that she was so proud of touched my leg. Before this dumb call for comfort I could have burst into tears, but though I patted and stroked him, my touch was not what he wanted, and after a grievous look the poor animal drooped his head and turned away.

Very gently I gathered his mistress into my arms.

Then I rose to my feet.

'Where is the smuggler?' I said.

The sergeant answered me.

'We have weighted his body with stones, sir, and cast it under the fall.'

'Very well,' said I. 'I am ready. Will you lead on?'

Without a word, he turned the way I had come, and when I began to follow, his fellows brought up the rear.

Half an hour later we came out on to the uplands by way of the bridle-path. And there I sat down for a little, to take some rest, with the wolf-hound crouched by my side and Lelia all slack against me and her beautiful head fallen forward and her soft cheek against my coat.

Some house was afire in Vardar. The big, red tongues of flame were lighting the neighbouring roofs and made a pretty picture of somebody's grief. As I got to my feet, I saw the roof fall in. But had Vigil itself been blazing, I do not think I should have given the matter a thought.

I addressed myself to the sergeant.

'I will go your way,' I said, 'in a little while. But first I must take – I must take her home. Do you know the village of Merring?'

The man consulted his fellows.

After a moment–

'I know the name, sir,' he said. 'Perhaps you can tell us the way.'

'I only know that it lies beyond Vardar,' I said.

'That is enough, sir,' said he. 'We will ask the way at Vardar.' He hesitated. Then, 'I hope you will believe, sir,' he said, 'that our hands are clean. We had you surrounded. It never entered my head that he would fire without warning. And when – when I saw what had happened...' Again he hesitated. 'We had reason to think it was her Highness,' he added jerkily.

'The crime is as black,' I said thickly. 'This was her deputy.'

Twenty minutes later I entered one of two cars that were waiting below. The police gave me this to myself, except that the sergeant sat by the driver's side. The wolf-hound lay on the floor with his chin on my foot. And I sat back, like some image, thinking of the pleasure which Lelia would have found in the drive and how she and I would ere now have been nearing Vigil but for that fatal darkness which had confounded our steps.

Now to get to Vardar, we had to cross the railway, and that by the level-crossing, whose light could be seen so far upon every side. When we reached it, the gates were shut, because some express was due, and we had no choice but to wait until it had come and gone.

On any other night we should have waited alone and, as like as not, have had to rouse the keeper to open the gates, but tonight he was up and doing because of the fire, and the spot was alive with people, some of them coming or going, but most of them doing nothing but stand around and argue abut the fate of the house, which seemed to have stood at some corner rather less than a furlong ahead.

I could have spared the check, for any delay seemed indecent, and my one desire was to bring my pitiful burden to those I was sure must have loved her and lay her upon the bed in which, but for me, she would have been lying asleep; the liveliness and the gossip into which we had been suddenly plunged seemed so ill-timed and outrageous as scarce to be borne, and, what was far worse, so bright was the lamp beside us that any moment some idle glance might discover that the car was conveying no ordinary passenger.

That the sergeant feared as I did was very plain, for after a moment he descended and stood by one of the doors, whilst I sat on tenterhooks, ready myself to murder the first that offended my dead.

So for five ghastly minutes. Then the voices declined to whispers, and I knew that our secret was out.

Presently the keeper of the crossing came up to the sergeant's side.

I did not hear his question, but I heard the other's reply.

'An accident,' he said shortly. 'An accident with a car. A girl has been run over. We are taking her to Vigil as fast as we can.'

The rumour went round like wildfire, and at a word from the sergeant the driver of the car descended and stood to the other door.

Very soon there was a crowd about us; but the train did not come.

I addressed myself to the sergeant.

'Can't he let us go over?' I said. 'I mean, this is not to be borne.'

'He dare not, sir. Someone was killed in Vardar? Why must she choose this night to hold back the Salzburg train?'

The gazing crowd was silent, but the press had swollen until it had reached the gates, and men were climbing on these to see over their fellows' heads.

The doctor sat back on his heel.

'Where is her home?' he said.

'At Merring,' said I.

'Then you must leave her here. I am the Coroner of the district and I must hold an inquest upon her death.'

'Sir,' said the sergeant. 'I beseech you–'

The other spoke over his shoulder to cut him short.

'As one of the police, you should be ashamed of yourself. This man here is a stranger, and how should he know the law?'

As he spoke, I heard the shriek of a whistle and then the swift approach of the train which was overdue.

'May I take her to some inn?' said I. 'I will pay any charges there are.'

The doctor raised his hand, as though to bid me say nothing until the express was by.

The next moment this passed, with a flicker of lighted windows and the shattering roar of a train that will lose no time.

As the racket faded–

'Were you driving the car?' said the doctor. 'I don't suggest it was your fault. That remains to be seen. But were you driving the car?'

Again the sergeant intervened.

'Sir,' said he, 'this is a political case. The matter will–'

'"Political case"?' snapped the other. 'You speak as a fool. I'm not concerned with your business, but this is mine.' He returned to me. 'Were you driving the car?' he repeated.

God knows how many ears were hanging on my reply. The cross-gates were still shut, and the thirsty crowd was standing twelve deep about the car.

'She was not run over,' I said.

The doctor stiffened. I saw his chin go up.

'What then?' he said sharply.

'She was murdered,' said I steadily. 'The sergeant will bear me out. We saw it done.'

For a long moment nobody seemed to breathe. Then the press seemed to rustle and quiver, and I heard the dread word 'murder' flitting from tongue to tongue.

The doctor moistened his lips.

'And the – murderer?'

'He is dead,' said I. 'I killed him. Summon me as a witness before your court, and I will tell you the truth from beginning to end. And summon also Leonie, Grand Duchess of Riechtenburg. Last night she passed through Elsa, and *if she is alive and well,* she will be glad to come.'

There was an electric silence.

Then–

'"Alive and well"?' cried the doctor. 'The Grand Duchess? What do you mean?'

I looked down at Lelia's face.

'She was not unlike the Grand Duchess,' I said. 'And it was dark. The man that killed her mistook her for Leonie.'

Again that curious rustle seemed to run through the crowd, but this time a definite murmur made itself heard.

The doctor frowned.

'Who are you?' he said sharply.

'I am under arrest,' I said. 'When I have seen to – to my friend, these officers will take me to jail. I think those that have ordered my arrest will do their utmost to prevent me from attending your court.'

The Coroner looked at me shrewdly.

'I will see to that,' he said. 'What is your name?'

'My name is Richard Chandos,' I said. 'The Grand Duchess is my wife.'

Ten minutes later I carried Lelia into the principal inn.

There, on a great four-poster, I laid her down, with the mistress weeping beside me, to see such beauty cut off, and the sergeant keeping the door against the whispering maids.

I turned to the doctor, who was standing at the foot of the bed, with his chin in his hand.

'I am helpless,' I said. 'If I could, I would watch by her side; but I can do no more because I am under arrest. And the sergeant has been very civil and I cannot abuse the lenience which he has shown. Will you see that her relatives are summoned? She lived with her uncle at Merring, and I know that she was called "Lelia", but her surname I never heard. And – and I would not like her disturbed if that may be. I will pay all the charges.'

'I will see to it,' said the other.

'And the dog,' I said, pointing to the wolf-hound, stretched dull-eyed upon the floor. 'He was hers. The poor brute cannot understand.'

'I will take him,' said the doctor kindly, 'and do what I can.'

'And you'll summon my wife?' I hesitated. 'It is right that she should be there. And I am very anxious that she should see this – this great-heart, who lost her life for her sake. She will certainly be at Vigil; I think she may be in Lessing Strasse, at the house of Madame Dresden of Salm. I'm afraid she is in great danger, but, as I have said, I am helpless. If she has been taken, they will say she is not in the country; but that is not true. She passed through Elsa last night about ten o'clock.'

The doctor said nothing, but stood staring straight before him, frowning and biting his lip.

I turned again to the bed, to look upon Lelia in her beauty for the last time.

She was very pale now and might have been made of marble instead of flesh and blood. All her loveliness was there, but death had so changed it that now she seemed to belong to some other and rarer school. And this, I suppose, was as it should be; but the veiled eyes and the grave droop of the lips that I had known so eager were like a knife in my heart, and I turned away blindly and stood to an open casement with the tears running down my face.

The window looked out upon the country which I had come to know, and though I could not see them, I knew it was commanding the meadows which George and Bell and I had traversed at this hour six days before. To the east the sky was paling, and the tops of the mountains rose up in a long, black screen, jagged and sinister, standing against the dawn. Very soon this would lighten their darkness, and the sun would clothe them with colour and make honest hills of them again. But not for me. I knew them for what they were. They and the clouds... Instinctively I lifted my eyes. *The heaven was clear.* Look where I would, the sky showed nothing but stars. The pall of cloud was clean gone.

After a little I turned again to the room, to see the Coroner stooping to Lelia's wolf-hound and trying to coax the poor dog to lift up his head.

I passed to his side.

'When will you hold the inquest?'

'At three o'clock tomorrow,' he said.

'I shall hope to be there,' said I.

'Never fear, sir,' said he.

I thanked him and bade him goodbye.

A moment later the detective-sergeant and I were descending the stairs.

There must have been three hundred people without the inn. As I emerged, I saw a general movement, and every man took off his hat.

Instinctively I put up my hand, to find that I was bare-headed. I think I had been so for hours.

As I entered the car, the crowd surged forward.

'Who touches her man, touches Leonie,' roared a deep voice.

An angry murmur answered, and the sergeant went something white.

I stood up in the car at once.

I could not let the man down. If he had not let me take Lelia, long before this he would have lodged me in jail.

'Sirs,' I shouted. 'I thank you. But we must be in order whatever we do. These men are doing their duty. They have treated me very well. And I am content to go with them. But listen. I have said that Leonie is in danger, and so she is. We will come to the court here

277

tomorrow – she and I.'

'At what hour, my lord?' cried someone.

'At three o'clock. But if we do not come – if Leonie does not come, you will know there is something wrong and that the danger I speak of has lifted its head.'

A long mutter answered me. Then the car moved, and they parted and let it go, crying out and waving and shouting 'Leonie'.

Fifty minutes later the car passed under an archway and into a court. The buildings rose very high upon every side, but there was light enough to show me two closed cars standing side by side in the shadows and their drivers, sick of waiting, asprawl on their seats.

From a doorway to the left of the court came a flood of electric light.

A moment later I was treading a long, stone passage, with a jailer going before me and another behind.

Then the door of some cell was opened, and I passed in.

CHAPTER 9

The Power of the Dog

They had taken away my wristwatch, but there was some clock hard by that chimed the hours, and I know that it was soon after ten that three or four persons came stepping down the passage and up to the door of my cell.

Till then I had seen no one but the jailers and a dreadful-looking barber who certainly shaved me well and would have ordered my hair, but I did not like the look of his brushes and thanked him to let that go. But now I was sure that somebody not of the prison was standing without the door, for there seemed to be some hesitation and I could hear whispers exchanged, and that was not the way of the jailers, who were downright in all they did.

Then the shutter of the grill was drawn, and behind the lattice of iron I could see some face.

Because, I suppose, I was so much troubled about her, the thought that it might be Leonie flung itself into my mind.

I started up eagerly.

'Leonie! Is that you?'

A snigger answered me, and I turned on my heel.

Only two beings I knew would have laughed in my face. And of these one was dead.

'"Handsome is as handsome does",' I said lightly. 'Can you really blame the Grand Duchess for turning you down?'

I know it was unpardonable, but the tongue is an unruly member, and the words were out of my mouth before I could think.

There was a dreadful silence. Then Paul, Prince of Riechtenburg, let himself go.

If the blow I had struck him was foul, be sure I paid for it.

His oaths and threats were nothing; the filth he spouted only dishonoured himself; but what he said of Leonie froze my blood. I have never heard a man so speak of any woman in all my life, and at last I stopped my ears, because I could bear it no more.

And when at last I put down my hands, I heard the footfalls retreating and found that I was alone.

The incident shook me badly, as well it might.

When Lelia told me that Leonie had passed through Elsa, my feeling was one of relief. Anything was better than that she should come up by the water and find the smuggler waiting on the Austrian side of the fall. This sense of relief was short-lived, and, as I have shown, I had already determined to take Grieg's car and drive to Vigil to find her, when our failure to make for Gola and the shocking events which followed took a startling and dreadful precedence of other cares.

All the time I was carrying Lelia – first to the car, and then to Vardar and then up the stairs of the inn, Leonie's peril made a distracting background to all my thoughts; and my feeble attempts to arouse suspicion in Vardar were made in the desperation of a man who sees his world slipping in the moment when he himself is beaten down to his knees.

Indeed, not until I had slept, was I able to focus the matter as it deserved.

At once three things became clear.

The first was that Leonie had entered Riechtenburg as the direct result of what she had learned from Bell. Of this there could be no doubt. Bell had arrived in the morning, and she had left for Elsa the same afternoon. She held no cards; she had simply come because of the danger in which she saw that I stood.

The second was that whatever were Grieg's instructions concerning my wife, the Prince would have held him guiltless if she had been killed. I put it no higher than that. Grieg certainly fired upon me, but my arm was about the maid he mistook for my wife,

281

and Leonie might have done as Lelia did.

The third was that if Leonie had been taken, no kind of pressure from Vardar would bring her to the Coroner's court. It was conceivable that, if the Coroner insisted, they might have to let me go. The man was strict and knew that I was in Vigil and under arrest. But when he demanded Leonie, they would laugh in his face. 'Go and fetch her from Littai,' they would say. And if they swore that she had not been seen in Vigil, the man must go empty away.

Following these conclusions, the beastly explosion of spite which I had touched off quickened my apprehension into a fever of fear, for though, so long as I listened, the Prince had said nothing to show me that Leonie lay in his power, I did not like the sound of his laughter and found an ominous confidence in his tone.

Still, there was nothing to be done. I was as cut off and helpless as any caged beast; and all my hope was in Vardar and the Coroner's shrewd, grey eyes and the hearts of the husbandmen.

Except that some food was brought me soon after midday, I was not visited again until three o'clock. At that hour three jailers came and took me along the passage and up a winding stair.

The room we presently entered might

have been called a court.

It was divided in two by a plain oak screen, between four and five feet high. Beyond the screen, the floor was considerably higher, so that such as sat on that side could command the rest of the room. Of this my side was bare, except for a bench in the midst and two stools against the wall, but the other was furnished with a table and four or five massive chairs of leather and oak. All around the chamber were curtains of dark green cloth, so that if there were doors or alcoves, they could not be seen, and, high above the curtains, a row of windows was casting a sombre light. At either end of the table, which stood lengthwise to the screen, was seated a stooping clerk, ready, no doubt, to record whatever took place; and behind the table were sitting two keen-faced men whom I took at once for examining magistrates. The one was older than the other and sat very stiff; his face was bloodless and might have been a wax mask. His fellow was almost lolling, with his elbow on an arm of his chair and his chin in his hand. For all his faint smile, I liked him the least of the two. They wore no robes, but were soberly dressed in black, and the only insignia of office that I could see were the bands of lawn which were fastened about their necks.

At a sign from the sergeant-jailer I took my seat upon the bench, when he and the other fell back and stood by the wall. The third jailer had not entered, but was, I think, remaining without the door.

The elder of the lawyers leaned forward.

'By our advice, one charge only has been preferred against you. I think you will allow that it is sufficiently grave. It is that of maltreating the person of his Royal Highness Prince Paul of Riechtenburg. This you are said to have done in the garden of a house in the Lessing Strasse six days ago.'

He paused there, as though expecting a reply, but if I said nothing, I was busy with my thoughts.

'By our advice…'

The advice was precisely that which a wise man-of-law would give. My stealthy entry into Riechtenburg, my theft of the Prince's car, my conspiracy with George and the Countess – all these had been rejected in favour of that offence which no motive could palliate, the penalty for which was most dire. If I denied it, the Prince would be called against me, and what Court on earth could be blamed for preferring his word to mine? Unless I betrayed my friends I could call no witnesses; and if I sought to refer to anything other than what had occurred in that garden, I should be instantly *and rightly* stopped. My trial was to be in order. The proceedings would bear investigation by the most captious of eyes. Yet my conviction was as certain as the midwinter snow upon the hills.

'Do you plead "Guilty", or no?'

'By what authority,' said I, 'do you question me?'

The man flushed under my tongue, and his fellow looked up.

'You are a stranger,' he said, 'and you do not know the law. An offence against the person of the Sovereign is dealt with *in camera* by a specially constituted Court. Be sure that you will have justice.'

'I see,' said I. 'I am before this – this specially constituted Court?'

'Yes,' said the other. 'You are.'

'I see,' said I. 'Very well. I plead "Not guilty".'

The words were scarce out of my mouth, when the curtains on the left were parted, and the Prince, who had been standing in a doorway, stepped to the table and flung himself into a chair.

His appearance was so abrupt as to give my judges no time to get to their feet, and they were plainly put out – as much, I imagine, by the blunt disclosure of the truth that the Prince had been eavesdropping as by his disregard of the Court and its dignity. But that was their master's way. The youth was a law unto himself and strained to breaking-point that fine tradition that 'the King can do no wrong'. But for his high estate, I can think of no company from which he would not have met with the shortest of shrifts; but, as things were, his insolence had to be suffered, and few beside Sully – the Lord President of the Council and a man of exceptional address – would dare to correct his behaviour and save the appearance which he was throwing away.

As the two were making their bows–

'Get on,' said his Royal Highness.

With what dignity they could summon, the Prince was sworn. Then the elder requested his monarch to give his account of what happened 'in the Countess of Dresden's garden six days ago'.

The Prince unfolded a paper and read aloud.

'My dog disappeared in the bushes, and I followed the animal in. Chandos stepped from behind a tree and told me to call the dog to heel. He had a pistol in his hand which he was pointing at me. I heard a noise behind me. When I turned I saw the man called "Hanbury", pistol in hand. He was the nearest, and so I knocked him down. Before I could call for assistance Chandos put his pistol to my throat. He spoke to Hanbury. "We must get out," he said. "I'm afraid." Then he spoke to me. "Will you tell your chauffeurs to drive me to Elsa?" he said. I told him to go to hell. At that, he said to Hanbury, "We must get rid of his chauffeurs and take his car." After some discussion the two of them seized me and started to drag me away. I broke free and swung myself into a tree. I expected them to fire, but I think they were afraid of the noise. I found another man in the tree and forced him down. Then I started to shout, and my chauffeurs appeared upon the scene.'

He folded the paper and stuffed it into his coat. Then he sat back in his chair and fell to biting his nails.

The elder judge lifted his head.

'Do you wish to question his Royal Highness?'

My spirits rose. I had never expected such licence.

'Yes,' said I, and rose to my feet.

The two clerks picked up their pens.

I folded my arms and looked the Prince in the face.

'Can you describe my pistol?'

The red-rimmed, watery eyes raked me from head to knee. Then their owner shrugged his shoulder.

'It was like any other pistol,' he said.

'Which was it – nickelled or blued?'

The Prince hesitated. Then–

'It was nickelled,' he said.

I could have thrown up my hat. I had scarcely dared hope he would make such a childish mistake.

I addressed the Court.

'I call for that pistol,' I said.

The younger of the judges leaned forward.
'What pistol?' he said, smiling.
'The pistol which I handed to the police.'
'But what will that prove?' he purred.
'You will see that it is blued.'
'No doubt,' said the other, 'no doubt. But the pistol of which we are speaking is the one which you pointed at the Prince.'
My spirits sank lower than before. That I was no match for these men was perfectly clear.
'I never had but one,' I said wearily.
With a gesture of infinite regret, the fellow leaned back in his seat. To this day I can see his raised hand and his pitying smile. The mockery stung me, and I felt as never before that I had my back to the wall.
'Have you any other questions?' he said.
I reflected dismally. Then—
'Was the Countess Dresden present?' I said.
The Prince's eyes narrowed.
'Yes,' he said roughly. 'She was.'
'Do you think her account of what happened would tally with yours?'
His Royal Highness reddened.
'D'you suggest I'm lying?' he blurted.
As his lawyers turned to soothe him—
'From beginning to end,' I said coolly. 'You know it as well as I. Everyone present knows it – because they know you. And now kindly answer my question. Do you think

Madame Dresden's account–'

I left the sentence there, because for the moment I had not the ear of the Court. The lawyers' hands were full. Beneath their lively entreaties the Prince was chafing and cursing and raving of 'exposure to insult' and 'royal blood'.

As the storm was subsiding, the younger of the judges looked round.

'Do you call the Countess?' – sharply.

'No,' said I.

'Then what she would say has nothing to do with the case.'

I swallowed desperately. No doubt the fellow was right.

I returned to the Prince, whose face was working with rage.

'You say you knocked Hanbury down?'

'So I – well did,' cried the Prince, 'you insolent swine.'

'Was he the only one you knocked down?'

'Yes.'

'Then why did you tell Weber that you had "laid two of them out"? Yesterday morning … when you were at Baron Sabre's … waiting for Grieg?'

His Royal Highness started forward.

'Where were you?' he said.

'Close enough to hear every word – *every single word.*'

Before the man could reply, the elder of the judges was making some fresh remonstrance with all his might. I think he was imploring his monarch to play the part of a witness and ask no questions himself. That the latter heard him with a scowl was, I am sure, because he had nothing to say.

A knock fell upon the door by which the two jailers stood.

Immediately one of them opened, to parley with someone without.

'What is it?' barked the judge who was not engaged with the Prince.

The jailer turned a scared face. Then he drew the curtains and let an inspector come in.

'What does this mean?'

The inspector stepped to the screen and opened his mouth.

'Speak up. I cannot hear,' said the elder judge.

'A Coroner's Officer, sir, is standing below. He has a witness-summons made out in the prisoner's name.'

With a gesture of the utmost impatience, the other sat back in his chair.

'Tell him to leave it,' he flamed.

The inspector quailed.

'He – he demands to serve it personally, sir.'

'"Demands?"' cried the other. '"Demands?" and how does he know that the prisoner is here? Send the man packing. Good God, must you come to us in a matter

290

like this?'

'The superintendent is out, sir; and the Deputy-Chief is away.'

'Have *you* no discretion – no power? An inspector of police that cannot deal with a peasant is best returned to the ranks.' He smote upon the board with his fist. 'Begone. Deal with the clown as you should. And if you cannot, call one of your men and ask him to teach you the way.'

The inspector withdrew, trembling.

As the door closed behind him–

'Who's dead?' said the Prince, frowning.

Now had his advisers been as wise men of action as they were wise men of law, they would have cleared the court and sent me away. But I think they thought the damage was done. Be that as it may, they instantly turned to the Prince, and the younger judge rose and passed to his other side.

I did not hear what was said, for their voices were low, but first one spoke and then the other, and I have no doubt that their talk was of what had happened at Vardar the night before. The detective-sergeant, of course, had reported what had occurred, but it had been intended, I fancy, to keep the facts from the Prince.

I watched the three closely…

'A demonstration?' said the Prince suddenly. 'What do you mean?'

The younger judge spoke very fast, but the

Prince cut him short:

'He said "demonstration",' he cried, with a smack of his hand. 'A demonstration means treason. It's a devilish curious thing that it should happen last night – *just when she'd entered the country*... Damn it, you're my advisers. Don't you–'

Another knock fell upon the door.

All eyes turned to the curtains, save only mine.

The lawyers were plainly uneasy. The elder's fingers were busy; the younger was standing up with a hand to his mouth. But for the look of the thing, I think they would even now have had me removed. Between them the Prince sat glowering.

A sturdy superintendent entered the room.

'What now?' rasped the elder judge.

'Sir,' said the superintendent, 'the matter is grave. I have but just come in. This Coroner's Officer from Vardar is not alone. He has brought six witnesses.'

'Witnesses?'

'Witnesses, sir – to see how he is received. They are, all six, men of Vardar. And the man himself is wearing the mourning sash. This makes him conspicuous. There is a crowd of three hundred, and I have closed the gates.'

Before the judge could answer, his master had snatched the reins.

'Disperse them,' cried the Prince. 'If you

don't know how to do it, send for the troops.'

The superintendent braced himself.

'They are orderly enough, your Royal Highness. But it – it is the impression conveyed. The obstruction of a Coroner's Officer is a most serious thing.'

'Who's obstructing the fool?' cried the Prince. 'Let him leave his – summons and go to his swine.'

'He has the right, your Royal Highness, to serve it himself.'

In evident agitation the elder judge half rose and lifted a hand.

'It is out of order,' he began...

'Silence!' roared his master, and stamped his foot. The old man fell back, shaking. 'What fool said the prisoner was here? Tell him he's wrong. Say you've looked at the roll and there's no such name.'

'It is useless, your Royal Highness. Himself saw the arrest.' The man hesitated. 'He – he has a second summons.'

The Prince stared, and the younger judge bent to his ear.

'Will you shut up?' blared the Prince. He returned to the superintendent. 'A second summons? Who for?'

'For her Highness, the Grand Duchess Leonie.'

There was an electric silence.

Then the Prince leaped to his feet.

'This is treason,' he mouthed. 'I said so. I

293

said so a moment ago. Witness-summons be damned. They want to get her to–'

'By your leave, sir.' The younger judge's voice cut through the sentence as a knife. As the Prince turned to rend him, 'The Grand Duchess is at Littai,' he added. 'At least, she left Vigil for Littai some hours ago.'

The superintendent replied.

'I have insisted, sir, that her Highness is not here. I think if he were permitted to serve the prisoner, the man would go.'

There was a moment's silence. Then–

'The Court will adjourn,' said the elder judge. 'Take the prisoner away.'

With his words, the jailers closed about me and carried me off.

I went, if not triumphant, yet full of hope.

The Coroner and his peasants were hearts of oak. And despite his advisers' efforts, the Prince had played into my hands. I had no doubt whatever that, had he allowed them to speak, they would have ordered my removal before I had heard what I had. But now it was too late. The younger judge's desperate interruption had been made because of those present who did not know the truth. *Leonie was in Vigil and under arrest.*

I waited the service of my summons with a hammering heart.

After a quarter of an hour I was brought to some waiting-room.

There stood a bent, old peasant, clad in his fine, white linen, with a broad sash of black and silver from shoulder to waist.

'Are you Richard Chandos, my lord?'

'I am, my friend.'

'Then I am to summon you to the Coroner's Court at Vardar tomorrow at three o'clock.' He touched my shoulder with the paper he held in his hand. Then he gave it to me with a bow. 'There, my lord. You are served.'

'And her Highness?' said I.

'My lord, I cannot find her. She is not in the Lessing Strasse, and I am assured that she left the country at noon.'

'It is untrue,' said I. 'She is here.'

'Come,' said the superintendent. 'You gave me your word that when you had served the prisoner you would go your way.'

'Ay, so I did,' said the peasant. 'God save you, my lord.'

With that, he was gone.

A moment later they led me back to my cell.

My elation was gone, and I was disquieted.

It now seemed certain that I was to go to Vardar, and there in open court to be given every chance of telling my tale. What this blunt recital would cost Prince Paul could not be measured. I was 'out for blood'; it would not be my fault if it did not cost him his throne. I was determined to omit nothing. His colloquy with Grieg in the greenwood should be rendered, word for word. But, though I should ruin her cousin, this would not help my wife.

To serve his summons upon me, the Coroner's Officer had been ready to wait all night. No lies could disconcert him – because he *knew* I was there. But Leonie's case was different. No one at Vardar had seen her, and the man had nothing to go on but my bare word.

And when the police confirmed this *and then went further than I,* his importunity had faltered, and he had gone empty away. When I went to Vardar without her, yet swore she was in the country, the peasants would disbelieve me – against their will.

I might swear that she was in Riechtenburg, but when they asked me to prove it, where was my proof? I had not so much as seen her; I had only heard say she had come in. *And the police confirmed this hearsay.* 'He is right', they said. 'Quite right. Her Highness did enter the country, and now she has gone'. My case would have been far stronger if they had denied that Leonie had ever come in. I might then have aroused suspicion instead of pity for a man that is beating the air.

'I am assured that she left the country at noon.'

I could not prove that she had not. And

Littai lay distant one hundred and ninety miles.

Far into the night I sat thinking – flogging my brain for some way out of the pass. But I could discover no means to help my darling, and at last I took to my pallet and fell asleep.

The dawn was up when I was awakened by the approaching footfalls of men in haste.

As I got to my feet, the door of my cell was opened; then the jailer stood back, and a fine, familiar figure passed into the small stone room.

'Sully!'

The Lord President of the Council took my hand.

'To Bell,' he said, 'the glory. Her Highness sent him for me. He has driven nine hundred miles in thirty-six hours.'

Here I should say that this was less than the truth. In fact, Bell had driven nine hundred and sixty miles in thirty-five hours and a half. In his journey to Vichy and back, he had crossed four frontiers, and his actual time upon the road was twenty-six hours. Considering that when he started he was by no means fresh, that never before had he travelled over the roads he used and that he could speak no tongue but his own, I think the feat was notable.

'Sully,' I cried, 'they have her.'

'Come,' said he. 'We will talk in the Commissioner's room.'

I followed him out, and two minutes later we were alone in an office, half full of a gigantic table and laid with as thick a carpet as ever I trod. As we took our seats–

'Where are we?' I said. 'In the jail?'

'No,' said Sully. 'We are in the chief police-office, and this is Weber's room. But Weber is sick.'

'He looked all right two days ago.'

'Yes, I don't think it's serious,' said Sully. 'But Weber is not very strong. I hope very much to be able to make him well.' He set his cigarette-case beside me and felt for a match. 'And now let me hear what has happened. Bell left you at Sallust, making your way to the bridge.'

I told my tale faithfully, omitting nothing at all.

The Lord President heard me out, with his elbow on the arm of his chair and his fine chin cupped in his palm. As was his way, he never interrupted me once.

As I finished, some clock struck the hour. Seven o'clock.

Sully rose to his feet.

'I will telegraph to Littai,' he said. 'I do not think her Highness is here. I have not yet seen the Prince, but those I have seen–'

'I know she is here, Sully. For one thing only, she would never have gone until she had seen my face.'

His brows drew into a frown.

'I will see the Prince,' he said. 'I have requested an audience at eight o'clock. And now about this inquest. They're bound to let you attend it. What are you going to say?'

'It'll take less time,' I said, 'to tell you what I'm going to leave out. I'm not going to say that Marya was married to Grieg.'

Sully's chin went down.

'Is that all … you're not going to say?'

'All,' said I, and lighted a cigarette. 'My statement will be a long one, but I don't think they'll find it dull.'

Sully lifted his head.

'It will never be made,' he said. 'You have the whip-hand, Chandos. The Prince will sign your pardon before midday.'

I laid down my cigarette and rose to my feet.

'My pardon won't shut my mouth, Sully.'

The Lord President met my gaze. Then he put his hands to his face.

'God forgive me,' he said, 'but I cannot blame you. Tell me your terms, and I will lay them before him at eight o'clock.'

'I will tell you my terms,' I said, 'when I have seen Leonie.'

I was not returned to my cell, but was led to a decent room overlooking the prison yard. To this some servant of Sully's was admitted within the hour. He had with him brushes and razors, as well as clean linen and towels and plenty of cigarettes, and he told me that Bell was asleep in the bed from which he had risen to let the Lord President in and that, when he had left the house, the man that washed Sully's car was washing the Rolls. When I had made my toilet, he served me a very good breakfast which he had arranged for some pastry-cook to provide, and when I had done, he brought me the morning paper and asked at what hour I would lunch. I told him at one o'clock. Then he wished me good morning and went his way.

Of the news which the paper gave, the inquest to be held at Vardar was given the largest print and the highest place. No names were mentioned, no doubt by order of the police, but I was referred to as 'a very high personage, for some extraordinary reason now lying under arrest'. Of the obstruction of the Coroner's Officer no mention was made, but the presence of the crowd was referred to, as indicating the interest which had been aroused, and indeed the whole passage might have been designed to make the most jaded of readers hungry for news.

Of Leonie nothing was said but the following words.

The grand Duchess Leonie entered the country by Elsa on Tuesday night. Her Highness is understood to have left again this morning. The object of her visit is not known. We see too little of the lady who, if not Princess of Riechtenburg, will always be the queen of our hearts.

This paragraph was printed immediately below that which dealt with the inquest which the Coroner of Vardar was to hold.

As the clocks were striking eleven, the door was opened, and Sully came into the room.

'She is not here, Chandos,' he said.

'Yes she is, Sully,' said I.

'My dear boy,' he began...

'I know it,' said I. 'I cannot prove it, of course. But they are deceiving you, Sully. Leonie is here.'

'She was here,' said Sully. 'She came in on Monday evening, driving herself. Jameson was with her. She drove to the Lessing Strasse, and there she passed the night. The Prince declined to see her, and she left again with Jameson before midday.'

'Why?'

'Nobody knows, Chandos. She received a trunk telephone call which cannot be traced, and she is believed to have left in response to that. I have seen the book which they keep at the Customs at Elsa. The car is entered as having come in at nine-thirty on Tuesday night, and the "Exit" column is stamped–'

'Show me a telegram from Littai, saying that she is there.'

'She is not there, Chandos. That I admit. But she may be at Bariche or Salzburg–'

'Or Vigil,' said I.

Sully threw up his hands.

'The Prince has sworn before God that she is not here.'

For Sully's sake I suppressed the obvious retort.

'Those judges know that she's here. And I think the superintendent, but I cannot be sure. And the men that took her must know.'

'Chandos, Chandos,' cried Sully. 'I have ways and means of finding the truth in this land. Where she has gone, or why, I cannot tell you. But I will swear to you that she is not here.'

'I do not say she is in Vigil,' said I. 'She may be at the summer-palace at Rothenthal. She was driving George Hanbury's car. Let Bell be waked and go with you to the mews. He'll know the car when he sees it. And if it is not at the mews, let him go with someone you trust to Rothenthal.'

'It shall be done,' said Sully. His hand went into his pocket to bring out an envelope. 'And now here is the pardon–'

'I'm sorry, Sully,' said I. 'But you know me too well for that.'

'My dear boy...'

Resolutely I shook my head.

'I am due at Vardar,' I said, 'in four hours' time. What evidence I shall give there remains to be seen. But I will not discuss the matter until I have seen my wife.'

Sully laid a hand on my shoulder and seemed about to speak. Then he changed his mind and turned to the door.

'I will come back,' he said. 'I am going to get hold of Bell and do as you say.'

When he was gone, I flung myself into a chair and stared at the floor.

Sully was wise. He knew the Prince and the country far better than I. He had his secret agents and he knew what men he could trust. Above all, he loved Leonie. And Sully was satisfied that Leonie was not here. Yet if she was not here, where would she be? She had set out from Littai, because she found my peril so instant that she could no longer endure to be out of touch – as I had feared she would do from the moment that the circus left Vardar, travelling west. That she should return because the Prince would not see her was altogether absurd. Besides, she had not returned. And what telephone call could lure her out of the country when once she was in? All the fear she had known was the fear of being stopped at the frontier – from coming in. More. She would have waited for Sully. She alone knew that he was coming, and all her hope was in him.

I rose to my feet, determined to stick to my guns.

The book kept at Elsa was faked. No telephone call could be traced, because none had been made. These things were the dust to be thrown into Sully's eyes. Leonie was here.

An hour and a half dragged by before Sully returned.

The man looked pale and worn, and I knew he had failed.

'Bell is below, Chandos. We have been to the Royal mews and to the summer-palace; but the car is not there.'

'So be it,' said I. 'Then it is somewhere else.'

'I do not believe it,' cried Sully. 'You know that I would not deceive you – or let myself be deceived. You know – you must know that I am as anxious as you … that she has been my darling for twenty years.' He threw himself into a chair and covered his eyes. 'When I was your age, I carried her in my arms – the loveliest baby-child that ever I saw. She was to be my mistress. Even then it had been arranged that one day those tiny hands should put on the Princess' crown. I watched her grow into a maiden, and I watched the maiden grow into a queen. And then my dream was shattered. You broke it, Chandos. She was to have been my mistress, and you – you took her away. And when I looked upon my master, I thanked my God. D'you hear? I thanked my God. Thanked him for sending you to save her from such a hideous fate. God made him a Prince. Had my father not seen him in the midwife's arms I would have doubted it. There are times when I doubt it now...' He broke off there, his voice thick and shaken with emotion as I had never heard it before. After a little he continued shakily. 'As Prince, I honour him. But I would give his royal body for a hair of her lovely head.'

'I know it, Sully,' said I.

'I honour the Prince. I serve him. I come to you as his ambassador. At this inquest at Vardar you will hold his name, perhaps his fortune in the hollow of your hand. He is young and headstrong, and the royal wine of sovereignty has gone to his head. In his way he loved the Grand Duchess. For years they had been betrothed. He had come to take her for granted, and his eyes were fixed upon the day when he would be Prince and she would stand by his side. And when you came, and she broke off her engagement – well, the blow might well have unbalanced an older and steadier head. His love was turned to hatred, his pride to bane. Jealousy strung him to madness, and all his thoughts were of vengeance for "the wrong which he had been done". Then, one day, he noticed Grieg ... Grieg had no cause to love you, and Grieg was out of a job... His Royal Highness was the cat's-paw – you know he is very weak. I was not there. Grieg played upon his baser nature, because it suited his book; and his was the will that rode his Royal Highness from first to last. I cannot defend him, Chandos. Had he not set up Grieg, the harm could not have been done. But Grieg was at once his familiar and his executive, and but for Grieg, he would never have lifted a finger to do you wrong.'

O rare and admirable Sully! Had ever so worthless a master so faithful a servant?

I found myself wondering for the thousandth time how it was that so true a man could endure to bear the standard of so false-hearted a prince. Sully was not ambitious and would have been happy to give up his seals of office and withdraw to some simple life. It was easy to say that having set his hand to the plough, so long as the breath was in him he would not look back. That, no doubt, was the way of his spirit; but what of the flesh?

His hand came to rest upon my shoulder.

'Chandos, time's getting on. Tell me your terms.'

I clapped my hands to my head.

'Sully,' I cried, 'don't press me. Don't draw the one card I've got. I know she's here. *I know it*. If you could have heard–'

'Do you think that when the inquest is over I shall rest until she is found? Do you think I could sleep–'

'Of what use will that be?' I cried. 'The Prince can dismiss you – banish you from the country by a stroke of the pen. If you are

306

inconvenient, *he will.* At the moment you are convenient. You alone can act as our go-between. Until the inquest is over, he dare not move. But once I have spared him – once I have saved his face, my hands are empty, and he can send you away.'

'He would never do that,' said Sully. 'I do not pretend he loves me, but the Council rules the country and rules it well. If he dismissed me–'

'If he has Leonie, he will. You're the fastest friend here she's got. Can't you see my point, Sully? At the moment my foot's on his neck. I can bring him, if not to ruin, to such disgrace and contempt that he will scarce dare to venture without his gates. He knows it – you've pointed it out. Very well. If I'm right, and he has Leonie, *if I make any terms which are not based on her release,* he will have won the rubber and got his way. Do you think he'll scrap his victory by keeping you on? By keeping on Leonie's champion, to cramp his style?'

The Lord President looked at his watch and rose to his feet.

'I will see him again,' he said. 'I know it is useless, but I will try again.'

I turned to the window and stood looking out upon the yard.

'I am sorry,' I said. 'I do not want to be unreasonable, and you have travelled all night and have scarcely sat down. If you–'

The sentence was never finished.

The sight of the prison yard had set me thinking, and a fact which I had noted, but never discussed, now rose up, staring and pregnant, to hit me between the eyes.

I was round in a flash, and trembling like any leaf.

'Sully, I'm right! I've got it! I've got the proof. Grieg ordered three cars to be in waiting from nine o'clock on. Three cars – on Tuesday evening. I heard his words. When I came here at dawn on Wednesday, they were still waiting down there. I saw them. The drivers were asleep. *But only two of them, Sully. The third was gone…*'

Sully was trembling, as I was.

'You mean–?'

'Where was the third?' I shouted. 'That's what I mean. Grieg never summoned it – unless he rang up from hell. I'm right, Sully. I told you. Take Bell to the police-station garage. Have every lock-up opened. But if you draw blank, I don't care. Three cars he ordered. I heard him. "To bring the prisoners in".'

But Sully was gone.

CHAPTER 10

Checkmate

Though I tried to make a show of tasting the excellent dishes which Sully's man had procured, after a little I laid my napkin down.

'I am sorry,' I said, 'but I have no appetite. Bring me some fruit, if you will, and give me a cigarette.'

I could see the poor man was upset, but I was beside myself, and, while the food choked me, the ceremony of his service was more than I could endure. And since pacing the room and staring out of the window afforded me no relief, I sat down at a writing table and took up a pen.

Time was short. It would be as well to be ready with such terms as I meant to impose.

By a desperate effort I brought my brain to heel and began to write.

The Inquest to be held at Vardar on August 8th.
In consideration of Richard Chandos' undertaking to suppress my name and to lead the Court to believe that Grieg was acting in these matters not by my express orders, as in fact he

was, but solely on his own account, I promise:-

(1) To be officially represented at the funeral of the murdered girl by one of my lords-in-waiting.
(2) To order and attend in person and in state a service of thanksgiving for the preservation of Leonie, Grand Duchess of Riechtenburg. This service to be held in the Cathedral Church of Vigil on Saturday next.
(3) Never to interfere with the liberty of the Grand Duchess again.
(4) To post sentries drawn from her Highness' Regiment at the house of the Countess Dresden and to put a royal car at her Highness' disposal until further notice.
(5) To reinstate immediately the Countess Dresden of Salm and never to molest her or permit her to be molested again.
(6) To grant and issue safe-conducts to the Grand Duchess, Richard Chandos, George Hanbury and their servants. These safe-conducts to be handed to Richard Chandos within the hour.
(7) To make over to Richard Chandos my wolf-hound called 'Aster'.
(8) To promote to the rank of inspector Detective-sergeant– and to maintain him in that rank.
(9) To pay to the police of Sallust the sum of five hundred pounds from my privy purse.
(10) To send to Ramon the smith, of Gola, a letter of indemnity signed by my own hand.

Such was my agitation that the drafting of these conditions took me a very long time, but the exercise had its value, for at least it fobbed off the emotions to which I was now prey.

Fear, hope, impatience and a shocking thirst for revenge fought between themselves for my possession as never before, and when my composition hung fire, fell upon my halting head-piece as curs upon a cur that is sick.

The forged telegram, the spy at Littai, the detention of the Countess, the efforts to prevent my escape – these things were all of a piece with a wilful and wicked attempt to bring Leonie into the land and into its ruler's power. I was the prize, certainly: but the horrid excitement shown by his Royal Highness the instant that Grieg had hinted that Leonie was on her way was most significant, and his outburst the day before rammed home the beastly truth. He hated me, but he hated Leonie more. She was lovely and worshipful – and she had 'turned him down'. She had declined a crown, because she could not endure to be his wife. And the country he ruled knew this and loved her no whit the less. He might be Prince of Riechtenburg, but she would 'always be the queen of our hearts'. His hatred had fed upon these things for nearly a year. Then Leonie had come to Littai, and Sully had gone away...

When I considered these things, I entered that state of mind in which I had put Grieg to death. My strength seemed to be resistless, and I could have sought the palace, forced my way into the presence and wrung the truth from the fellow with my hands on his sacred throat. Because this course was denied me, my passion fed upon my flesh, to set me shaking and sweating and staring before me like a madman cooped in his cell. Indeed, there were times when I thought I must lose my mind, for the vials of wrath seemed to be flowing over because they were not poured out.

Some clock struck two.

In half an hour I should be due to leave for Vardar, if not before.

The sands were running out.

If Sully failed again, what should I do? I had broken one of his dreams. Was I to break another and bring the throne he had done so much to dignify into contempt? What if I did – and then found Leonie at Bariche, alive and well? I must be fair with Sully: but I must first be sure that I was being fair with myself.

I read through my 'terms' again, folded up the paper and put it away.

Then the door was flung open, and the officer the Prince had called 'Candel' was ushered into the room.

Something to my surprise, his hand went up to his cap in a formal salute.

'I am commanded, sir, to ask you to come with me.'

For a moment I sat irresolute.

This was the Prince's man.

I glanced at the open door, to see the detective-sergeant that I had come to know. Our eyes met, and while I was looking at him, he nodded his head.

At once I rose to my feet.

'Lead the way, please,' I said.

As I passed the sergeant, I asked his name…

The passages seemed unending, but presently we left them behind and came to a carpeted corridor, very wide and lit by electric light. On one side of this were so many doors in the wall, and on the other, recesses with doors in each of their sides. There were, I think, five recesses, but when we came to the fourth, Candel entered and opened the right-hand door. Then he stood back and saluted, and I passed into the court in which I had stood at my trial the day before.

But this time I was ushered on to the dais, and there, half-sitting on the arm of one of the chairs, was Leonie.

As the door closed behind me, she flung her arms round my neck…

I do not know how long it was before I could find my voice, but when I had done so, I could only say over her name.

'Leonie, Leonie.'

'I had to come, Richard. I had to.'

'I know,' I said. 'I would have done the same.'

'You'd have come before, Richard. I waited six awful days.'

'You're safe and sound, Leonie?'

'Yes, yes. But they were ready. There was a spy at Littai – I threw him off the scent. I let him believe I was going in by the path. But they held me up at Elsa for half an hour, and I hadn't been gone five minutes when a police car met and ditched me on one of the bends. I knew it was a trap – *knew it*. But what could I do? They pretended they were frightfully sorry and put the car at my disposal to go where I pleased. I simply had to risk it. And once I was in, I found the doors had no handles upon the inside.'

'But you stayed at the Lessing Strasse?'

Leonie shook her head.

'They brought me straight to this building, and I've never been out.'

Another door was opened, the curtains were parted, and Sully came into the court.

He stepped to Leonie and put her hand to his lips.

'I thank God, madam,' he said, 'that your husband is stronger than I. He has saved the light of my eyes.'

Leonie took both his hands.

'We both thank God, Sully, for the finest friend in the world.'

'For a broken reed, madam.' The fine head went down. 'I took my master's word.'

'As you were bound to do. But between you and me there is no need of oaths. I'm sorry not to be your Princess, but I am very glad to be the light of your eyes.'

She put up her mouth and kissed him, and poor Sully held her and kept calling her 'his darling' and whispering 'Thank God.'

Then he let her go and stood back and folded his hands.

'I have come for your terms, Chandos. I am, of course, quite helpless. But if I held a sword in my hand, I have told his Royal Highness that I would break it in two. Ask what you please, and I will make it my business to see that your price is paid.'

In silence I sat to the table and copied my document out. When I had blotted the writing–

'Let him sign that,' I said, 'and return it to me.'

I like to remember that Sully never looked at the sheet. He simply nodded and took it and left the room.

Five minutes later he was back, and, if further proof were needed, I knew that the Prince must have been but a few yards off, for the signature *Paul P.* was not yet dry.

I blotted it carefully.

Then I put away the paper and handed Sully the draft.

'You will need that,' said I, 'to be sure that the terms are fulfilled.'

The Lord President took it with a smile which came nearer to being grim than any I ever saw come into his gentle face.

'I read them aloud to him,' he said. 'I do not think either of us will forget them so long as we live.'

Five minutes later Leonie and I were in the Rolls, which Bell was driving to Vardar as hard as he could. By his side sat Jameson, prim and correct as ever, despite his two days in jail.

And as we went, I told my darling of Lelia and how she had lived and died.

Of our reception at Vardar I scarcely know how to speak.

Despite our solemn errand, the demonstration of affection for Leonie was so moving and played such havoc with the feelings that I did not know where to look, while Bell and Jameson had tears running down their cheeks.

This may sound foolish, and not the way of grown men, but I can only say that such as have not been subjected to such an ordeal can have no idea at all of the onslaught upon the emotions which such a demonstration provokes. Indeed, when later I mentioned the matter to Marya, she seemed surprised to find me so simple and said at once that royalties themselves and those in attendance upon them were specially schooled to subdue the impulse to weep which any outburst of loyalty was bound to excite.

Of the inquest there is little to be said, except that I kept my word and made Grieg out the author of all the ill that was done: and if, as I think, it was suspected that the Prince's hands were not clean, that was due to his reputation and not to any word that fell from my lips.

My arrest I alleged was due to Grieg's false deposition that I was practising treason against the throne – a charge of which, I avowed, I had now been formally cleared. And if I suppressed some truths which might have startled the Court, I think that those I made known were shocking enough.

Indeed, I had but one aim – to dignify Lelia's memory as it deserved, raise her a monument which no weather could ever corrupt, and make the fair name by which I knew her a household word. Whilst I was seeking to render this poor return, Leonie watched by the side of her beautiful deputy and only came down when I had spoken, to tell of the spy at Littai and how she had led him to think that she would seek to go in by way of the bridle-path.

Whether his Royal Highness read the report of the inquest I cannot tell, but if he did so, I cannot believe that the last of Leonie's statement failed to bring a blush to his cheek.

'By virtue of the position which Major Grieg so much abused, he was able to intercept the calls which I naturally made upon my cousin, the Prince. When his Royal Highness was made aware of the conspiracy, his indignation was great, but, since the principal is dead, he has graciously consented to pardon those others who were so foolish as to become accessories.'

Long before the proceedings were over, I was brought the six safe-conducts which I had required, and, when the business was done and a verdict of wilful murder had been brought in against 'the late Major Grieg', I sent out a note to Bell and we left the inn by a garden which lay at the back of the house.

The Coroner overtook us and led us to where he lived, and there we received the wolf-hound, who seemed very pleased to see me and took to Leonie at once. Then Bell came up with the Rolls, and five minutes later we left for the Sabre estate.

I stopped the car in the drive at the spot at which Lelia had crossed it almost at this same hour two days before: and there Leonie and I alighted to walk to the mill.

As before, the sun was low, the clean,

sweet air was radiant, and the steadfast peace of the landscape ministered to my mind. Beneath this influence, the memory of Lelia took on the semblance of a dream, and ever since then I have constantly asked myself whether Fate did not hear my wife's prayers and lay upon Lelia's shoulders her precious mantle of love. It cannot, I think, be denied that Lelia took my wife's place and played out that very part which, had she been present, Leonie would have played: and it will be remembered that I never set eyes upon Lelia till Bell had reported to Leonie and made her suspense too heavy for her to bear. From that time on her one idea was to be with me, and help me and save my life: and all these things Lelia did.

With her eyes on the wolf-hound before us—

'You are thinking of Lelia,' said Leonie.

'Yes,' said I. 'At least, I am thinking of you both. I cannot separate her from you, and I have a curious feeling that what she did she did at your instance because you could not do it yourself.'

'I think you must have loved her,' said Leonie, taking my arm. 'I do not see how you could have helped it.'

'No,' said I. 'I never loved her. I could not, because of you. There is no word for the feeling I had for her. "Like" is useless: and "fond" is not what I want. I am "very fond

319

of" Marya, but Lelia touched my heart.'

'I do not mind if you loved her, my darling.'

'I know. I would tell you, if I had. But I did not, because I could not: and I could not, because of you. It is no credit to me – I felt very badly about it. For all she gave, I had nothing to give her back.'

Leonie stooped to gather a flower.

'She was very lovely,' she said, and set the flower in my coat.

'She was,' said I, 'and she had the prettiest ways. But though I could feel her charm, I could not answer it, my darling, because I have kissed your lips.'

She put up her precious hands and set them about my head.

'I wish I had known her,' she said. 'She took my place. But I would not call her back, if I could. For her sake – not for my own. She died in your arms.'

'She was not like other women,' I said. 'I told her plainly that I loved you again and again.'

'That was very – very strict of you, Richard.'

'My darling, I had to. I could not let her be nice to me without knowing where she stood.'

The magnificent eyes lighted, and I felt absurdly rich.

'I am very fortunate,' said Leonie.

The thing was too hard for me, so I gave it up and kissed the beautiful mouth.

'Did you … kiss her like that?'

'Once. I'm so glad I did. It was just at the last.'

Leonie nodded gravely.

'That's right. I'm so glad you did, too.'

'I did not mean to be unfaithful,' I said.

'Neither you were, my darling. You gave her something that was mine – something that was not yours to give. You drew a cheque upon my personal account. Do you think that I question your signature? Do you think I would not honour it blindly, as you would mine? I asked you, because I am a woman, and women are very curious where the man they love is concerned.'

I put my arms about her and held her close to my heart.

'There is no one like you,' I said, 'in all the world.'

'Lelia was like me,' said Leonie.

'She was – in her way. I think that that was the reason why I liked her so well. And now, as I tell you, she seems to belong to you, and if I am to focus her clearly, I have to shut my eyes.'

My wife put her arms round my neck and looked at the sky.

'I think,' she said, 'you have added her love for you to mine. I have never loved you so well.'

Then again she gave me her lips, and we went on our way.

Four hours had passed, and George and I sat on the terrace of Madame Dresden's house.

The night was warm and starlit, and the breeze that had risen at sundown had died away. In the distance some band was playing, and now and again a slant of music stole to our ears; but Vigil is quiet of nights, and, except for that sound and the brush of tyres upon the boulevard at the end of the twinkling street, we might have been deep in the country which we had left. From time to time the measured tread of a sentry rose from the pavement beyond the garden wall, and the dog lying crouched by my side would lift his head. The rooms behind us were dark, and the lights of Marya's bedroom were laying two squares of silver upon the dew of the lawn. Leonie and she were there, talking. Now and again the shadow of one or the other would darken for a moment one of the pools of light. Bell was below stairs, asleep: and Rowley and Jameson were on their way to Littai – the former to fetch us some clothes, and the latter to order the lodge against our return.

'When we left you,' said George, 'at the mill, Rowley took Marya's line, and I made straight for the house. Marya and I had left by the door in the cloister, and so I knew how to get in. I had a look round about first, but as Grieg didn't stand up and wave, I had to hope for the best. I got it, almost at once – in the shape of the biggest let-off I shall ever have. I'd just started across the turf when a bullet hit the barrel of my pistol which lay as usual in the right-hand pocket of my coat. It hurt all right – it was like the kick of a horse – and of course I thought I'd been hit: but that didn't stop my running, and I was within that cloister before you could think. When I found that I wasn't bleeding, I thought I must be funny like that: I couldn't believe I wasn't wounded, but I couldn't think why I was standing, feeling rather bored and thirsty, instead of writhing in pain and biting bits out of the flags. Then I had a look at my pistol and got it in one. That bulwark was done in all right, but I couldn't really complain. Where the bullet went on, I don't know. The point is, it wasn't in my groin. All the same, I was pretty well fixed. I was disarmed, and Grieg knew all about me and where I was. And as this was not at all what I wanted, I thought very fast. Then I entered the house, whipped to the hall and shouted Marya's name in a tone which suggested that I'd less than a minute to live. When she didn't answer, I knew she wasn't there. The blood and tears in my voice would have fetched a she-bear. So I entered the dining-room, threw a window open, got out, shut it and bolted like any rabbit across the girdle of turf. Then I picked a good covert and sat down to think.

'Considering the new position, I found it good. That of course, was because I was comparatively safe. As a matter of hard fact, the position was exactly the same. But because my hide appeared to be more secure, I found it immensely improved. Of such is courage. Never mind. Grieg didn't know I was disarmed. All he knew was that he had missed me and given himself away. I thought it unlikely that he would enter the house. He believed me to be in possession, and possession – complete with pistol – is more than nine points of the law. If he didn't enter the house, he couldn't ring up the police and tell them to pick him up. I found it extremely likely that he would withdraw. The neighbourhood was unhealthy. He had lost you and Rowley, and now he had as good as lost me. What was more, by opening fire he had, so far as he knew, put all of us wise about him. His game was to make himself scarce. His game was to walk to Vardar, or some such place, take the rest he needed and turn up all bright and smiling at dusk and the bridle-path. And that, I believe, is what he did. I never saw him again. What was so trying was that I never saw Marya.

'To do as I then tried to do needed at least six men – two to watch the house, two to scour the park and a couple of connecting-files. For two long hours I hovered between these duties like a lost soul: then, when I knew that Grieg must have left if he had any hope of reaching the path before dusk, I let the house go and started further afield.

'For all the good I did, I might have stayed where I was. I not only didn't find Marya, but I finished by losing myself. Talk about a dark night... It was Rowley that found her just as night was falling, utterly lost, of course, and only too ready and willing to do as he said. But as soon as he started to take her back to the mill, he knew that in darkness like that he could never find the way: so, while they had time, he steered for one of the drives. Rowley's no fool. He was afraid of the house, but Marya had to have shelter and he was going to put her to sleep in Grieg's car.

'When he found the car gone, he told me he could have cried. But Marya was ready to drop, so he chanced his luck and took her into the house. He found some woman-servant and made her get ready a bedroom and light a fire, and when he had seen Marya eat, he sat down outside her door, pistol in hand. And I spent the night in the open, for the simple and excellent reason that I was in the open when night came down.

'I'll pass over the next eight hours. How many times I fell I've no idea, but when for the second time I'd walked bung into a tree,

I lay down on one of its roots and tried to forget. I failed signally. My memory was brutally active, and my imagination was worse. I was like a sick man, seated between two hearties who take it in turns to slap him upon the back. After several years, the sky began to grow pale...

'Well, Rowley saw me from a window at seven o'clock, and five minutes later I was in Marya's bedroom and being desired to go out. I consented – on one condition. That was that she was dressed in ten minutes' time.

'"What for?" says Marya.

'"Well," said I, "you can't cross the park like that."

'"I'm not crossing the park," says she. "I'm staying here."

'"We shall leave in ten minutes," said I. "Not ten and a half. Dress or not, as you please. But at least put on your slippers. Not that you weigh very much, but I'm rather frail this morning, and Rowley's tired."

'Then I withdrew.

'I went to the chapel and found the register. One glance was more than enough. Marya's writing was that of a child of six, and the rite had been witnessed by Andrew, whose surname appeared to be Jove. I had meant to cut out the page, but I changed my mind, took the book to a fireplace and burned it leaf by leaf. It was very thin, and the leather cover was limp and burned with the rest.

'I found Marya cold with rage, but I found her dressed, and half an hour later we were back at the mill.

'Well, there's nothing much more to tell. Marya was wild with me, but, now that I knew she was safe, I was wild with her. When she spoke of "her husband" I said that if you hadn't killed him, I damned well would, and that if Rowley wiped my eye, I'd kill him, too. And I told her I'd burned the book and was going to poison the priest. I told her that, thanks to her folly, you'd had to go out alone, and I asked her to try and guess why you hadn't come back. In a word, I was extremely brutal. And, such is woman, brutality had its reward. When it was evening again and I suggested that I should take her back to "her husband's" house, she burst into tears, said she was sure Grieg had killed you and added that, if he had, she'd kill herself. I give you my word, Grieg's star had fairly set. The mill fairly reeked of murder. And if he'd looked in at that moment to ask the time, I believe we should have fought for his body like so many beasts of prey. Thus was order restored. But when you didn't fetch up, I was frightened to death. By this morning we'd given up hope: that you were either dead or under arrest was painfully clear: with the optimism of his class, Rowley favoured your decease. But in any event the only thing we could do was to try and get Marya out and then come back. Of course she stuck in her toes, but the farmer's wife from whom I'd been drawing rations was getting inquisitive, and the mill as a residence left a great deal to be desired. I decided to move tonight. The bridle-path, via Gola and Ramon the smith. And then you blew in at sunset and called it off.'

Lelia was buried at two o'clock the next day. Two royal cars were berthed in the shade of the chestnuts without the old churchyard, and Leonie, Marya and a sad-faced lord-in-waiting stood by the open grave. And with them, the Lord President of the Council of Riechtenburg. Though Lelia's uncle and two cousins were all her kin, the peasants came in for miles to honour their dead; and, when the service was done, Sully pronounced the oration with the silver tongue for which he was justly famed.

Lelia, it seemed, was well known in the countryside. The postman being infirm and the post in those parts being a casual business, she had often carried his letters, rain or shine; and though she seldom used villages other than her own, there was not a farm for miles round which was not familiar with her beauty and pleasant ways. If she had had swains, I never heard of them, and it was the good-wives that sobbed the loudest when they passed by the grave. And that was, I think, a rare tribute to a maiden of Lelia's years.

When all was over, I followed the royal cars to Janes, and there Leonie descended and all of us changed at an inn. There we bade goodbye to Sully, who passed his word to visit Littai within the month, and then we drove to Gola, with the servants following after in George's car.

Ramon, the smith, was at work in the little forge, and Marya and I alighted to bring him out to the Rolls.

When we said the Grand Duchess was come to thank him for what he had done, the poor man was quite overwhelmed, but five minutes later Leonie and he were discussing the craft of shoeing as though he had been in her service a score of years. His wife being out, Leonie would not leave till she had come in, and whilst we were waiting, the letter of indemnity arrived.

By the time we were ready to go, all the village of Gola was standing without the forge, and, a second demonstration being more than I felt I could bear, I took my leave of Ramon and made my way out of the crowd and down the road. And there they took me up a furlong away. George driving the car and cursing and dabbing his eyes and swearing that I could have no conception of 'the brutal assault upon the feelings which an outburst of devotion commits'.

Then I took the wheel again, and we came into sight of Elsa at five o'clock.

The frontier-post had clearly been told to expect us and ordered to speed our party upon its way, for the cars were not examined, but the guard was out and waiting to pay my wife the compliments due to her rank.

Slowly we passed the guard-room. Then I drove on to the bridge and into Austria.

It was a curious moment – I think, for all of us, and to me it seemed as though I had ended some chapter which did not at all belong to the book of my life, but was now to go up to some shelf and lie there alone for ever until the Judgment Day. And that made me think of Grieg and remember that the water we were crossing was that which a few miles up had been raging about his grave.

Here I should say that the Coroner of Vardar had told me that Grieg's body would never be given up, but would be held and pounded, as I was used by the mill-race against the wheel, until the flesh fell away and the bones broke loose and were scattered about the bed.

Fifteen minutes later we sailed by *The Broken Egg*...

When we were forty miles from Littai, the sun went down. At that moment our road lay high on the breast of a hill, and seeing in the foliage a gap that gave to the west, I brought the car to a standstill and sat looking back to the country from which we had come.

Below us lay new-mown meadows, with the swathes as the scythe had left them, in long straight lines; beyond, stood a miniature hamlet which the sober cast of evening was melting into the landscape before our eyes; and, far in the distance, over-topping all other country, rose up those sable mountains which kept the bridle-path. Above them, the sky was flaming, and every peak and ridge stood up a sombre monument against the red.

Whilst I was gazing, as though to correct my humour, not twenty feet away a nightingale burst into song. I never found music so grateful, and, as I listened, it seemed to round our venture and add another fable to Æsop's treasury.

Twice over that lonely bird sang his rare song, whilst we sat still and heard him and forgot the world. And had he sung for an hour, I think we must have waited until he had done, for all his song was for us, and, so far as I was concerned, the comfort his notes distilled was beyond all price.

Half an hour later I switched the head-lights on, and, twenty minutes after, we ran through the village of Littai and on to the lodge.

This was open and in order, as though we had but left it that morning and now had returned from fishing some distant stream, for Jameson was a good servant and had left undone nothing which might in his eyes contribute to our relief. The rooms were ready and lighted and gay with flowers, the table was laid for dinner beneath the limes, and he was waiting as usual to usher us out of the car.

So we came back with the guest we had gone out to seek nine days before.

And that is all my tale.

When I sought for the artist-spy whom Grieg had employed I found that he had left Littai the day we came back. I can only suppose that he thought his work was accomplished, for no telegram was sent him to bid him return.

What priest it was that married Marya to Grieg we never knew, but I am inclined to think that he belonged to no parish, but was some hedge-priest or other that Grieg had found. Be that as if may, so far as I know, the fellow held his tongue, and, indeed, if he had spoken, nobody would have listened, for Andrew's wits were failing and the register was gone.

That she should now marry George was only logical, and though, because of her mourning, the engagement was not announced, it was an open secret that they would be joined together before the winter was out.

This meant that she would leave Vigil for good and all, and since my wife now shrank from so much as treading the ground of which her cousin was lord, it seemed unlikely that, so long as he lived, Leonie and I would ever revisit the country of which she was still the Grand Duchess, in which she was so much beloved. For this I now was sorry as never before, for I had not known how much she meant to the people, and to disregard such a friendship seemed graceless indeed. Yet, there was nothing to be done, and, I cannot pretend that I myself would have cared to enter the country again. Stream and forest, high hill and pasture, city and peeping farm – for me the place stank of its ruler and all his works; and, as I have said, it is to me a mystery how that fine gentleman, Sully, can continue to do his duty on the steps of so degraded a throne.

Though we seldom speak of them, the burden of those nine days will stay with me while I live.

While I live, I shall see the garden of Marya's house, and the Prince white-faced and trembling against the green; I shall smell the reek of the circus, and see the Jew standing in the horse lines, drooping his faithless eyes; I shall see the police-officer at Sallust and the faces of the men about me, and shall hear the noisy slam of the door of

Grieg's car; I shall see that deadly spinney and the furtive flash of the coachwork and hear the roar of Grieg's pistol directly ahead; I shall feel the thrash of the mill-race upon my back, and see standing out of the darkness the sheaf of foam; I shall see the flame of the shot that took Lelia's life and Grieg's hands slipping from the girder from which he fell…

And that out of the stress and tumult of which these things were part will rise up for me two figures – the one so close upon the other that sometimes they seem one flesh. Both came for my sake to share the peril in which they were sure I stood; and one of them was taken, and the other left. That ever a man was more honoured I cannot believe; and though it will always seem shocking that so lovely a life should have been given for mine, I cannot forget that if I had died in the mountains, Leonie would have had no one to save her from the power of the dog. So Lelia passed over the river to save us both, and if ever the trumpets sounded, I think they sounded for her as she came to the other side. For her ways were as lovely as she was, and she was of good report.

This Large Print Book, for people
who cannot read normal print,
is published under the auspices of

THE ULVERSCROFT FOUNDATION